PROCLIVITIES

A POP CULTURE ODYSSEY

JAY ALAN REEVES

ARCHWAY
PUBLISHING

Archway Publishing books may be ordered through booksellers or by contacting:

Archway Publishing
1663 Liberty Drive
Bloomington, IN 47403
www.archwaypublishing.com
1 (888) 242-5904

Because of the dynamic nature of the Internet, any web addresses or links contained in this book may have changed since publication and may no longer be valid. The views expressed in this work are solely those of the author and do not necessarily reflect the views of the publisher, and the publisher hereby disclaims any responsibility for them.

Any people depicted in stock imagery provided by Thinkstock are models, and such images are being used for illustrative purposes only. Certain stock imagery © Thinkstock.

ISBN: 978-1-4808-1635-0 (sc)
ISBN: 978-1-4808-1633-6 (hc)
ISBN: 978-1-4808-1634-3 (e)

Library of Congress Control Number: 2015904913

Print information available on the last page.

Archway Publishing rev. date: 4/9/2015

INTRODUCTION

I am not sure why there needs to be an introduction to my work or why people who write books like this one need to explain their writing before anyone actually starts reading what the author wrote. I think most books are pretty much self-explanatory once the actual reading process begins. But in the interest of formality, I will write my own introduction to my work. Normally, an introduction is written by a someone other than a book's author. Unfortunately, everyone that I know who is literate refused to be a part of my writing. Cowards!

I freely admit and take pride in the fact that what you are about to read ain't your average book. In fact it probably deserves a little explaining more so than an ordinary book. Most writings start at a certain point, flow to a specific destination, and have a *Big* Close and you are supposed to get all squiggly at the end and feel enlightened. Let me know if that happens!

As you will soon realize, I have little respect for convention. You can really pick this book up and start reading it about anywhere that there is a break in the page. The thing is confusing anyway so it won't matter. What you will find is actually a series of essays on various topics such as *"background thinking"*, as well as just plain random comments and thoughts with many *"Words that start with N"*. You will also find that as far as convention is concerned, nothing is sacred! Not even those who believe in the *"Mono God theory"* are spared. I offend everyone equally. I do not discriminate based on race, religion, or creed. Actually, I specifically condemn all of those things. What the hell has creed got to do with discrimination anyway? You can kiss my ass if …

actually, I never found having my ass kissed all that particularly pleasing. Anyway, if you are so damn touchy that you can't handle a bit of objective criticism then you can suck my … if you are female. Actually, let's make that *attractive young* female, preferably with full lips…... This brings us to "*The Most Compelling Proclivity of All*" which is, of course, sex. You may well ask, what is the point of all of this? The point is I have made an honest effort to explore the current "*Pop Culture Talking Points*" and the related proclivities of the American population, and if you insist that I honor your sensitivities, you "*Might Be A Sociopath*" and you are gonna be damn disappointed.

I originally intended my writing to be timeless but that challenge proved to be beyond my wisdom and skills. I had visions of purveying a higher level of

consciousness when I started my writing but quickly abandoned those visions when reality checked in. I do believe that I am more or less objective when considering the realities of many of our most controversial and current social issues. You are going to hear me picking on liberals as you read this. I know that bashing liberals is a bit to easy these days considering how outrageously ridiculous the current leftist dogma is. The Obama administration is on the verge of collapse (as of this writing), and cheap Nancy Pelosi shots are embarrassingly easy as her case of "*Liberal Psychosis*" worsens.

The undeniable truth is that most of the relevant comments regarding pop culture and politics are commonly said daily and my opinions do not represent an "*Original Wealth*" of ideas. What I do think is unique about my perspective is my exploration of the whys of what conservative pundits are saying. I do explore "*Liberal versus Conservative* " at a deeper than normal level .

As for the rest of my book, a lot of BS occurs in the section "*Men*," where I discuss the nature of the male of our species. BS is a natural thing for men. I also spend lots of time addressing the nature of the pop culture issues concerning "*Women*." The section "*Vaginitis*" refers to a small minority of constantly complaining women who will never be satisfied with their lot in life, no matter what. Keep your standards low and your mind open and try my "*Recipies.*"

I hope you enjoy a perspective that I believe you will find very different from the usual book written by some anonymous ghostwriter while the "asshole" on TV takes credit for it. If you don't realize that such things are a normal happening, you are probably a brain-dead liberal (BDL).

Also, I give credit where credit is due in "*Footnotes,*" as this is a part of any writing. My writing is no exception though I do take a different approach! For the most part, everything I have written is my own, so footnotes, per se, are not really an issue. I call the section footnotes, though it should probably be called endnotes. I choose foot notes because end notes sounds so final. I assure you this is not the end. So be sure not to skip footnotes because I have tried to make them interesting rather than something you would normally ignore. "*Krib Notes*" is another departure from writing convention. *Krib* is spelled my own way which means that it can be whatever I want it to be. What you will find in this section are the things that I wrote which did not make it to the actual main body of text. When random thoughts of possible content would pop into my head I would record them in "Krib Notes" so they wouldn't be forgotten. They would eventually either be transferred to the relevant essay topic or dismissed as thoughts consistent with an alcohol-induced semi-comatose state. I have a lot of time invested in "Krib Notes," and simply deleting these extensive efforts did not appeal to me. Rather than dump them I decided to include them as just what they are: random thoughts. I also included a "*Glossary,*". You are gonna wanna read it.

If you are a fan of "Global Warming" and "Climate Change." I suggest you take a deep breath before you start reading my two separate observations of this political phenomenon. You are about to get a whole new prospective of the issue. I am seriously asking for and welcoming challenges to my thoughts. I'd also like an actual scientifically based discussion of the realities of man-made changes in weather and the related facts. I would like to propose this factual discussion to demonstrate the physics as utilized by scientists who are willing to stake their professional reputations on the results of their studies. Hopefully there are scientific experts out there who are willing to come forward and circumvent the attempted tyranny of the climate change agenda.

About me.

Jay Alan Reeves is not my real name. Most writers use a pen name. I am not sure why. I assume it is intended to assure a bit of privacy as far as the author's personal life is concerned. For me, it is a matter self-defense. I don't want the people I have maligned to have an easy time finding me so I've used a pen name just in case! In the meantime you can send your death threats to my website: www.iamnotamused.com.

Also, feel free to add your ideas to "*The National Register of Things That Suck*." I ask only that your suggestions be unusual calamities consisting of only one or two words! If you have suggestions for "*Lowlifes*" I will take them under advisement.

As I've already said, what you are about to read is actually a series of essays written to be relevant as stand-alone separate documents. Accordingly, there is some duplication of comment and information.

When I originally conceived the concept of Proclivities as a book I assumed that most people understood the meaning of the word. I have found this to be not necessarily true. A dictionary definition of "proclivity(s)" is;

A human tendency or predisposition toward a particular behavior"

The concept is about how a person will react under a given set of circumstances.

For example, when a man encounters a woman he finds very attractive; almost every straight man will smile at that woman if not briefly imagine a romantic encounter as in, OMG I sure would like to ++++ her!) Compare that reaction to coming upon a woman who is extremely unkempt and slovenly. Most men will look away or make no eye contact. It is our proclivity to take joy in an encounter with that very attractive person while being perplexed by the apparent choices of the repulsive.

Disclaimer:

Any similarity to actual real persons as represented in this writing is a mistake. I sure as hell did not intentionally mean to portray anyone that I actually know as referred to in this book. I could get my ass kicked if someone actually thought I was talking about him or her. I think we can safely assume that the ass hole guy is not going to get a hold of me and apologize for his rudeness and incompetence. Anyway, the business he lost by pissing me off has been well more than the cost of his bungled repair. He is the actual looser, not that losers are bad! Also I suspect Sara Pelosi[1] has some highly paid low life lawyers … … not that lawyers are *Low Life's*, but if they were, I could spend all of the $127.00 that I will get when I sell this book on phone calls to hire a hit man to shut them up; not that a hit man would do such a thing. Oh, and then there's the Jon Stewart thing; I was actually referring to a guy I knew many years ago named Jon, that is now dead. He truly was lacking in the ability to generate spontaneous humor so was condemned to using snarky sarcasm as a substitute for cleverness. There is no reason to think that I was referring to the least funny person on Comedy Central named Jon. You can send inquiries regarding your dissatisfaction to 1600 Pennsylvania Avenue, Washington, D.C.

A prominent element of what you are about to read is the frequent reference to the thinking and behavior of the previously mentioned BDL, (Brain Dead Liberal.) I think it is necessary to fully describe the BDL concept so that you will be under no false assumptions as to my meaning. The phrase is not a reference to your average liberal. It *is* a reference to liberal extremists who just can't help him or her self because they have their heads rectally oriented. It also does not refer the liberal do-gooder who never considers that the money confiscated from the public to fund social programs is actually the result of someone else's hard work and dedication. The proclivity of the BDL is to give no regard to the fact that this hard--working person may have a compelling personal need to keep those funds for their own compelling purposes. It also does not describe a person who has never understood the real cost of federally borrowed money to our culture and the inevitable economic stress of repayment. Nor is it a reference to the average young social worker who has the notion that they can make a real and lasting difference in the world. I also don't mean the ordinary recent High school or college graduate who has been indoctrinated by the liberal educational system for a decade and a half. Such a person will likely grow to the point where real- world living will give them an actual education. Another innocent category of the BDL is the person who simply lacks the wisdom to realize what the effect of every day exposure to liberal values, as presented by the media and other ranting BDL's, has done to their personal understanding of cultural issues.

BDL *is* a reference to those liberals similar to California Democrat Nancy Pelosi; meaning, people who may have suffered a major trau-matic loss of cerebral blood flow at some point in her/his life. BDL also refers to those who are so far off the deep end politically that reason and practicality have ceased to be an issue. Their thinking becomes focused on successfully advocating an unworkable principal so much so that common rational thinking is sacrificed in the name of that principle. Be warned that symptoms of liberal brain death may also appear intermittently. At times, the apparently afflicted are able to present "them-selves" as more or less normal, if not rational. As an observer you must be careful when assuming a person is a BDL given that an outburst of political absurdities might be only be a temporary psychosis. You should never make an assumption based on a random vocal emanation advocating completely unworkable social policy. This person may simply be weak-minded; or he or she may have recently watched *"Meet the Press"* or '*Good Morning, America"* on TV. Brain- dead liberalism in its truest form is always irreversible. Once a rational mind crosses the threshold into extreme liberalism the mind becomes completely clouded by the concept. Like crossing a burned bridge returning to the other side is not possible. Therapies have been tried and successful recoveries' have been rumored, but not documented.

If you have an acquaintance that is a BDLs, you should not judge them too harshly. The BDL mind-set is similar to an addiction: in that once a person becomes hooked on advocating liberal policy it is very hard, if not impossible to stop. The BDLs differs from drug addicts in that there is little or no social pressure to stop "using." Liberalism to any degree is the dark side of social advocacy and is seductive by nature given that the afflicted "self- assume" a higher perceived social status. Most forms of any psychosis and other states of delusion have significant negative consequences and often carry the stigma of the social outcast. The BDL mind-set is actually mainstream thinking as the media is concerned and is therefore validated and encouraged as a normal daily thought process. Given this fact it is easy to understand why liberal brain death is normally permanent once the victim crosses this bridge. It is also true that high- profile public figures are those most likely to be targeted by the BDL as a means of compelling a certain social agenda. Those in social positions that garner mass exposure frequently tend to be liberal by proclivity and therefore are more vulnerable to such pressure. Another prominent component of the affliction is the compelling need to pressure public figures, (using guilt against ego) as an effective tool for manipulation, —assuming that media types are likely ego oriented. A component of liberal brain death that I find fascinating is that while victims appear to be universally simple minded they actually have the same characteristics intellectually as the population at large and similar to that of conservatives. You may ask how it is that a mind completely overwhelmed by a social concept; —a concept that has historically and repeatedly failed over the centuries, and with tragic consequences, —can be anything but of low mental functioning status or is simply illiterate. As unlikely as it may seem, many BDL's are often very capable intellectually. It is an oxymoron[2] for sure that some BDLs are intelligent but behaves as if simpleminded at the same time. This is where the brain-dead component comes in. The casual observer could easily assume that a part of the mind is either diseased or has died. The BDL is liberal psychosis, Axis I or Axis II afflicted.

Let's get you warmed up with an easy topic that everyone can relate to:

Low Life's.

LOWLIFES

Most of us occasionally encounter those who don't necessarily understand or choose to follow the rules of life as imposed by our culture. I am not necessarily talking about criminals or social derelicts. What I am talking about is the ordinary everyday asshole; the person who just can't help but be a jerk, dickhead, bitch, ho, etc. You get the idea: a person who takes advantage of others without regard for basic common decency. The most common type of asshole is the accidental asshole. This is someone who might make a random social blunder while not trying to be an asshole. Other people appear to be intentional assholes and actually get a kick out of the behavior. I have also found the person who believes everyone else is an asshole is usually the biggest asshole of all. I also think those most likely to flip the bird frequently are those most likely to the meet the previous description.

I understand that the standard meaning of flippin' the bird is "F—you." It is intended as a quick and vulgar insult that everyone understands instantly. It is a very effective and useful tool when the need arises to quickly express your opinion of someone at a distance. It is direct and to the point and not ambiguous. It is normally given anonymously and in passing but it can also be useful one-on-one in close quarters. Not too long ago, I had the need for a different sort of insult delivered to a classic jerk who had wronged me. I was very tempted to pass along the aforementioned brief thought by gesture but he was much bigger than I and clearly the type who would overreact to an accurate description of himself.

An insult should be fast and clever if not scathing. But sometimes insults are just a simple social faux pas, where a person just says the wrong thing, the unintentional insult. I am more concerned with the harsh and vulgar insult like you might say to your former spouse: the intentional insult, but there are different degrees of insults. Insults can be just a playful joke you say to a friend just to get under his or her skin, all in good humor. We also have international insults, "Your country sucks"; regional insults, "Your state sucks"; local insults, "Your town sucks"; and personal insults, "You suck." In the situation mentioned previously, I had a great need for an appropriately harsh insult. Since that incident, I have had time to give it much thought, mostly during those endless hours alone in my combine cab, with little else to amuse me beyond the radio and thoughts of vengeance.

Clearly at the time I wrote the following, I was really PO'd. The asshole in question had ripped me off on the repair of a fuel-supply pump. Not only did he not fix my pump twice, he also lied to my face about the nature of the problem. It was a blatant bold-faced lie that could not possibly have been true. He eventually became angry and threatening when I politely pointed out his lie. He simply had no capacity to admit he had made a mistake, no matter how obvious the truth. Of course, he would not return my very expensive and still not correctly repaired fuel pump until I overpaid him. After pondering this fellow's basic nature, I was inspired to write the following.

"I witnessed the satanic rape of the feral bitch that bore you."

Translation: "I watched the devil rape your mother, who was a skanky, female, wild-dog whore, and you were born as a result."

Yes, I was really pissed off, really really pissed off. My goal was to condense a comment to the fewest number of words and still be as insulting as possible. This insult isn't very quick and is admittedly, a little vague. It is not the kind of thing you could pop off in a bar at the guy who offended your girlfriend so it lacks any real useful value. It is more about being really offensive as the harshest of statements. I think being told you are the son of the devil is bad. I think being told that your mother was an actual bitch dog who was raped by the devil is *really* bad. How much worse could it get except that I stood by and watched while it happened and didn't care. I think it takes the term "son of a bitch" to a whole new level. (For all I know this guy's mother might be a very kind person. She may well not deserve these harsh comments. She may have actually been too kind to her son who figured out early he could get away with anything as far as his mom was concerned. My apologies to her if this is the case!

When considering lower life forms there are many levels of rectally challenged people. Clearly the worst human behavior is murder. But there are degrees of murder. The person who kills randomly for no just reason is the worst. The law recognizes declining levels of the crime and punishes accordingly. Those who kill in war are not thought of as murderers at all. I could go on and on about criminals but this is not my point. The people I am thinking about are those who, when given a chance to do the right thing do not necessarily take that chance. I like to use my dear departed uncle as an example. He was a part of the Coast Guard during World War II, and in that there is honor. Beyond that and as best I can tell, he had no track record of ever doing anything of value for humanity. To the contrary he was a person humanity supported surreptitiously. For most of the time I knew him he lived off our culture's generosity. He was a bum when he was a younger man. Over the years he *was* eventually promoted to "homeless."

He did have jobs occasionally. At one point in his career he took to selling lots on a local residential lakeside development property. As it turned out the developers were less than ethical (imagine that!) and those who bought into the scheme were cheated. My uncle made a lot of cash on the deal and actually bought an expensive Cadillac with the proceeds. He lived well for a while but eventually reverted to his natural state so much so that the car became his home. The punch line is that when a local news program did a story on the plight of the homeless he was found living in his car in the back alleys of downtown Des Moines and became the subject of the story. It was his ten minutes of fame but he found himself so embarrassed by the story that he left town and drove to Dubuque and rented a room in an old motel that had been converted to one-room apartments. How he paid for the room I don't know, but the likelihood is he lived there at the expense of the public or that of the motel owner. He once told me "It ain't so bad; they feed ya and you don't have to do anything", referring to a recent weekend in an Omaha jail.

It went on and on with him as to how he lived. It was his proclivity not to support himself more comfortably though he clearly could have. Was he a lowlife? All I can say is; his entire family shunned him over the course of his life for his aberrant deeds.

A list of other forms of the lowest not likely to be convicted of a crime.

Computer hackers: They sit in absolute safety and wreak havoc on the lives of others. They steal time and wealth from people and with no personal gain except to satisfy their own self-loathing. They are so cowardly and slothful that they lack the courage to steal from us face-to-face which involves personal risk.

Scam artists: Internet and otherwise.

Politicians: Self-explanatory.

Socialists: It is impossible to exist in a socialist society without enslaving the productive. In spite of good intentions, socialist societies have always lived in poverty.

Dictators: The ultimate criminals; people die, nations suffer.

Local drug dealers: Yes, people want the drugs but that does not make it right!

Global warming/climate change extremists: What they really want is power and social control. Real or not the changes demanded will have little if any effect on our climate.

Televangelists: They use people's fear, ignorance, and compassion to fill their pockets, often at the expense of the elderly and poor.

Union bosses: Not your local representative but the kind of guy who end up in a building as part of the foundation.

Welfare scammers: Not the truly needy, but the person who isn't trying though capable of earning a living .

Telemarketers: They intentionally mislead potential consumers with verbal bait-and-switch language providing mostly useless products and making millions in the process.

Lawyers: The more exposure I have to the legal system the more contempt I have for lawyers, including the ones who work for me. I have come to see the legal system as the ultimate scam far worse than the worst of what you may think.

Honorable mention!

ASSHOLES
ATHEISTS
ANARCHISTS
AUDITORS
ANTAGONISTS
ANTICHRIST
AGNOSTICS
ATTACKERS
ATTORNEYS
ANTISOCIALS

BIKERS
BUMS
BASTARDS
BELCHERS
BORES
BITCHES
BANKERS
BILL COLLECTORS
BULLIES
BIGAMISTS
BOSSES
BUNGLERS
BURGLARS
BOOKIES

CON ARTISTS
CANNIBALS
CREEPS
COCKSUCKERS

CALIFORNIANS
COMMIES
CROSS-DRESSERS
CU—TS
COPS
CARNIES
CAPITALISTS
CRONIES
COWARDS
CROOKS
CHEATERS
CRIMINALS
CEOS

DIVAS
DRUGGIES
DRUNKS
DOPERS
DICKHEADS
DIPSTICKS
DOUCHE BAGS
DEADBEATS
DORKS
DULLARDS

EVANGELISTS
EMPERORS
EGOMANIACS

FORNICATORS
FREAKS
FASCISTS
FULKERS
FONDOLOGISTS
FINKS
FARTS

FAKES
FLAKES
FUDGE PACKERS

GOSSIPERS
GANGSTERS
GRINCHES
CURMUDGEON'S
GAMBLERS
GEEKS
GOONS

HOOKERS
WHORES
HARLOTS
HERETICS
HOODLUMS
HEDONISTS
HYPOCRITES
HEELS
HOMOS

ILLEGALS
INDIGENTS
INTERLOPERS
INDIANS
INFIDELS

JOKERS
JUMPERS
JOCKS
JERKS
JACKOFFS

KOOKS

LIBERALS
LIARS
LOUSES
LECHERS
LEECHES
LOWLIFES
LOUTS
LOSERS
LEPRECHAUNS
LAWYERS
LEFTISTS

MOTHERS-IN-LAWS
MO-FOES
MALINGERERS
MALCONTENTS
MIMES
MORONS
MOLESTERS
MONGERS
MONSTERS
MISFITS
MUGGERS
MISCREANTS
MASOCHISTS
MASTURBATORS

NYMPHOS
NAZIS
NARCS
NEANDERTHALS
NARCISSISTS
NECROPHILIA'S
NINCOMPOOPS

ORPHANS

ODDBALLS
OLDSTERS

PIMPS
PORNOGRAPHERS
PUKES
PROSTITUTES
PANHANDLERS
PUSHERS
PARANORMALS
PARANOIDS
PRIMA DONNAS
PRICKS
POACHERS
POLECATS
POLACKS
PICKPOCKETS
POLLUTERS
PROCRASTINATORS
PSYCHOS

QUEERS
QUEENS

REDNECKS
ROWDIES
ROOKIES
REPORTERS
REJECTS
RAPISTS
RAPPERS
RUMPELSTILSKIN
RACISTS
ROCKERS

STEPMOTHERS

SPEEDERS
SHOPLIFTERS
SLUTS
SLEAZEBAGS
SOBS
SUCK-UPS
SKANKS
STOCKBROKERS
SLACKERS
SCOUNDRELS
SCUMBAGS
SCOURGES

TRIPPERS
TAUNTERS
TAX CHEATERS
TAX COLLECTORS
TERRORISTS
TARTS
TROLLOPS

USED-CAR SALESMEN
USURPERS

VANDALS
VOYEURS
VAMPS
VAGABONDS

WUSSIES
WIMPS
WOPS
WACKOS
WELCHERS
WITCHES
WENCHES

WASPS

X-WIVES
X-HUSBANDS

YAHOOS
YANKEES
YO-YOS

ZOOKS

And, of course, me, myself, and I

More on "f— you" and the famous gesture;

I was thinking; Under different circumstances, this gesture could actually be good news. It could actually be seen as an invitation for sex. Possibly we, as a culture would get along better if it became a friendly message saying that, "I would like to have sex with you." Yes, I would "F" you. Instead of insulting people in traffic we could actually be flattering them by demonstrating, by gesture that we would like to have sex with them. If I am driving down the road and eyeing a hot chick in the next car over and she flips me off, instead of being heart broken, I have just been told "Yes, I would do you." At the very least this event would give me a smile that would last all day. How about in a shopping mall? If I were walking along and saw an attractive woman and then flipped her off, she might actually smile given that she has just been told by gesture, "You are so hot that I would gladly engage in sexual relations with you even though we don't really know each other." "*Kumbaya.*" In the same vein the verbal version of the statement could actually become an offer for sex; usually good news. The emphasis needs to be on the second word to have the desired meaning. Say it to yourself as a question:; "f**-—k *you?*" Emphasis needs to be on the second word to get the desired response. Emphasis on the second word equals sex. Ya! Emphasis on the first word? … Okay … possibly I need to rethink this but I still have to ask, why is the phrase "f**---—k you" considered an insult anyway? Almost everybody wants to f---—***.

Back to the topic of lowlifes

What else can I say about lowlifes? We all know um. In looking back at my list I think a little explanation would be appropriate. For example, whores! I don't mean to criticize the promiscuous females. Actually promiscuous females have put a lot of smiles on my face not to mention given me a good night's sleep. Some people on my list are just trying to make a living; others are real bags of crap. For example, pornographers. The percentage of men who watch porn is very high but as you may notice I am not much for statistics. Having said that most men and a lot of women watch porn which should justify producing a high quality product that continues to guarantee strong audience. Yet those guys doing skin-a-max are just crap. How in the hell can anyone make something as fascinating and as universally desired as sex and its image seem dull. Have you seen this stuff? Dull, Dull, Dull. If you are going to go to all the trouble to get naked people and get a studio and then get it on TV and all that goes with it the least you could do is make it interesting. They write bad scripts with terrible actors but we expect that. After all it is porn. Just a hot naked chick is usually enough of a reason to watch porn but not for these bags. It must be intentionally bad. This can't be a mistake. It is on purpose! They are trying to give porn a bad reputation!

Others on the low life list are the iconic hated and my favorite is ex-wives/spouses. Not just mine, but ex-wives generally. I have seen dreadful behavior from an X-wife toward her X- husband and she was my current love interest. All I could do was agree with her when she speculated that her ex- husband hated her. Still others on the list are just intrinsically corrupt, liberals extremists for example. Liberalism always assumes that the public needs to be centrally controlled as its primary motivation. Individual freedom must be sacrificed for liberalism to succeed? Gossipers? I have a theory that says gossipers are actually acting out their own socialist proclivity when gossiping. They focus on other people and other peoples' lives. It is all about the social group and the component behavior of the "people" that motivates gossipers. Con men prey on the gullible and weak-minded and those info-mercial guys are the lowest of the legal low, except possibly for personal injury attorneys. If you're a lawyer and can't make a living any other way you practice in personal injury. The social cost of personal- injury judgments has been devastating to our economic efficiency. Infidels? I think that term includes me. Also; I have been known to speed. Some on the list are just naturally slothful people who follow the path of least resistance as an income and life are concerned. Our culture, too often, magnanimously supports those who choose to follow this easiest path in life without prejudice, —and supports them in the same way as those who are obviously incapable. By supporting such people we as a culture advocate the mind-set.

Some thoughts on sociopathy!

You might be a sociopath if;

- You frequently belch in public.
- You actually think your fecal matter does not smell.
- You like getting into a good bar fight.,
- You think everybody else is a dickhead/ bitch.;
- You can't understand why people don't get out of your way when you are driving.
- You think your life is all about you.;
- You don't care what people think about you.
- You have an overwhelming urge to strangle all the dumb shits around you.
- You see no reason not to steal or cheat when you get the chance.
- You think your mistakes are not your fault.
- You think other people frequently get pissed at you for no reason.
- You think you are hot even though you are 100 pounds overweight.
- You think about you frequently.
- You are serving a life sentence in prison.
- You don't understand why people won't do as they are told.
- You are running for political office.
- You see other people as objects that are in your way.
- You flash the bird frequently.

- No body messes with you.
- You would force yourself sexually on another person.
- You think you are "bad."
- You are a bitch, and proud of it.

After further thought on the "f— you" thing while it may sound like a really bad idea I thought of something that might actually make it work. What we need to do is not point the middle finger *up*. Possibly it would work if we pointed the finger sideways or better yet *down*. Think about this. Really. We could start a whole new cultural revolution of harmless unintimidating flirtation and silent sexual innuendo. This would always be nonintrusive and flattering and also easy enough to ignore. It has potential!

WOMEN

My best and most valued friends have always been women.

It's a matter of propriety.

In the company of a woman of letters; —an accomplished professor of her chosen trade; a woman who never knew how much I admired and respected for her accomplishments; argued that a country-music act known as the "Dixie Chicks" should be supported and defended for controversial comments made by lead singer Natalie Maines during a concert in Texas many years ago. These comments ended their pubic appeal as musicians, comments condemning the president of US. My admired friend defended Natalie's comments, not based on the circumstances of the situation but on the fact that she was a woman and her given default right to speak her mind. She has and had the right to speak her mind of coarse; no question about that. But freedom of speech requires a prudent discretion as an obligation of that freedom. Natalie's comments were grossly inappropriate. Chick A ignored the fact that half of her paying audience was likely conservative or right leaning if not proud of the fact that the current president was indeed a Texan and, she insulted her home state by declaring her shame as a native Texan and her geographic connection to the president.

My friend saw this as a woman's issue; and a woman's right to speak her mind. In truth, it was a matter of propriety. My friend could not or chose not to separate the two things. The same mistake was made at the concert by the lead Chick. People loved their music but that love does not translate to expertise as politics are concerned. Chick A imagined that her fame as a musician gave her license to proclaim her leftist politics to a crowd of paying fans. They had no future as a musical act at that moment not because of Natalie's politics but because of an extreme presumptuousness that anyone gave a damn about her politics. Propriety was disregarded in favor of an assumption based on a very inflated ego. "I like your music but who the hell are you to stand before me and condemn my president! "Up yours, lady!!!" My learned friend had placed her priorities so much so on advocating for women that she did not judge the Chick for her choices rather supported her for her gender. My friend eventually submitted, by consensus of opinion to the thinking of an uneducated farmer, me, to add clarity to the situation. I will mention again that I admired her greatly. There was no need for her to convince me or anyone else present that we should honor her gender as status and rights were concerned. I took no pleasure in this event for it gave her an underlying and subtle contempt for me personally. Unquestionably clever and brilliant her advocacy as a pseudo feminist was her compelling issue and her lack of insight regarding the issue was her personal glass ceiling.

I want women to live as equals to men as women's rights are concerned. As no two people are equal, the genders are also not on average equal. It is not about being exactly equal as persons; it is about having equal rights and equal opportunities. I can guarantee equal rights for women but how can I guarantee equal opportunities? Of course I can't. Nothing can. No person or government can guarantee equal opportunities to anyone no matter who that person is. As long as any group or person thrives by the advocacy of any entity, there can never be equality for that group or person. When you become dependent on the results of an organized advocacy you are now not equal and never can be. It will never be true that any group is equal if granted a compensating grace.

I grew up with and supported the notion that women are a protected class of people. It is ingrained in me not by demand but by an understanding that women were to be protected given their physical vulnerabilities as compared to men. It is a universal sanction that I except with honor and a personal desire to comply. It is understood that those of us who are stronger are little less than fearful cowards when we prey on women. I am no coward and I will suppress as necessary those who are such cowards. Defending any one woman from harm has never been a necessity in my life thankfully. I am not a big or powerful man and would be more or less defenseless against a person who was. In reality the most I can do is support the defense of women generally and advocate those sentiments to those who would be influenced by me. I see this notion as universal among males except for an extremely small minority. Oddly enough the feminist movement that I so happily supported many years ago actually had the effect of making women more vulnerable culturally. Once largely homebound women now traveled freely and widely without the bother of a male companion. Women put their physically vulnerable selves in situations that they were previously culturally protected from.

Clearly the feminist movement had its righteous calling. One must consider how it ever became culturally popular that women were expected to be socially submissive to men. A bit of a no brainer actually given that the more physically powerful men prehistorically dominated all of the assets as sustenance was concerned. Women became dependent on, if not servile to the men around them for their daily needs. It is very likely that larger more powerful males procreated through "forced reproduction". As a result what's now known as *natural selection* took place. Eventually women became dependent on men for their survival. It is natural that the sustenance-providing men would demand servitude from the dependent females. In the modern age of easily available food and shelter women can depend on their own skills to provide for their needs and can also satisfy those needs at a level that far exceeds the basics of life. Women are no longer dependent on men but culture has taken a long time to catch up with need. Having lived through the feminist movement as it was happening I passively participated in the support of women. I saw no reason whatsoever to deny those quests so apparently important to my fellow sisters.

Is it true that a woman can survive by the efforts of others without guilt or public condemnation? Has "she" been a protected class for so long a time that it is ingrained in our collective psyche for her to survive based on the generosity of a magnanimous entity? Is this proclivity the reason why so many women count themselves as liberals as compared to men? Is that why women are often outspoken supporters of government stipends which support the public not at large but as individuals? There was a time in our nation when women could not vote. The founders of our nation did not consider at the time that there was any reason for women to vote. It was more than a century after our nation was founded that a concentrated national effort was conceived to gain voting rights for women. Women were not actually granted the right to vote for yet another forty years. It is a historical fact that there were a lot of pissed-off women who pursued extreme measures to gain voting rights. If I were a woman I think I would still be pissed off about that fact today. How the hell is it possible that this nation existed for nearly 150 years with half of the population ineligible to vote? And I am not counting immigrants and blacks both free Negroes and slaves. This was a profoundly different mind-set as compared to our collective social psyche today.

There is much potential controversy as to the nature of our country today and the effects of women voters on our politics. Actually it's a hornets' nest. For example, there are those who will tell you that the social welfare state began when women got the right to vote and that national budget issues are exacerbated by the proclivity of women to accept money and other support that they have not labored to earn. There is nothing in it for me to piss women off at that extreme level. Clearly this topic; "women" is at best inflammatory as far as politics and women are concerned. It is actually true that my greatest desire is to offer the women of our culture clues as to how the group can evolve to the next higher social level as the perspective of men is concerned. The most profound and most obvious clue is that above all else men value character. The Marine Corps is the extreme and absolute permutation of this notion and it is the best example of my meaning. *Character* meaning "doing the right thing at the right time without regard for personal gain in an easy and obvious situation." Character meaning that the person can be trusted to do the ethically correct thing no matter the temptation or situation.

For most of my life I have assumed that women just needed a chance to step up and find their place at the top. I assumed the women's movement would be an evolution that would play itself out over time as women climbed the ladder of success and social status. As the decades have passed I have become less confident in this eventuality. I have begun to understand the scope of an inherent disadvantage that I did not previously see and would prefer *not* to see now. I want women to succeed in their desires and the same as men. There is no downside to the success of women as men in general are concerned. That said, the inherent disadvantage I perceive is not clearly defined in my mind but I know it involves emotional self-satisfaction as a priority to social accomplishment. It involves the lack of the ability and desire to succeed as a social group. It's about the conniving mentioned above as a priority to integrity. Its goal is self-actualization as the greatest achievement if at the expense of another woman—and, better yet, a man. I know very accomplished women successful and smart who are blocked from the next step up and not by culture but by their own lack of vision regarding an understanding of themselves and their actions and thinking. The greatest impediment to the cultural success of women is *emotion-based reasoning!* The glass ceiling is often self-imposed and not cultural. My examples are of women I respect and admire not because they are physically desirable but because of their natural talents. "Don't hate me because I'm beautiful" summarizes the problem from a different point of view. It unintentionally points out that women are in competition with each other and as a priority to society generally. It explains cattiness and the shared misinformation that I have seen as common among women and I have suffered as a victim personally from those intentional miss-directions—and suffered a great deal.

Today, for the first time in my life I heard a woman admit that women are diabolical and conniving, something I never thought I would hear from a woman though I already knew it to be a fair statement. Sometimes I wonder if it is true that women actually have any real friends. BFFs[3] might be just a myth. The ongoing competition among women mentioned above is cultural and woman A is using woman B to gain a leg up or some random advantage and without regard for the personal welfare of woman B. Women will join forces to condemn men if a particular man or group of men fail to honor women. This might be the only time a woman can trust another woman. Women relish the opportunity to bash men as a group. I think that this is why "MRI" (Men Are Idiots) advertising is so popular. Male popular advertising involves beer, sports, and hot chicks in bikinis. Female popular advertising also includes romantic fantasy scenarios, but MRI advertising is more common. Why are women drawn to images of men as dullards who can't do anything right? Mostly, these images portray bungling husbands. Clearly the appeal is that advertisers place women in a superior status to men by comparison using the feminine ego as a target of manipulation. The woman/wife is smart and the guy/husband is a moron—(yet she married him.) I personally have no desire to feel superior to women. I don't care. An advertisement showing women as idiots has no appeal to me. Beautiful young women in bikinis works just fine for me; it is very appealing and will keep me focused on your advertising.

GOING FOREWORD;

The future of women is not what a *fondologist* would imagine it to be. Success is not about complaining and bitching until you get what you want. Men dominated culture through evolution as women chose the preferred male for breeding stock. It is women who made men what we are and we are not motivated by your complaining. We will never honor those who choose to control men by manipulation and as said, honor is everything to men. We may play women's games so we can have sex or have a family to care for but women will never really own us in our minds if women choose to use surreptitious manipulation as a means of control.[4] I will hold a woman as a goddess if her heart is true and she is not conniving, as "we" (i.e., men) are concerned. Also, women should not assume we men don't see it coming. Men are not necessarily fooled by feminine manipulation. For the most part we do know what women are up to—we just don't see any reason to create conflict by exposing this behavior. For women to be "equal" in men's eyes, women must abandon the notion of underlying manipulation and be a true person. We men place our priority on a woman's physical appearance much more so than her character. This is because our desires place her physicality as the greatest value she could have to us as a man. I will be cautious when I decide to rely on a woman as a person given the possible manipulations mentioned above. As long as she is available sexually it is a compromise I will accept. I have also have known many very unreliable men but I can easily detect them and am not vulnerable to or influenced by their other charms. I am vulnerable to the charms of women. I will also add that the person I regarded most highly of all in my life; was a woman.

Bashing men had become a popular form of exercise for women in the 1980s and 90's

Today was the fruition of a multiyear plan. The plan was conceived to correct an injustice inspired by a woman. My guidepost was doing the right thing ethically. There was no deception but to direct in the right direction, those who would misdirect by their own proclivity. All concerned were given ample opportunity to do the right thing of their own free will. Those opportunities passed undone. I pursued a course intended to benefit those deserving while sacrificing some personal wealth in order to gain larger wealth, both originally intended mine. All intended benefited. Those unintended and conspiring suffered by their own hands and it was an unjust woman and her contemporary who were responsible. A woman also recognized me for my accomplishment in spite of the fact that she who recognized me was unaware of the scope of the plan or the lack thereof. The plan was not preconceived entirely, but was the result of following a true course toward an intended goal that led to an unintended retribution. Not that I didn't intend retribution, but that it came in a way I did not expect and was much more harsh. I am admittedly proud of this accomplishment.

Old movies are like a written history of our cultural heartbeat but not by the story line or script specifically. Any screenwriter is likely to write a script that reflects the values and concerns of the day. Public thinking of the time is unintentionally included and reflected in the movie even when it is a period movie. A movie about the old west made in the 1930s reflects the thinking of the 1930s. Movies made today inescapably reflect our current cultural values. If they didn't, today's movies wouldn't be accepted by the public and they wouldn't be profitable. When I watch these old movies, as I commonly do I see a distinct difference in the portrayed role of women. Movies made in the 1950s portray women as housewives or as lustful, single, desperate-to-catch-a-husband connivers. A 1960s episode of *The Twilight Zone* portrays one particular female character as empty-minded to the male lead ("Darrin Stevens"[5]), who has been granted the temporary ability to read minds. When leaning in close to hear her thoughts all he hears is silence. This is intended as a humorous joke poking fun at women as empty-headed. Any male producer using this portrayal of women today would be condemned harshly, if not burned at the stake.

I have lived through a tremendous redefinition of the role of women in American culture. Starting in the 1960s there was an uprising of dissatisfied women. This uprising was the genesis of the "feminist movement. These women were not at all pleased with their lot in life and took to the streets to make their grievances known. Personal rights were the primary issue. History will not remember them fondly! Genders need to be partners in culture, not combatants. The feminist movement gained tremendous momentum by the late 1970s as females were burning their bras in effigy. I had no reason to object. The young women who were part of my life at the time were for the most part not feminists. Feminism was more of a coastal issue. In the meantime mid-western women were successfully advancing in the world of business and politics and with a minimum of bitching. Midwestern values have always been sought-after as far as coastal employers were concerned. The era was a very good time to be from the Midwest. As time passed feminism evolved to what sounded like, and looked like, an angry bitches' club of lesbians. This is an exaggeration of course but not far from how they were seen by many. Feminism is really a classic example of a growing social movement that gains too much momentum and is then overrun by extremists who seek influence and power. The time was right for a redefinition of the role of women who were no longer the masters of the home but copartners in supporting the home. The social pendulum has swung. This swing was a backlash from the often publicly maligned female character. Not the female characters as portrayed in movies, but the personal character of females generally speaking which was frequently portrayed as questionable. This had become a current cultural phenomenon of the mid-1900s. I see little or no evidence that such thinking was pervasive earlier in the century, but it is clear that women were expected to assume a submissive role culturally that is not expected today.

Feminists have required that we men should honor women for their social value beyond physical beauty, but; like it or not the physical form of the female body is a highly prized and driving force in the advent and future of humanity. It is so powerful that Arab cultures cover women as much as possible to suppress the power and resulting reaction of the male response. This covering up actually has the opposite reaction in that a woman with an unfortunate face is still assumed to be desireable because we can't tell at a glance whether she is or isn't. Also, the enticement factor goes through the roof: "I just gotta see what's under there." Actually the girl in the bikini takes away the mystery and after about an hour or so we men stop staring at her and start looking for the next chick in a bikini. Women should never underestimate the power that is theirs by natural causes or discount this power in favor of advocating for compensation due to a perceived disadvantage.

CHOICE?.................

Choice my ass; take a stand. You either believe that abortion should be allowed or that it should not be allowed. The choice thing is crap and a cop-out. It is also patronizing. I fully understand that this "choice" affects women profoundly more than men but I would like to see another example in which only one gender has the power to determine social policy—a social policy that is about human life and death. Personally, I favor allowing abortion but it is a very close call for me as it is for our culture. I am 50.01 percent in favor of legal abortions. I am 49.99 percent opposed. It is inescapable that only a pregnant female can make this decision but to freely publicly advocate in favor of the validity of the decision is soulless coldhearted manipulation in favor of a personal agenda having nothing to do with the social morality of abortion. Abortion will never be a good "choice"! It will and should always be, a hard "choice."

This morning, I woke to a tweet promoted by an e-mail from Twitter. There were several prominent story lines presented as bait to encourage my use of the social media site. I clicked on an article showing a beautiful woman elaborately displayed and surrounded by sparkly glamorous designs and extremely feminine, highly flattering clothing. Oddly enough the article was about feminism. I was curious as to how a display of artificially enhanced feminine beauty and an article on feminism could be tempered together as one and the same. Isn't it true that a primary principle of feminism is that women are more than just objects of desire? Aren't we men supposed to honor and respect women for their abilities? Aren't we supposed to honor the notion that women have value beyond physical appearance? This bait flagrantly violated that principle. I had to investigate!

This post focused on the rights and free choices and opportunities of women as compared to. ... Actually, I don't know what these comments might be compared to. There are no choices that can be made by anyone today that are not equally available to anyone else regardless of gender, race, or sexual orientation. Women have a very high profile in every venue of society. I am not sure what inequality this post is focused on. After much thought I came to the only conclusion I could make. When all other possibilities have been eliminated whatever remains must be the truth. My conclusion must remain my own private opinion for fear that I might be tracked down and executed by a horde of feminists! Post your answers to this puzzle on my website: www.iamnotamused.com. If you guess correctly I will donate a trillion dollars to the Foundation for Disingenuous Exploitation of Women. (iamnotamused.com)

MEN

This should be fun! Rated R, for Repugnant, Raunchy, Ridiculous, Rude, and Right!

While writing the previous section on women I was very reluctant to be too hard-hitting. I don't necessarily want to offend women as a group though there *is* a hell of a lot of easy fodder flying in all directions. It is a target-rich environment actually. Cheap shots are embarrassingly easy. Women willingly admit that they are emotional, inconsistent, mysterious, and intentionally troublesome. Men think these things are bullshit. They don't work for men. We don't play those games. We have better things to do such as getting drunk, picking our noses, and scratching our butts, all of which are important daily activities for men. I almost forgot to mention the satisfaction that comes from a generous fart and a deep long belch. We actually score our belches. It *is* a contest. There is a pill that that will stop gassy anal releases but I have to wonder why anyone would want to stop something that was crude, stinky, and flammable. Men are competitive when it comes to foul offensive odors and classless vulgar sounds! And we like pussy but that does not necessarily mean that we like cats. Actually, men tend to not like cats at all. I think this is mostly true because no one has come up with a good recipe for cat.

Yes, we are always looking for something to eat, including the aforementioned pussy. It is ingrained in the very roots of what it means to be a man in that we go out and hunt our prey, then bring it home and eat it. Our cookbooks are in our memory and are recipes are about how to make beaver taste good. Yes, I have eaten beaver. It didn't taste all that good, but in a little while I wanted it again. Be careful not to get it too hot. This is not the sort of odor you want coming out of your kitchen. Also, a lot of the beaver these days, comes with the fur missing. Personally, I prefer a nice pelt. I hear some men say, "It tastes good if you cook it right." I say, "If you have to cook it right, I don't want to eat it." Going hunting isn't just about going out in the woods and killing something. The successful kill proves us worthy as men and worthy of the little woman at home. We gain status as men from the successful hunt.

Fishing is the same thing. Fishing and hunting trips are so much better in that they are also an adventure for men. Men seek adventure. It is manly to wander the woods and avoid being eaten by a bear or getting lost. It is even better if you can bring home a moose or a bear. Plus you can drink all the beer you want and no one will be giving you crap because you drink too much. Speaking of crap, no flush toilet? No problem! Poop in a hole and wipe your ass with a squirrel. Just don't let it bite you.

Another thing men really like is the f-word! The f-word with -*ing* added has got to be the word most frequently used by men. Men in a group isolated from women will use the word almost obsessively. Men gathered in a peer-group setting can and will be extremely vulgar, with frequent references to sex and bitches and pussy. It is fun to let go when no one cares what you say or how you say it especially when you are sure it will not be repeated. It is also a great opportunity to be a racist! Only a real lowlife would dare repeat what is said in the private company of men.

Explosions are also manly. Nothing makes a man happier than blowing the hell out of something and it is best if there is a big ball of fire in the process. Dynamite is fine for destroying things but it can't compete with a boiling flaming cloud of blackened greenhouse gases billowing in the sky. It is as much fun as you can have with carbon. We like guns for the same reason. You can use them to blow things up from a distance. It's cool to see what happens to something when you shoot it. Boys and their toys! Speaking of toys, any machine is cool. Anything that is powerful, fast, and noisy is cool and dangerous is a plus. That is why we like fast cars and Harleys! The relationship between men and rolling vehicles is legendary. It must have begun the day after the first successful test of a wheel. "My wheel rolls down the hill faster than yours and it goes farther and It looks cooler!" I suspect the evolution of the wheel was pretty fast given this competition for having the coolest-looking wheel and the best-working wheel and the fastest wheel. It was probably a hundred years before men thought of using the wheel as a tool for hauling heavy loads, which is not cool or fun or fast.

BEER?

Beer must taste better to men than women. I see women drinking plenty of beer but women don't normally drink it obsessively. If it weren't for obesity and pending alcoholism I would drink lots and lots of beer. It is a very satisfying beverage and it keeps your system flushed out but who would drink it at all if it weren't for the alcohol! The near-beer products gather dust on the store shelves. Getting drunk with your buddies over a keg of beer is a lot more important than just getting drunk with company. It is about sharing a common experience. When we men drink we are testing and learning about each other. If you want to really know a man, know him drunk. Getting drunk isn't just fun for men, it is a necessity. It is also true that there are certain times when we need to get drunk more urgently. This occasional need is mostly dependent on whom we are married to and it can be sort of a monthly issue. Getting drunk is also used as a marker in a man's life. We use alcohol when we are sad or when we are happy or when we are celebrating or when we strike it rich or when we need to drown our sorrows. It is multipurpose stuff and damned effective for killing a cold virus. It should also be noted that beer automatically tells you when to stop drinking.

Men like sex a lot. Sex is about anthropology but most men are just horny and want to get laid. We *must* get laid actually! This can be a hell of a problem for men. One of the most challenging things that we men face is that women control all the available supply of vagina. It can be a very closed market and a man needs to try hard to penetrate. Women can be very reluctant to share, and they use our driving need for sex to manipulate us. Men can get damn frustrated with women and we would not put up with all the crap if it weren't for sex. Women would not put up with men if it weren't for all the money! It is a fair trade-off that keeps everybody out of trouble. That is why the direct transaction of cash for sex is illegal. It takes away the power of women to use sex to control men. And again, the beer thing: most women are impregnated under the influence of beer. Why are you here? Why were you born? Because your dad was horny and got your mom drunk which she willingly did and after the proper amount of alcohol-based lubrication she woke up the next morning pregnant. Today, wine has become the popular "excuse" of choice for women!

Women like to mention male bonding which is also crap. Men don't bond unless we are gluing a house together. We have friends and groups of acquaintances and everyone is welcome but there is no bonding. For the most part men are solitary creatures except for when the family group comes into play. We do hang with other guys but in the absence of the family we will spend a great deal of time alone. Older men are like old bears in that we tend to wander the woods aimlessly and alone. We avoid crowds. Pop culture would suggest that men are not family oriented. In truth it is very rare that a man does not want his own family. Extremely attractive men get lots of free uncommitted sex, but after a "cum-n-go," or a "bag and shag" or an "ejaculate and evacuate" he tells the girl/woman that he is just not interested in a family, which is a lie. For the right babe, he would commit.

Speaking of lying to women, does anybody really think the sexes could get along if men didn't lie to women? Women know we are lying to them. They expect us to lie. It is a rite of passage and a tradition for men to lie to women. Women pretend not to know we are lying because they think we will say something that they can use against us later. It's a workable system.

It is still about sex. Actually, it is *mostly* about sex and the resulting procreation. Men don't trust women sexually because we men are naturally whores and will almost always cheat when we get the chance. We assume that women think the same as we do and will cheat on us as available. If a woman is sure that her husband would never cheat on her it is because he doesn't have a penis. *But,* be reassured ladies. In my opinion most men never stray sexually and not because they don't want to but because they just don't get the chance unless they are willing to hose a "very unfortunate looking" woman which is normally not worth the risk.

If you're a woman telling a guy you're pregnant the first thought in his head is, *"Is it mine?"* I suspect that this is true for almost every man. It is not because he thinks *you* can't be trusted, it is because he knows *he* can't be trusted! The random meeting of two strangers in a bar makes a good story line in a movie but is mostly a myth. Unfortunately, only a few women are that slutty, which is a damn shame.

"I am such a tramp! I let that woman have sex with me and I don't feel a bit of shame. I just need to have more respect for myself!" This is an example of something no man has ever said. Something else no man has ever said? "I don't like your boobs."

Real men don't like to dance either. Real men dance with women to get next to women. Dancing is not a proclivity of men except as a prelude to sex. Real men don't need to dance to get a woman's attention. Dancing is for cowardly wimps who are afraid to take what they want and when they want it. Women don't find cowardly wimps attractive. Why do women dance? No doubt they just like doing it. Anthropologists will suggest that it is about women putting their "stuff" out there so we men can check it out and it works. Talk about a guy getting a good look! Spinning and shuffling—rhythmically I might add—definitely puts the woman on display, definitely gives a man sufficient information to decide whether or not he would like to see her naked. It doesn't say much about personality though; but we really don't care about personality as long as she is not a raging bitch or a psycho. … Actually a raging psycho bitch is okay if she's hot enough. Such a woman can't be "contained." We definitely lust after these women even though we know that it will take a lot of balls to score. The rewards are high so some guys are willing to risk it. It is common knowledge that men have a genuine need for a sexual release occasionally. Some poor unfortunate men don't have access to sex for years and years. Going without sex for long periods of time leaves a man traumatized and depressed and feeling isolated. No man *should* have to go without sex. We need a government program!

Another thing; Real men don't do poetry. Real men kick ass. The guy who does poetry is a candy-ass. He is soft and mushy and spends too much time thinking. He needs to go eat a snake raw and he is probably gay or will come out eventually. If you're a woman going after a man who does poetry you better bring a set of cahoneas with you just in case he doesn't have any of his own. Real men don't spend much time hoping either. Real men believe in taking action to get the desired results. Wishful thinking is for the weak!

Male aggression? Seeking wealth and power? Men are famous for it. Men are scorned for it. Liberals hate us for it. Why do we do it? It's a hobby. It gives us something to do when we are bored. Wealth is seductive and it gets you laid. Wealth is power. Poor people admire wealthy people. Wealth gets you a private island in the Bahamas that you can stock with partially naked young women. You can afford to give them whatever they want so they will be *very grateful* naked young women. You could actually start a free college for hot babes. This would guarantee a continuous stream of fresh "students." You could educate them in a non-liberal environment and they would eventually become a super race of highly practical and capable hotties. They would eventually run the world! Um, … let's think about that last part for a while. Anyway, I still think a Caribbean island sounds like a great idea and you could fly to your island paradise in your own helicopter with a really hot pilot named Candy.

Quote from a friend of mine: "I want to keep my daughters away from guys like me!"

Men don't care about clean so much either! What is it with women and clean? I have known women whose lives were controlled by keeping everything clean. Their lives were a mess, but their houses were clean. My house is clean enough and I can easily find all my clothing that would otherwise be hidden away in a dark closet. My shoes are also out where I can find them and the kitchen cupboard doors are open for easy inventory control. And I know for sure that my vacuum cleaner and washer/dryer will not be wearing out for years and years. I also don't have to clean my countertops every week because the stains and dried food blend in with the mottled stone. I am saving money on cleaning supplies. I also sequester carbon with the inside of my oven. My house is environmentally friendly. Things are growing in the refrigerator! Layers of dust on the windows improve the R value of glass. You need to use my habits as a guide to save the planet.

Men don't remember every thing that we ever did together or ever said *to* the women in our lives! How is it that women always want to trap us with this? "I remember your name and I come home every night." Isn't that enough? And just see what happens if the guy forgets her birthday. You'd think women liked having birthdays. "You told me you were thirty-nine. Your sister says you're forty. Why is it Okay for YOU to forget a birthday but it's not okay for me?"

And don't test me to see if I love you! If you constantly doubt me loving you is going to be a challenge. BTW, ladies if your man doesn't lie to you it means that he doesn't love you. If he tells you the truth it is because he isn't afraid of losing you. Every man does things he doesn't want his woman to know about. He is actually trying to protect you from the truth. It is better that you don't know everything!

Sports? A man identifying with his favorite team gives him a chance to win at something even though he didn't actually participate. It is also about trashing the other guy's team and being better than they are while our women cheer for us. Women eagerly cheering for their men has happily evolved to the point where we actually hand pick the most desirable females to lead the cheering process. It only gets better in that we put them out front for all to admire and in skimpy outfits to boot. Three cheers for cheerleaders! The practice actually created a whole new category of male sexual fantasies in the same way that it added an additional attraction to sports competition. You should also note that ticket prices for sporting events can be very high; so high that only the financially successful can actually afford to go to the big game. It has become a status symbol to attend an important game and it is great to have a chance to feel good about your college or town or state no matter how useless and unskilled you personally are.

Now she wants me to throw out my porn collection. OMG! These magazines are classics! It took my years to get all these. I'm not going to just burn them. They're valuable. …"

Yes, guys like porn! We like to look at photos of naked women and watching a video of a super-hot woman getting herself thoroughly ++++++ is never gonna get dull as long as it a different woman every day. I have known women who liked porn also; obviously, smart, practical, sensible women. What would be the point of a stag or bachelor party if there weren't porn? Men also like strippers. Who doesn't respect a hot chick that has the courage to get naked in front of a bunch of drunken guys? What've you got that's better than that? I have known a couple of strippers personally. For the most part they love what they do for a living and it's tax-free income. Hookers are another matter altogether. I have a hell of a hard time criticizing a girl who is willing to trade sex for cash. It seems like a practical thing. She needs cash; I need sex. It's a win-win though there is something ingrained in me that such a thing is just a little over the line. Could there be a hint of decency buried in me somewhere? *Hmm.* … That would be seen as a weakness!

It is a rare man that doesn't have a decent streak in him. Most men are just looking for a chance to do an act of decency and be recognized for it. This is a part of who we are also. I'd like to be a hero. I want to be a hero. I don't want to get shot doing it but I do want the glory and am willing to take risks. Most men don't hesitate to commit to danger when the need presents itself. Wars are fun until the killing starts. Still, we will eagerly line up to do our duty. This is also instinct. It is instinct to protect our necessary resources at all costs. It is an instinct of survival. Yes, we men have our faults but the good things we humans have created as a race are largely the result of the impetus of men—and our desire to please our women.

VAGINITIS

Women are fond of complaining? Is that a real thing? Is it true? Possibly it is a proclivity! I have never personally known a woman I would describe as a complainer. I have known a few men that liked to complain; not real men, liberal men. A friend of mine who worked for the public works department of the city of Minneapolis once told me that as the complaining public was concerned, "the last thing you should do is give them what they want." By that he meant that once people got the idea that complaining would get results they became more likely to complain. The fact is, women have a reputation for complaining

Enter a famous, wealthy, well-connected woman born of a famous family!!!!!!! I won't mention Maria Shriver by name because I don't need another woman mad at me! Let's just say that it wasn't her but it was a woman extremely like her who publicly announced the results of groundbreaking new research. What was the focus of this most recent assault on our culture? What was the new and profound revelation? Women are paid less than men! OMG not again! I thought we had addressed this lie decades ago and that it had lost it legs as a social manipulation issue.

It was last year if I remember correctly. I was watching one of the Sunday morning talk shows hoping to get fodder for this writing. As luck would have it I struck gold in the form of a woman extremely like Rachel Maddow. For those who don't follow feminism, she has a show on MSNBC. It would not surprise me to know that you have never heard of her. The ratings for her show and for MSNBC generally are terrible. Still, she is another example of a very successful well-placed, talented female who just can't stop complaining. This particular female happens to be a lesbian. That fact is not an issue but it does play into the story. Rachel's comments focused on the same notion that Maria had addressed: women are paid less than men! This is a complaint that has been around since the days of Gloria Steinem (1970s), and it is likely based on historical facts. Today, it is one of those "facts" that can be spun either way. It is true that women earn less than men but it is not true that women are paid less than men. Actually it is against the law to pay less based on gender. What is the difference between *pay* and *earn*? *Pay* is your hourly compensation for your time. *Earn* is the amount of money you make over a measured period of time—one year for example—and can change depending upon the number of hours you work or the normal pay scale for your job. The ruse created by these two women is that *earn* is deceptively substituted for *"paid"*. Oddly enough, Rachel said women were paid seventy-seven cents for every dollar men were paid, while Maria said women were paid seventy-two cents for every dollar men were paid. Apparently women have taken a pay cut that men didn't take in that one-year time frame.

Okay, now that we have background, I have some thoughts! (Betcha can't wait for this!) Where can I hire women who are willing to do the same work as men for 25 percent less? There is a factory nearby that would be delighted to fire all the men and replace them with women willing to do the same job for 25 percent lower wages. I could act as an agent and provide labor for the factory. I could make a lot of money doing this. I could become a rich Republican. Send an application please. Clearly this is never going to happen and the women currently working at the factory are paid the same wage as men and all according to union mandates. I imagine there are a lot of nonunion employees paid much less than the production employees at this factory. This would include those who work in the offices at the factory, both men and women. Also I know of some highly placed women at there who are making a damn good living as upper management, but the fact is, women are more likely to be employed in the lower-paying office jobs. It is not discrimination. It is not bias. It is proclivity. These office jobs are not likely to be career positions and the employees assume this fact when they are hired.

Back to Ms. Maddow. I have already mentioned that my pretend

Rachel is a lesbian. It is also clear that Rachel is a lot on the masculine side (as a lesbian). She has a very authoritarian and aggressive persona. Is there a different pay grade for that? Her bio mentions a domestic partner named Susan. Given the natural attraction of mating, meaning that masculine attracts feminine and feminine attracts masculine, —as a proclivity, I assume that Susan, is indeed much more feminine than Rachel. If this assumption is true, is Susan paid less than Rachael?

Our non Marias public announcement of a new political push to even the wage scale between the sexes was the result of yet another study." It was presented in the media as a report from an obscure "commission." I am forced to speculate that the report was funded by and the commission was "commissioned" at taxpayer expense. My heart sank when I heard this story. Not because I felt sorry for women but because I knew this report was designed to do nothing but exploit women. Yes, this sham is intended to incite women to a false cause that will ultimately benefit the actual cause which is a liberal egalitarian culture. The very people who are supposed to be the benefactors of the agenda are actually pawns in a much bigger game perpetrated by feminist extremists. This report is a blatant bold-faced lie. It is based on false assumptions. The premise and theoretical foundation and assumed purpose of this report have not been factually established. It is an intentional deception that can serve no other purpose but to deceive. This report is now known as the "Shriver Report." I really doubt that Maria had much to do with the report but that she was likely recruited on behalf of women's groups in order to add celebrity to the profound new book on the topic—a book supposedly written by Maria. As I watched Ms. Shriver speak to the report she had a very uneasy look on her face. I would like to think that in her heart she knew the report was bogus which made her uncomfortable. Possibly this is just wishful thinking on my part but I would like to give her the benefit of the doubt and assume that she was morally conflicted with this report which she knew to be false, but could not refuse its public support.

What fallacies? The report is based on the false premise that we are a socialist economy in which everyone is compensated equally no matter what. This report ignores that there is no ethical premise in which an employer is required to ignore supply and demand as labor is concerned. This report is based on the false premise that there should be no differentiation for skills and experience and seniority. This report makes no allowance for the fact that some jobs are just better suited to one gender over another. It makes no allowance for supply and demand in that some jobs just don't require much skill or training and those jobs are considered secondary part-time income to the family. There is no consideration of the fact that the wages of the higher-paid men are benefiting the wife or the mother or the female children of the higher-paid earner. This is clearly not about wages. It is about advocating for women to not be dependent on men. It is about women getting jobs that they haven't earned or that they do not deserve. Are female employers exempt from paying female employees at a rate equal to men? One woman gets more, and the other woman ends up with less. Who makes that decision? This entire report is a hoax that is not accurate and not true. Those responsible for this report are desperately corrupt and are committing an act of fraud to foster a personal false agenda. They are cheating in a game-playing quest for perceived equality, and in the process, have abandoned any possibility of ending the game as equals!

I admit to watching a report about this sham on the CBS evening news. Don't condemn me for watching CBS news. I watched it in the name of research! Watching it was necessary for my work. The report included a profile of a Latino woman with two young daughters. ... If you have just assumed an image of an impoverished Mexican American family you would be mistaken. This woman was well spoken, very well educated, and almost certainly well paid, and she did not live in poverty. No information was given about her income but she had earned two master's degrees. I can only assume that she is *very* well paid. Her living environment appeared to be very nice and comfortable. But I have to ask two questions: Where the hell did the money come from to pay for the extensive and very expensive college education? And; who was raising the children while she was taking classes and studying? The point is, this woman had it all. She was not a victim of gender discrimination by any fantasy that I have ever had and yet she was presented as a "harmed" woman who only needed wages equal to men to prosper!

My thoughts this issue; No one, no one, *no one,* wants women to be discriminated against. The quality of my personal life depends heavily on the needs of mothers, sisters, daughters, friends, and lovers, all of whom are very important to me. There are no troglodyte men left alive who want women to be barefoot and pregnant. There simply is no discrimination against women beyond free enterprise, and my heart is saddened when I think of a twelve-year-old girl who in the company of her own family might have seen this story on TV and, for the first time in her life, has been led to believe that she is valued less because she is female! It is sickening and it came from a woman not a man and not the culture at large.

I do have one more question that has been troubling me. Possibly my question has been addressed by Rachel, Maria, and their allies; possibly it is something that is assumed to be true. Possibly it has not been considered at all but I gotta know Just *how* are they gonna convince every man to take a pay cut so that women's pay will be equal to men's? Equal pay is the goal, isn't it?

There is another controversy that I would like to address as a side note. Only this time the subject is feminine beauty. Apparently I am not supposed to enjoy the sight of a beautiful woman if she would prefer to be enjoyed for her accomplishments more so than her beauty. … I am not sure if that is Maria's true intention but it is definitely an inevitable result of the concept as advocated. The premise is yet another principle of feminism in that women should be more highly regarded for their talents as people rather than for their beauty. I have no problem with that but, how do I know which women to admire for their skills and which women to lust for? Other than beauty is there a method that I can use to tell the difference at a glance? We are going to need to establish a quick and obvious signal that shows whether a particular woman is worthy of being admired for her accomplishments, just in case she also happens to be beautiful. I would not want to dishonor women by making this mistake.

And; Maria was a serious hottie when she was young and I admired her accordingly. If I understand correctly I am now supposed to regard her for her accomplishments which are assumed to be more valuable than her beauty. I am willing to do so but when was this transition made? Is there a cutoff age or is it a matter of opinion? Older men would still find her very attractive! Also, are there other forms of beauty that are off-limits? Humans have always treasured beauty not just in each other but also in all physical aspects of life. And I think most every woman would choose to be beautiful if she could. As I have mentioned elsewhere, beauty is power. I should note that Maria did not choose her X-husband Arnold, for his acting or his intellect. She chose him for his fame and form.

Also; If you are an attractive young woman who would prefer to be admired for your accomplishments rather than your beauty; just wait about forty years. You are eventually going to find out just exactly what that feels like!

THE NATIONAL REGISTER OF THINGS THAT SUCK

The first fifty, in no particular order:

1. Getting up early and going to work
2. Old age
3. Disease
4. Flat tires
5. Rich people
6. Politicians
7. Snow storms
8. Taxes
9. Speeding tickets
10. Power outages
11. Cleaning
12. War
14. Warps in the fabric of space and time
15. Government
16. National registers
17. Stupidity
18. Rejection
19. Losing weight
20. Winter
21. Loneliness
22. MSNBC
23. Traffic

24. Shingles
25. Smart-asses
26. My X-wife (her best skill actually)
27. Cold
28. Leeches
29. Vacuum cleaners
30. Obama Care
31. Car wrecks
32. Afghanistan
33. Poverty
34. Losing
35. National Public Radio
36. Depression
37. Rules
38. Celibacy
39. School
40. Fat
41. Internal Revenue Service
42. Jail
43. BDLs
44. Losing;
45. Employees
46. Putin
47. Lawyers
48. Hemorrhoids
49. Politics
50. Lawyers

You have my blessing to add to this list and you can do so on my website, www.iamnotamused.com. Trying to come up with things for this list sucks.

I hope the point is clear that I am mocking the concept of a national register—*any* national register. BDLs will give you an endless line of crap as to why such things are important. I don't have a problem with that as long as it is privately funded. One thing that really sucks: the notion that there is an office somewhere in America (probably Washington, DC) that is managing national registers! The general welfare cannot possibly be served by such a list which makes it unconstitutional. What makes me want to vomit is that are hundreds and hundreds of such constitutionally illegal government offices. There is actually a register of smokestacks and silos and borrowed federal money is paying for it. The toilet of the federal government desperately needs to be flushed—and the lid put down and the water turned off and the door locked and the room quarantined and the building that houses it destroyed. ... But that will never happen because there is a group of BDLs siting around somewhere proclaiming the glory of saving our heritage for future generations and saving their government jobs in the process. And they are singing "Kumbaya," all the way to the bank at our collective expense; And that *really* sucks.

LIBERAL PSYCHOSIS

There was a time in my life when, as a volunteer, I was commonly exposed to such documents as follows. Included in these documents were many clinical diagnoses used as references to determine needed treatments and possible courses of action for those afflicted with mental health issues. I had access to professionals who could translate the documents for me and offer insights as to their meaning. In the course of these events I was made aware of *axis levels,* which were used to categorize the severity of an emotional disturbance. These axis levels also served as clinical and diagnostic standards for health-care professionals.

I am aware that the game has changed in subsequent years and I assume the definitions and standards that I learned are no longer current. I know that many common diagnoses of the time are no longer recognized at all. *The Diagnostic and Statistical Manual* (DSM) is still the standard and it is where any such references could be found. The descriptions provided in the format that follows were a part of that manual—sort of.

Given that the mental health community has yet to recognize the affliction of liberal psychosis I offer my observations. These symptoms are rated I through IV, Axis IV is the least afflicted, and Axis I is the most severe. All mentioned symptoms accumulate as the severity of the psychosis progresses.

LIBERAL PSYCHOSIS: CC SOMATOFORM; DELUSIONS, GRANDEUR

Axis IV: Votes for left-of-center politicians and supports policies accordingly, though does not necessarily understand those policies. Experiences self-gratification about political choices, with no regard for fallacies of those choices. Supports high taxes, with tax deductions as a form of social management. Accepts other liberals' arguments without question. Supports labor unions. Ignores failed liberal policies. Not normally religious;

Axis III: Openly advocates for Left-leaning politicians and their programs. Not concerned with unintended consequences of liberal policies. Argues liberal political points publicly. At times, displays a tendency to grin for no apparent reason (mild self-induced ecstasy). Believes in man-made climate change and high taxes for the rich. Is willing to kill a fetus but not a murderer. Openly condemns peaceful Christians but not violent Muslims. Cowardly. Vegan. Agnostic.

Axis II: Is sympathetic toward socialism. Doesn't care about unintended consequences of leftist policies. Doesn't care if climate change is real or not but advocates for social change accordingly. Political theory more important than political fact. "from each to each" economics. unlimited abortion. Harshly judges notions contrary to liberalism. Abhors capitalism. Mature females leave gray hair undyed. drive old Volvos. Advocates animal life but not human life. Supports minimal punishment for criminals who are assumed to be victims of their environment and therefore innocent. Vegetarian. Atheist.

Axis I: Ongoing advocacy of liberal policies, with no regard for human welfare. Believes all wealth is evil. Prays to Mother Earth. Assumes intellectual and cultural superiority to contrary viewpoints. Advocates ends-justify-the-means politics. Repeats statements in unison (group function as required behavior). Spouts negative cause-and-effect relationship of social policy as punishment for human failings. Occupies public parks as a means of public protest but doesn't know the reason for the protest, nor care. Condemns Christianity. Thinks Nancy Pelosi makes good sense.

Generally (and as best as I can recall) Axis I symptoms are considered life altering to the point that all other factors in life become secondary, as is true with any severe mental illness. Axis II would represent a very troubled mind with little hope for recovery. Both Axis III and IV have progressively less impact on the victim's' life. You might describe Axis IV as "a fully functioning person with a noteworthy proclivity." You would see this person as just your basic liberal.

Axis I and axis II Intervention is normally useless because the victim is always in denial. Another impediment to treatment is that the psychological community is also predominately liberal so it tends to under diagnose this disease.

We all know of a few Axis II liberals. They are the ranting extremists of public discourse. Treatment for these people is unlikely to occur because they remain capable of rational conversation; and at times can appear to be symptom free. To determine if an acquaintance is Axis I or II liberal psychosis afflicted, try vocally expressing, and with conviction, some absurd conservative notion, such as "everyone should be expected to make an effort to support him- or herself." If the subjects turn red, they are Axis II afflicted. If they show symptoms of passing out, they are Axis I. Simply repeating the words "free health care" "free health care" over and over is the best way to help the victim recover quickly. Axis II liberal psychosis is considered a significant mental health disorder. It is treatable as with any psychosis but delusions are rarely given up easily and treatment is a task best left to the professionals. Treatment could take a long time and most likely will involve public funding.

I have great sympathy for anyone suffering a mental health disorder. The Axis I victim is truly living a terrible inner battle of the mind. Liberal psychosis carries its own special burdens. If you know such a person, you might provide them with the occasional verbal rhetoric of an MSNBC commentator. In their psychotic state they may assume that they have transcended to, or are in the presence of, a liberal, "next life," godlike icon. This can have a very calming effect but I believe the condition to be otherwise irreversible. Good luck!

I think, therefore …?

I like to make the analogy that thinking is like a train track: every now and then the switch on the track is flipped the wrong way and we are directed to the wrong track. That isn't normally a problem for most people. Once you figure out that you have made a bad choice you just back up a bit, flip the switch the other way, and then your thoughts will flow in a more productive direction. All too often, forward progress down an incorrect track has been extensive and backing up becomes a very undesirable option. A great deal of time and much energy can have been invested in the wrong direction and we feel the need to proceed no matter the apparent fallacy. It becomes a choice to move on or to abandon the prior progress. Abandoning our investments is never an easy choice. Continuing to invest can also be a difficult choice. Conflict creates anxiety, doubt, and stress. Unless the mental traveler is supported by a strong roadbed, the track can fail to carry the load and a train wreck is inevitable. It's probably time to stop and ask directions if you find yourself meeting this description!

YOU MIGHT BE A BRAIN DEAD LIBERAL IF ...

You would fight to the end to keep a soulless murderer from the death penalty, but believe that random abortion is a reasonable "choice."

You will spare no expense to save a patch of weeds or a mud hole, calling it an "environmental victory," and never consider the environmental cost of your efforts.

You believe that because you drive an ugly car you are saving the environment.

You believe in global warming and man-made climate change, but have never personally seen a single bit of science to prove it.

You believe that conservatives are ignorant, selfish, mean-spirited buffoons, though these same people are often your close friends and co-workers.

You see the people in your society as a single group and not as individuals.

You believe that most people will naturally do the wrong thing unless people like you guide them.

You will support any social program, without regard for cost or efficiency.

You believe that the "wealthy" aren't paying their fair share, in spite of 40 percent income-tax rates.

You believe that all wealth is really owned by the community at large and that those possessing too much should give it back.

You believe that most wealthy people got that way because they were crooked or somehow cheated the poor, rather than due to their own personal diligence.

You use phrases like "food insecure" when what you really mean is "gas insecure"—as in, not having enough gas to drive to the food bank.

You are, thought challenged."

You don't explore alternatives to failed government programs intended to fight poverty and hunger, no matter how obvious other options are.

You don't question the ethics of successful and wealthy rock stars, rappers, politicians, or athletes, but somehow businessmen are intrinsically corrupt.

You will applaud flamboyant parading gays in drag, but are concerned that Cookie Monster sets a bad example.

You are not concerned about the ethics and legality of a political rally held by illegal criminal aliens held on government grounds in Washington DC.

You have no idea why so many people are so concerned about our national debt.

You believe criminals are actually victims of circumstance, and that there are no naturally corrupt people.

You would never use the term *Negro* or *black* but the inaccurate term "African American" to describe those of apparent African descent, and then assume you are culturally enlightened or being sensitive.

You have no regard for the notion that the terrible harshness of prison is the primary deterrent to crime.

You will vote for a political candidate based on gender or race, and with no concern for qualifications.

You believe that reading and understanding a document proposed as a new law is not necessary before voting in favor of that new law.

You believe that *equal rights* actually means the unequal right to force people to make the decisions you want them to make.

You see no ethical problem with condemning hardworking people to a life of servitude to the lazy and slothful and corrupt, (unconditional welfare).

You use terms such as *overrepresentation* regarding groups and crime when what you really mean is that they are a bunch of damn criminals!

You understand the concept of a "*food desert*".

You would drive ten miles to buy an energy-efficient light bulb.

You can't distinguish between an evil corporation and evil people.

And the number 1 way of diagnosing whether your brain is damaged as politics are concerned: You voted for the most unsuccessful, corrupt, and incompetent president in US history—twice— and have no idea what went wrong!

ORIGINAL WEALTH

Borrowing enormous amounts of money no matter the source then seeking out public works projects and other social expenditures as a means to infuse capital into the economy, which would then be "turned over" several times to create tax revenue which would then be used to repay the debt, is a notion completely without any theoretical economic plausibility at all. There is no science, there is no previous positive result, there is no math, there is no anything that would suggest at even the most unlikely level that such a thing is in any way possible. Not only is the previous statement true but any person with an interest in economics, any first-year non-liberal college student, an Iowa farmer, an unusually bright child would know without asking that such a plan had no possibility of success whatsoever. It's a fool's game. It is a Ponzi scheme at the highest level, the second-greatest hoax in American history. Yet in 2009, it was the driving concept of a widely supported, highly popular program of the Obama administration.

It seems clear to me that the worst legacy of the George W. Bush administration was the concept of the economic stimulus package. The plan was so incredibly terrible and unsuccessful that the Obama administration decided to adopt it as "policy," only bigger—much bigger. Indeed, it became the political rally cry of the Obama presidency. Paraphrasing his words, the only reason that the stimulus didn't work is that it was not big enough. After multiple years of absolute failure Obama still insisted that we as a nation needed even more stimulus-package funds to grow our economy. How could it be that such an otherwise intelligent man, a man who as a little known political figure managed to get himself elected president of the United States, a man who electrified the voting public, a man who would lead us out of the doldrums of the Bush administration—how is it that this "savior" could have been so desperately wrong? My personal opinion? I don't think he was wrong.

I think it was never his concern that the economic stimulus would work. *If* it worked? … Fine, so much the better, but that was never Obama's goal. I simply refuse to believe that this obviously worldly and well-educated man would bet everything, including the future of our nation, on such an incredibly and obviously unlikely plan. What was he thinking? What *was* he thinking?! … Can you say, "orgy of socialist spending"? How about "redistribution of wealth", Or "spread the wealth around"? Or "a step to the birth of the new world order". Yes, this would be the long prophesied time when humanity would evolve to a one-world status in which we all shared equally in the world's resources, a world where no one was too wealthy or too poor. A time when, at last, we would live in a culture in which everyone was truly equal. Not just financially equal, but socially equal.

Are such notions are on the edge of political thinking? They are not necessarily my conclusion regarding the current administration (as of the time of this writing). But this being a book on proclivities I mean to suggest that a part of our current president's thinking includes the aforementioned notions. According to Joe the Plumber[6], Barack Obama is a socialist. Obama did say the words "spread the wealth around." It was recorded by reporters and reported on widely. Yes, I understand that politicians say whatever the crowd they are speaking to would be most likely to respond to favorably by proclivity. In this case, "spread the wealth around" is a very incriminating statement having much more weight than a more innocuous statement such as "I will protect your free health-care plan until we are all equal" and "I will do what I want with your tax money and if it's not enough I will support social programs that will ruin the economy by borrowing fantastically absurd amounts of cash and then I will use the money to buy your vote again through social programs that give money to you that we as a country don't have and eventually all our national wealth will be dissipated to a level where you will all be equally poor as a result." God bless Obama! Yay for equality!

But I digress.

In the world of economics, *utility* refers to the useful or desirable value of anything. It is not necessarily a reference to the company that provides your gas or electric supply. For example, gold has both desirable utility and useful utility. It is shiny and pretty. Gold is also a great conductor of electricity and does not corrode which makes it the perfect material for use in electrical switches. It is at the same time, a luxury and a common commodity and has long-term value both static and intrinsic. Conversely, consider the utility of the one-cent piece commonly and incorrectly known as the penny. Its economic value is almost nothing. I have stopped keeping pennies because they have no value to me. Also, they cost more for the government to make than they are worth. So stop making them right? Wrong! It is not about the monetary value of the penny; it is about the utility value of the penny. It can be used thousands and thousands of times to create an exact amount in a monetary transaction which *is* a legal necessity. It is true that the one-cent piece is nearly obsolete as a monetary amount but I hope you see that it has more utility value than currency value and I hope you understand the difference; and also understand why our government keeps making pennies.

Most man-made products lose value over a period of time; houses for example. Other products are consumed all at once such as beer. Beer has utility in that it is refreshing … and produces intoxication. Twenty dollars spent for beer can be a good investment. Oftentimes the intoxicating and refreshing effects offer a much-needed break from our daily drudgeries. (Plus, beer is actually very nutritious.) But don't forget that beer's purchase will only return a small percentage as tax revenue. The total value of the beer becomes consumed wealth. When you drink the beer it ceases to have value and utility and the wealth value of the beer ceases to exist. The sales tax collected from the sale and production of the beer is used to support local government and an ongoing revenue stream is continued that actually started with the ingredients used to make the beer (grain, hops, yeast). Every transaction leading to the consumption of the beer benefits someone and each of those someones has a job and pays taxes. This is not true for a stimulus package. Yes, taxes are paid but they are paid from money (wealth) that we as a nation don't have. That money does not yet exist as part of or social collective wealth. It is borrowed money, and that money, (wealth) will need to be repaid with interest, eventually.

Every time a taxable event occurs the stimulus package total is dissipated because at every transaction some, if not most of the wealth is consumed for essential needs and conversely wealth ceases to exist. In a functional healthy economy it is the economic interaction of all these events that puts the beer in your hand and benefits everyone involved— and also keeps the economy moving and (hopefully) growing. Economic growth is absolutely necessary due to the mathematical realities of an ever-expanding population if we are all to share in "THE wealth."

The economic stimulus could not succeed for the reasons mentioned above. There is no mystery as to why the plan failed. The only mystery might be why the plan was attempted in the first place. Any non-liberal economist knew by obvious example that success of the stimulus was not possible. Leftists will claim that the plan was a success in that things would have been much worse without the economic stimulus package. I know of no feasible economic concept that can be applied to validate that argument. (Sort of has a lot in common with climate change doesn't it?) Success was never an option. Success could never have been the goal. Economic redistribution of wealth was the goal. The only possible outcome of this ongoing federal program is/was long-term economic recession and in this case the program has the potential to suppress the global economy for decades. Why? The wealth of the future is being spent now! At some theoretical point in time the cost of borrowing the wealth will equal the value of the wealth borrowed. Extreme devaluation of the currency is the only way to repay this debt. When this happens, the viability of our economy collapses.

The extremely low interest rates that were a result of the economic stimulus package have benefited the wealthy far more than the poor. Why? Because the cost of borrowed money (interest rates) is making capital investments much cheaper for capitalists and evil capitalists' profits are higher as a result. Expensive houses cost much less accordingly. On and on. All the fundamental behaviors of capitalists become more viable under the concepts of the economic stimulus package because capitalists will take advantage of low interest rates to improve evil profits. The legislative intention of the stimulus package was to create more cash flow for the economy which would then "trickle down", and it has but the economic chasm between the haves and have-nots has only been widened. The wealthy class has benefited and the middle class has benefited but the poor are still poor. There is no form of legislation in which economic equality can be mandated. There is simply no scenario in which an egalitarian culture can exist in prosperity for all and the common wealth that many people believe should be equally shared is always the result of an individuals sacrifice and hard work. There are no exceptions. Taking it (wealth), no matter how you receive it is stealing from if not enslaving those who created it. The economic stimulus as presented by the Obama administration was conceived to circumvent this reality. The poor get money that does not belong to anyone—yet.

GOVERNMENT WASTE

It is easy for me to think of an example of ridiculous "government" waste. Many such programs are funded through the Department of Agriculture and I have been the benefactor of the grossly inefficient programs and wasted funds given that I farm for a living. The most offensive examples I frequently ponder are the Conservation Reserve Program (CRP) and the Wetlands Reserve Program (WRP), which are having virtually no positive benefit to our environment or to our climate. The theories that guide these programs don't have the potential to benefit our environment equal to the wealth consumed at the expense of the environment. They also have the effect of reducing supplies of available grain. Lower supplies of grain will always produce higher prices for food. In taxes paid and higher food costs the public loses twice. The Soil Conservation Service has long since become obsolete in terms of having any real benefit to the environment and to saving soil. Also its cost-effectiveness is desperately poor. It has been many decades since farmers became profoundly aware of the intrinsic personal value to the individual farm as protecting soil is concerned and as a farmer myself, it is in my best interest to maintain the soil in as healthy a way as can possibly be done. Also as a perfect example of misguided thinking, wildlife benefits were touted as a great benefit to habitat. Yet in recent decades the population of pheasants in my area has plummeted to historic lows to the point that hunting them has become a forgotten pastime by many would-be hunters. Quail have virtually disappeared from the landscape while millions of costly acres have been put to supposed quail and pheasant "habitat." Why have those game birds disappeared? Because of environmental factors having nothing to do with grass land habitat. Vast public funds have gone for nothing as is typical of "collective" thinking and public funding.

As mentioned farmers and agriculture have been the darling of tax-payer-funded support for many generations. Does America need farmers? Of course we do! What is assumed by the previous question and what is not true is that if any one farmer goes broke, there will be less agricultural production. Virtually every farmer wants to expand his or her operation. Any unsuccessful farm will be quickly and eagerly absorbed by the surrounding neighbors and the available farmland will likely be more efficiently farmed and accordingly more profitable. Production will not be decreased by the lack of farmers. A cycle of recent profitability in farming has led to a very aggressive if not a conflicted climate among farmer neighbors. Increasing land values has made even modest-sized farms financially healthy. There is a great deal of wealth in agriculture. America needs us and we need America but subsidizing farmers through tax dollars has only one effect on agricultural production; the cost of production goes up by the amount of the federal subsidy. Rental incomes of wealthy retired landowners go up. The price and value of farmland goes up. Demand for tax-deductible equipment goes up and so does the price of equipment accordingly. Seed, fertilizer, chemicals—and on and on—all go up when the suppliers know we can afford to pay the increase. Higher profits also lead to more planted acres which increases demand for inputs which leads to a higher cost for those inputs. Farming lives or dies by supply and demand on both sides of the equation. Your taxpayer subsidies are not helping farmers become more profitable, and they are not producing greater quantities of cheaper food for the world in the modern day of agriculture. The only groups that really benefit are the already moderately wealthy landowners and politicians!

The real value of farmer subsidies is the political brownie points for liberals who convince the voting public, and themselves that they have made a difference for the betterment of the world. It's another Kumbaya moment for liberals. I assume that you can think of many such examples of absurd government waste in your own life assuming you are not a liberal. The more of our national resources the government controls the less national wealth there will be for all. Government by proclivity spends wealth very inefficiently. The more national wealth the government is spending, the greater the waste and the less collective wealth the nation will have and it has a multiplier effect. Why? Because the wasted funds could have been used by private enterprise to create more wealth. Government does not create wealth. It consumes wealth! Government cannot operate at a profit. It can only consume the wealth and the resources of the nation. Even if we assume that there is no government waste it is still true that government can only consume resources. The disposition of these resources is at best a hopeless and futile battle carried out by Congress and congressional efficiency is historically very bad. Government building national infrastructure is still government consuming resources and is conversion of wealth to utility. Converting wealth to utility is a good thing normally but when wealth is consumed it cannot be used for profit-making purposes. It either ceases to exist or it is converted to other purposes or it is stored as a static form of wealth. Gold in a vault for example, is a static form of wealth. So is your house.

"Wealth is not finite." This simple statement is the most important thing any non-capitalist can know about economics. If more wealth is created nationally than is consumed nationally the nation becomes more wealthy. When there is more wealth nationally there is more wealth to go around for everyone. Poor people are not poor because wealthy people are rich. If all the wealth of the extremely rich were given to the poor the wealth of the rich would soon be dissipated and consumed by the poor and therefore cease to exist. Eventually the wealth is going to be dissipated one way or another—either by the excesses of the wealthy or by the necessary consumption of the poor. Wealthy people spend a lot of money. That is the motivation for becoming wealthy. This money mostly goes to working people who make the things the wealthy consume.

Just because someone has a hundred million dollars doesn't mean that they have that much in available money to spend. Typically great wealth is in the form of static assets such as homes or commercial buildings. It is about total possessed net worth: income cash and other assets which collectively describes "the wealthy." Only creating a continuous and expanding stream of new wealth will help the poor and the wealthy are very likely to do this. The less fortunate will always need added resources to provide for their needs but only by adding to their personal economy through productivity can the cycle of poverty be broken. As long as the poor are dissipating wealth beyond what they are personally creating—and also dissipating wealth created by others—the entire economy must suffer. This is a simple and indisputable fact. Accordingly, less wealth will be available to support the poor. Less tax revenue will be available to support government. Again, wealth is not finite. Wealth results from an endeavor of human activity that creates something of value, usually as a result of exploiting the resources of the planet. The food we eat is an obvious example. It is the food that I create as a farmer in quantities well beyond my personal needs that I sell for cash to add to my personal wealth. I will eventually buy farm equipment with some of these funds and when I do an economic stream is begun. This describes the notion of original wealth. Liberalism and a socialest mind-set cannot thrive if these facts are commonly understood. There is no public forum where these ideas are taught and these ideas lie in direct conflict with a centralized social control mandate.

Wealth, or things of value are constantly being created and consumed. That's what economics is and all wealth is in a state of transition. There is no such thing as completely static wealth! The value (utility) of a pound of apples has never changed, only the price.

I could never to pretend to capture all the subtleties of an economy. It is a concept far too complex for me, or the experts to pin down. What was true last week might not be true next week. It is dynamic and constantly changing and the economic power brokers are tipping the scale. Politics make it worse.

The grossly wealthy make news because of their extreme excesses and assumed corruption. The poor make news because we as a culture sympathize with their plight and normally with no regard for the cause. Not all the wealthy are corrupt. Not all the poor are slothful. Not all the poor are ambitious.

Government spending cannot create original wealth, no matter how that money is spent.

Much of the crop I produce is sold to foreign nations which brings foreign original wealth back to the US. Again; the only way to create wealth is through some form of active productive effort.

Wealth can also be gained from a foreign source by the production and sale of "value added" items. Chopping up a log so that it can be burned as firewood is an example of "value added." In this case, value was added when personal labor processed an otherwise useless log into conveniently useful firewood. As a nation wealth is created by the free enterprise of its people to produce something that increases in value and that did not exist or was not available before they made it so. Turnover in currency wealth does create tax revenue but this process dissipates the investment by the percentage of wealth that is not returned as tax revenue per exchange. Taxes should be collected given that the resources of the nation have been collectively consumed and it is reasonable that a portion of those consumed resources support government.

Only original wealth can replace previously consumed wealth at its original value or utility. If the money was borrowed cash from a foreign nation wealth is lost twice because the money is now not available for future conversion to utility and interest must be paid on the funds, which is the process of direct dissipation of wealth that can never be converted to utility. This is one more reason that the economic stimulus package did not work. This is the reason Obama should not have been reelected. The plan never had any potential to work. It was well known among those with the simplest grasp of capitalist economics that such a thing was absolutely impossible yet those who would gain personal wealth through government redistribution of wealth voted in favor of continued support of this failed political agenda. Our economy could only falter in that less wealth is being created than is being consumed. And again the only thing that could make this scenario worse is that the wealth being distributed and consumed is *borrowed* money. You should be very pissed off about this fact unless. ...

Confused? So am I. The fact is that every politician knows this scenario or something similar to it. This ain't rocket science. It is basic knowledge and understanding among educated people who are not liberal extremists. In the era of economic stimulus packages we are compelled to ask the $20 trillion question, what in the hell were they thinking? It is a sad fact that George W. Bush just didn't know better and the Democratic (socialest) Congress ran with the notion. By the time it was known to be not working Obama was the president of the united states and had a rubber-stamp Congress in his pocket. The two levels of power determined that the only reason the stimulus didn't work is that it was not big enough which led to an ever-expanding increase in economic stimulus funds and years of recession inevitably followed.

The tough question for me is this one disturbing scenario: was it always about redistribution of wealth for Barack? He had to know that the stimulus scheme would not work or was at the very least, mathematically unlikely (read: "impossible"). He had to know this. He is by proclivity and as described by Joe the Plumber a socialist. He is a socialist of color, a socialist of color whose people had been victimized for centuries, held in poverty and repressed at every level of society in modern times and also held as slaves historically. Such a thing must not be easily put aside even for a man of his wisdom. It would appear logical that his decision-making might have been jeopardized as a result of these facts, and possibly the nation has suffered accordingly.

The trump card in any economy is and will always be "what people believe." When the social-oriented government (i.e., the Obama administration) came to power, investment in our economy faltered.

Why? Capitalists—those who held available investment capital—believed that the likely return on investment would be less and responded with caution. Absurdly expensive social programs absolutely would dissipate wealth and accordingly, returns on investment would be less likely to produce a profit worthy of the risk. Our economy faltered because capital investment slowed. We can disagree about the dissipation of wealth and its effect but it does not necessarily need to be true. Our human proclivity is based much more on what we believe to be true than any other factor. We capitalists believed that any investing would become riskier and responded accordingly. Worldwide flow of wealth slowed and like the fall of dominoes the global economy faltered. Our American economy is one of the two largest economic entities on the planet and is still the most influential. If dissipation of wealth exceeds creation of wealth in the United States we will spend less in China and their economy will have less wealth as a result. Accordingly, they will buy fewer of my soybeans and the monetary value of my beans will go down. They have been buying a lot of my beans and with American money! Production and sale of original wealth as crops recaptures our original "original wealth" when China spends our money with US.

It is rarely reported in the media (liberal by proclivity) that the Chinese economy also made the same sort of stimulus investments that we did in the USA. Ultimately like many other countries, they have an enormous and looming public debt to repay and have fantastically overbuilt residential and retail properties that are a burden to their economy. They also have an enormous advantage over our nation in that they have a nearly endless pool of cheap labor to draw on. Also, they are not financially supporting masses of unproductive citizens through government programs or encouraging the poor of other nations to come to their country and share in "the wealth," as we are.

Labor is the primary source of original wealth! Ultimately, all wealth has its beginning with the endeavors of human activity. This activity can be fostered as an individual entity or organized as a collective (a.k.a., corporations). Capitalists organize human activity to create original wealth and everyone benefits. The less the cost of human activity—labor—the more wealth created for the evil capitalist. The balance between labor costs and excess exploitation of labor is a never-ending issue socially. The Chinese and have a great advantage over the United States in that the production cost of labor is less; this is well known. Apparently union organizers don't speak Chinese. It is a very popular argument that capitalists make too much money and that labor is exploited accordingly. No one will publicly argue against a well-paid labor force. There is little debate. What is also not debated is that the fewer people who are laboring, the less wealth of all forms there is that is being created. In summary; The more people not laboring the more the social cost to those who are laboring in the form of redistribution and as a percentage of their income as taxes. Less wealth will be available to invest in the creation of new additional wealth. The results are what happened during the Obama administration and its Democratic Congress.

Leftists claim the Obama recession started while George W. Bush was in office and it did. What the myopic Left will never accept is that once it became apparent that America would soon have the most liberal government since the FDR years. Capitalists and capital funds with all their perceived profits, became less certain of profitable and reasonable risk. Again; capitalists pulled capital from the economy and the increasing snowball to a world wide recession was unstoppable. The timing is absolutely undeniable and the recession began when Joe the Plumber declared that the person who was most likely to become the next president of the United States was a socialist.

Government investment is different than private investment in that it does not concern itself with profit! The measure of risk does not follow normal convention. Government might invest in a solar-panel project without determining if the project is likely to be successful and profitable. The administrator of the project will not focus on cost controls and necessary profitability with the dedication that a free-enterprise capitalist would. Wages paid might be "above scale." The results of this non-theoretical project are now a matter of history. Much wealth was consumed and dissipated. It was wealth that we did not have as a nation. It was borrowed wealth. No utility was created by this wealth. The project was a scam and the cost of this scam must be recouped by future tax revenue from original wealth that has yet to be created. Why have no criminal charges been considered? Why hasn't our president owned up to these mistakes? Liberals supporting Obama will not concern themselves with this costly political failure given that in their minds all wealth is public property and/or all wealth is gained with the permission of the state. I also have to point out that this project was conceived on the notion that solar panels would help the environment which is a favored cause of leftists who will spend freely for such programs. For them, funding was a no-brainer and the project was funded without regard for feasibility. Not only did the project consume wealth, it also had the effect of creating a tremendous amount of pollution. Consider all the fuel consumed and coal burned to make metals and endless resources wasted—all at the expense of the environment. Trees cut and oil wells drilled and tires created and used up and on and on and on. It was an environmental lose-lose and would have also been a political lose-lose if we had a Republican administration.

Conservative economics is not a perfect world by any means. Capitalists tend to be the financially aggressive among us by proclivity. Aggressiveness generally speaking, breeds contempt for the "rules," and may abandon social convention in the name of enhanced profits, also known as *greed*.

Aggressors commonly try to stay one step ahead of the rules. Rule books tend to get thicker over time as society attempts to regulate the latest schemes of aggressors. Blatant theft and corruption make headlines and the left condemns capitalism again. The media love such stories knowing that most of its listeners are not wealthy and will be unsympathetic to news stories condemning greedy capitalist aggressors. The financial bailout of the banking industry was another fabulous mistake for the Obama presidency. While it appears to have been directed to save troubled banks the actual benefactors were those consumers holding loans with those troubled banks in that they were able to walk away from overpriced upside-down properties with no continuing obligation. It was the house-buying public at large that apparently benefited from the banking bailout. Obama will not receive leftist political points for this nor will he be condemned. Do an Internet search today and you would assume that the bank bailout was not an Obama administration event. To a fault, those websites are mostly liberal media renditions of the events with no easily discernible notion that the bailout was a result of an Obama administration policy and decision. This is bias that under any other circumstances would be considered corrupt!

These capitalist banks needed to fail at least to the point where investors' assets were lost. It was capitalist banks that were also saved by the bailout. The pop culture Left-leaning media condemned capitalists for their political and financial gains at federal expense all while proclaiming the glory of a successful federal mandate. (AKA, Duplicity)! In this case any search you did on this historic event would also be dominated by Left-leaning media articles and those articles support the notion of successful bailout results. As a capitalist I want those banks to have failed financially and the personal assets of the investors and owners of the banks to be lost. Liberals/socialists actually missed a chance to nationalize banks. Fortunately their lack of understanding of economic issues saved this country from a further faltering economically. Capitalism is made more viable by the risk of failure. Failure must be part of the equation. This failure should never be at public expense. Failure at public expense is known as socialism and socialism is best known for its poverty. It was a lose-lose for our nation yet it was supported by both political parties.

It is absolutely shocking how little understanding there is of the basics of economics among the general population. It is rare to hear liberal media conversations that accurately reflect the realities of economics. Also, a liberal agenda cannot concern itself with economic principles. Liberalism can only exist in an environment in which a priority to social policy circumvents the needs of an economically strong nation. The principles of either are in direct conflict with the other. The only possible result of this fact is that any given economy will be lessened by a ratio equal to the percentage of the non-self-supporting population as compared to those who do profit enough to provide for their own needs. Liberalism cannot thrive in or sustain a prosperous economy if a liberal agenda is the national priority. Liberalism will always self defeat its own intended goal.

BACKGROUND THINKING

LIBERAL VERSUS CONSERVATIVE

She believed, no she justified the decision that it was okay to ride my bike not because she didn't regard me but because in her background thinking, (as a liberal/socialist by proclivity), she didn't make a distinction as I did that it was my personal property and that I had total autonomy over what and when things; (if any), would happen to my bike which does include her riding it. In her mind the bike was an autonomous object, an independent thing, a component of the universe like air or the stars. She by proclivity did not give my ownership of the bike much due when the urge to try the ride became her dominant thought. It wasn't that she meant to defy me, it's that the culturally imposed expectation of compliance with my ownership was less of an influence upon her than the notion of the "no one person completely owns anything; share and share alike" idea that is her background reference point and is the "socialest" notion of the collective human experience.

I prefer to use my self-styled word, *socialest,* which means "the way in which a socialist behaves." I don't want you to get caught up in the classic conflicted definition of the term *socialist.* Far too many people ("liberals") scoff at the very sound of the word "socialist," as if there were nothing real to the concept. Given that fact, I would like to revisit the actual meaning and concept of the word and give you a fresh perspective on the "one and all" notion of earth and society and the human group and individual components of the group. Of being born of a background proclivity that is the basic reference point to all personal thoughts that make us liberal, centrist, or conservative. Social*est* is a notion that places its priorities on the group and not on the individual. It is the idea that everything of value to the group is the resource of the group equally and available to all individuals of the group as needed. It assumes that all individuals of the group will participate equally in the group (or as appropriate). The social-*est* differs from the social-*ist* in that the dictionary definition of the socialist is different from the common meaning that we give it today. We think of the socialist in the way that I have described the socialest but the socialist is more accurately described as a person opposed to free-market capitalism. The social*est* is meant to describe a blend of socialist and communist. Karl Marx called socialism a transition between capitalism and communism.

In our daily lives we unconsciously use our background thinking as a reference point to our thinking and decision making process. Our background thinking is our personal computer program. It is literally what makes us who we are and directs what we say and do. You can't learn to be a liberal, centrist, or conservative. No amount of lecturing and preaching can convert any of us from our natural cultural reference point. No matter your education or other influences you will eventually adopt a liberal, centrist, or conservative political viewpoint as is consistent with your proclivity.

Nancy Pelosi is the perfect example of this proclivity. She was born with a severely liberal mind. Nothing can change that fact. While making an observation of her thinking as she is speaking, it is easy for me to understand why you may assume that the woman is ignorant. It is quickly clear when she speaks that she has no concept of the simplemindedness of her politics but she is actually a very smart woman who simply places a greater priority on the short-term benefit of the group generally speaking, as and when she is advocating her political policies. It simply is not a part of her understanding or concern that she is confiscating the wealth of others both current and future and sacrificing the prosperity of those others in the process. It is shortsighted and naive, yes but is not a lack of intelligence. A case might be made that the people voting for her are dim witted but she is not. She is compelled by an inner need and emotion-based reasoning to provide for her social group and its perceived immediate individual needs. As a politician she unconsciously sacrifices the long-term good of the group to meet her personal need to gratify her own proclivity immediately; and she is personally rewarded by the fruition of a self-aggrandized plan. The woman genuinely believes she has changed the world for the better though she is only creating a much bigger problem with tragic social consequences that others will need to solve eventually. She is actually the conspiring government agent though she has magnanimous intent. This apparently sweet and simpleminded woman is actually the unintentional tyrant. It is an amazing contrast that the apparently selfish and harsh conservative mind-set so commonly maligned by liberals actually describes the person who will give you the best chance to prosper.

As for the BDL, it is my observation that the average "very liberal" mind appears to be unusually uninformed if not ignorant of and suffering from a systemic absence of ordinary knowledge and a functional understanding of the daily workings and mechanics of our social group. Decisions and opinions involving cultural issues are motivated by emotion rather than by pragmatic facts. The BDL will advocate right or wrong based on feelings and not practical functional application.[7] The objective evaluative thought process has apparently failed or never existed. I can confirm that the "very" liberal people that I know personally are also very if not profoundly naive and show no tendency (i.e., proclivity) to expand personal wisdom. Instead such people advocate in favor of theoretical principles that have not necessarily been validated. Thus, efforts to increase their own social knowledge have also been stymied.

I feel I should recognize at this point that it is only a matter of time until some BDL condemns me for being insensitive because I use the term brain-dead liberal. This phrase could be seen as offensive to the brain-dead! Yes, there are families whose loved ones are brain-dead. I don't intend to slight their tragedy and I don't intend to insult the brain-dead by comparing them to liberals.

It is clear that President Obama's proclivity is/was toward socialism.

He is also inclined to copy the European economic model of government, one in which the government controls most of the nation's resources and only the social elite have any real wealth which results in a relatively small middle class. The bulk of the population leads an austere yet comfortable life but has little in the way of an opportunity to climb the rungs of the socioeconomic ladder. BDLs often refer to Europe as an example when debating US government policy. It is considered tawdry in this economic/social model for the non-aristocratic class to possess conspicuous wealth.

Personally, I was born a conservative with a centrist slant. I can't be changed. I was born this way. It is my proclivity. I will have moments where I waver back and forth between the social boundaries of my tendencies but when challenged I will always come back to my personal center. Like most people when I was young I might have been considered a Left-leaning centrist as my schooling in the liberal education system ended. As I aged I evolved to see the travesty of liberalism as manipulation-free thinking became my daily experience. This happened in spite of the fact that conservative advocacy was not politically popular at the time. This was a very liberal period in world history. It was the 1970s.

My personal value judgments;

1. It is and always will be up to me to decide when and where I share the fruits of my endeavors through charity. I believe in charity and I agree that we all should practice it given the appropriate time and place as based on our personal values and discretion. To require me by law or social fiat to participate in charity against my will and discretion is tyranny. A political program that requires my contribution to any charity indefinitely enslaves me especially when it is obvious that no long-term solution to the charitable need is feasible.

2. I shall do nothing that will hinder the life of another person for my own personal gain.

3. I will respect the religious beliefs of others no matter how absurd those beliefs might be but only when no one is likely to be harmed because of those beliefs.

4. For me it is a matter of ethics and fairness. The collective can't

exist without someone giving more than his or her fair share and/or without someone receiving more than his or her fair share. Both shares will be determined by personal proclivity to produce or consume not by ability unless otherwise controlled through state autonomy. It is impossible that we will all contribute by equal effort or receive by equal need even if we would all choose to do so.

5. There will always be those who choose not to fend for themselves beyond the here-and-now need. This proclivity will leave them vulnerable to an eventual need that is beyond their personal acquired resources. That is not my problem.

6. I may eventually need socialest help to survive. That *is* my problem. I will live my life as best I can to sublimate the eventual need of a socialest solution for my own issues. I hope I will be able to help supplement the needs of others who are important to me as necessary. I expect everyone to do the same.

7. There will always be those among us who will need help to thrive or survive. It is unthinkable to let such people falter and we should collectively help them but they have no right to choose that level of help by government-imposed fiat. If circumstances require it, I will live my life by this same standard.

As a capitalist I have assumed the responsibility of providing for my own needs as best as I am able. In fact I am almost daily working toward excess funds needed so that in a time of greater personal need such as medical problems I will have the funds available for this need. No other person has been deprived of anything because of my pursuit of excess wealth. I would not pursue such excess profits if it were not for the benefit of reserve profits. If I were not profiting from my endeavors I would pursue a different means of providing for my needs and for the needs of those most important to me and I would still maintain a reserve. I will never demand or vote that anyone else must provide for my needs. To me the notion of voting to confiscate the wealth of others for my own needs is morally corrupt and morally corrupt to the same degree as theft at the point of a gun no matter the need.

I have to ask what might the personal value judgments of a leftist extremist look like if listed as I have listed mine? I offer some possibilities:

1. I will fabricate whatever reality is necessary to foster my personal agenda.
2. The ends justify the means.
3. You didn't do that alone.
4. I will do whatever I can to eliminate individual prosperity.
5. Your money is not really yours. It belongs to the state and you have taken too much of it.
6. I will suffer unless the wealthy support me.
7. Even though I am wealthier than you are I still think you have too much money so I am going to take some of it and give it to other people so that they will vote for me. After all who besides me should have wealth, power, and control?

Over the top, maybe, but real and true—absolutely!

It is inescapable that there are many among us who will simply choose to accept—or who are resigned to accept a social charity minimal wealth living. We have as a component of our society a subculture that expects nothing more of itself.

BDLs like Vice President Joe Biden take great pleasure in condemning capitalists for their unethical proclivities. Practices such as price gouging, price fixing, exporting jobs, making employees work all day, etc., etc., are some common examples. Joe would never make a negative value judgment against the notion that once a potential employee accepts a job he or she doesn't have the right to determine compensation for that job. Personally about me—I am doing this writing for profit! I think I will take … $25 million as compensation. Sounds about right. I only want a living wage! I just want a very good living wage. On second thought, I think I will need a private jet. Better make that $50 million. (Oh, and income taxes will take half of that money so I will actually need $100 million.)

"Ask not what your country can do for you, but what you can do for your country."

John Fitzgerald Kennedy, former Democratic president of the United States of America.

Some *current* political principles?.

JFK, the lost hero of the Democratic Party of the 1960s, would today be persecuted by the current (liberal) media culture as a right-wing extremist. How dare anyone suggest that we should not ask what our country can do for us? Today the issue of what the government can do for you *is* the standard way a politician gets elected and it is the only campaign strategy for demoncrats. Can you imagine how very harshly any politician would be criticized by the Left-leaning politico for suggesting that we as citizens should expect less from the government than we are willing to give to the government? That we should be expected to do more for our country than our country would do for us? Can you imagine what President Obama would say as a "quotable phrase" given the same historical parameters that existed during the historic Kennedy speech? It might go something like: "Ask not what your country needs form you but what you will get from me after I take all the money from the rich."

And I think, "Your government money will be coming soon.," is definitely Obama's most utilized political strategy.

Some other liberal possibilities:

"Ask not what your country can do for you, but what your politician can do for you!"

"Ask not what you can do for your country, but if your country is really worth helping."

"Ask not where you can find a job, but how much money you will get in food stamps and housing subsidies.".

"Ask not how to succeed on your own, but how to survive on the generosity of others."

"Ask not where to find the welfare office; the welfare people will find you."

"Ask not what your health care will cost; you can get it completely free."

"Ask not what your country can do for you! Wait a minute; yes, ask what your country can do for you and we'll use your money to do it so that you will vote for us. Oh, and don't worry if we don't have any money left over; we'll just borrow it from foreign nations. Yes, we leftist politicians will actually borrow money from the Chinese to buy your vote! Isn't America wonderful?"

LABOR UNIONS

How do we justify the politics of the labor union, the longtime financial backbone of the Democratic Party? I know for sure that the average laborer just wants a job—a good job yes, but the main priority of laborers is the job itself and these loyal employees have little if any concern for leftist politics. And we may safely assume that as many of these employees are conservatives as are not. Yet labor union leaders traditionally fund politicians of a Left-leaning nature and do so with a certain absence of concern for the choices half of the union members would otherwise make, and will do so while proclaiming capitalist management to be unethical.

I have friends who work for a local John Deere factory. Some are hard-core union supporters and all workers at the factory benefit from the union's presence regardless of whether or not they are hard-core leftists. Typically these workers have little if any knowledge of the politics that their union dues support. Also these skilled laborers typically tend to be conservative when questioned about the sort of politics their personal political beliefs would advocate. If you want to have some fun with union members enlighten them about some of the political policies and candidates that their union is supporting. Gun control is usually good for a hot reaction and they tend to hate Obama! Keep in mind that to work at this factory you must be a union member. Your participation is not optional. Union dues are not optional and your personal politics are of no concern to union leaders. If you are a hard-core right-winger and want a job at this factory you have no choice but to support liberal politics whether you like it or not. Is that tyranny? I will look up the word *tyranny*: "arbitrary use of power and control." *Hmm!* Possibly I should have looked up the word *corruption*.

I won't criticize unions for trying to get all the money they can in the form of wages but it must be true that the concept of exporting jobs had its genesis with labor unions. I am not sure exactly how a job can be exported. The notion sounds like babaloney to me. We can export cars or corn but I am not convinced that exporting a job is actually possible. Is there a cargo ship that exports jobs and is it profitable for the shipper? What does this ship look like? Clearly the notion involves moving a factory to another place to reduce labor costs and increase capitalists' evil profits and probably evil corporate profits. Exporting jobs sounds very much more sinister than moving a factory and BDLs commonly exploit this ploy. Could this be a ruse to influence public opinion in favor of labor unions and the Democratic Party? Surely not! Here is another description: "Relocating an out-of-date production facility." The unions have a long history of corruption and greed of union bosses. The union format fosters a single-minded self-serving policy that has no regard for the national economy as a whole. Some employers will exploit the needs of available labor at a minimal compensation level creating hostility and resentment among workers. Eventually the workers revolt. No surprise there. There is definitely a need to prevent repressive exploitation of labor. The unions originally formed as a result of this exploitation and eventually became a powerful political voting bloc. The Democratic Party adopted unions and their cause but the party exploited labor by confiscating wages in the form of high taxes. These taxes were used to pay unemployment benefits when the workers lost their jobs because the market could no longer support the high cost of their labor and the companies eventually relocated. Labor is screwed again only this time it is voluntary—sort of. And yet the labor unions claim capitalists are corrupt!

In some cases, union labor comes at a cost of as much as fifty dollars per hour or more to the employer. I could never justify my job as a skilled laborer at a rate of fifty dollars per hour. I am not worth fifty dollars per hour given that the job I might be doing would be eagerly filled by thousands of people willing to work for half that rate. I would willingly work for less except that my union has an all-controlling death grip on the evil, greedy, corrupt capitalist owners of the company that my organized labor union works "for."

Labor unions are also a socialist microcosm of our culture. The collective organization known as labor unions is the best example of what happens in a socialist economy. The masses (a.k.a., labor) demand their fair share. Also nonworking (i.e., retired) members require ongoing support at the expense of the collective funded by the payer, which is the company and in this case is equal to the socialist state. State funds require replenishment from the collective (a.k.a., taxes/union dues). The bosses (politicians) gain power and control and require their "cut" from the union dues/taxes. It is only a matter of time until the power and the cash breed corruption (as in our current form of government). In the meantime the cost of labor and therefore the cost of production goes up through external union (collectivist) manipulation. The sale price of produced goods goes up as a result of increased cost of production as labor. All who consume union-produced products pay more for these products and therefore need to receive additionally higher wages to off-set the increased cost of buying union-made products. It is a hopelessly closed loop except for the external influences of non-collectivist and much cheaper foreign labor. This is what happened to American labor in the last decades of the twentieth century.

EVIL -CORPORATIONS?

If your proclivity is to the hard Left you are likely fond of condemning evil corporations. For the record corporations are not evil; people can be evil but corporations are a form of business. Corporations are actually the "collective" notion of doing business. It is literally the masses that support an organization—usually for profit so that the collective may share in the evil profits. Yes, capitalists are actually leftists, as corporations go. It is also true that if you are running or managing a corporation and you are paying taxes on corporate profits you are doing it wrong. Corporate stockholders pay their taxes as personal income or as capital gains when actual funds are transferred to the owners as income or when the stock is sold. A well-run corporation should normally show a min-imal profit. This is intentionally done as a means to avoid being taxed twice commonly referred to as *double taxation*. Yes, there is corruption in corporate management and it is carried out in despicable ways that the average person never hears about but mostly as a means to avoid paying taxes, which for most of us is an American tradition. Here is an example of another leftist deception/lie: Why the hell should any American corporation doing business in another country pay taxes on profit from that country to the US Treasury? Do we expect corporations in France doing business in the United States to pay income taxes to France for profits earned in the USA? *No-o-o-o!* Your leftists pundits would have you believe this is true and that American corporate taxes on profits from foreign sources are underpaid to the US government even though those corporations have already paid taxes on those profits elsewhere. Again, the ends justify the means as leftist pundits go. Is it a blatant political lie or just common ignorance when leftists claim corporations are making billions in profits without paying taxes, also referred to as *corporate welfare.* In truth, the United States is the only nation that does collect taxes on foreign profits. Without the option of a profitable corporate structure the non-wealthy would never have a chance to participate in a profitable large-scale business. It is a lie on two levels. Did you vote for these people and their agenda; an agenda that claims it is capitalists who are corrupt! To me the people who make these claims are cultural trash. What do they really want?

I don't think I need to spend my time pointing out the pitfalls of unethical capitalists. These pitfalls are well documented and are a constant source of media chatter in our daily lives. The proclivity of the media, as I have pointed out is to advocate leftist politics using capitalist methods for corporate profit. Leftism sells. The same is true of talk radio with an opposite twist. Making fun of BDLs is fun and entertaining. It is very easy to point out the fallacy of leftist politics from a humorous and ironic perspective. On the other hand right wing bashers are anything but amusing. They assume a posture of a superior intellect and a more evolved wisdom which is rarely seen as funny. Were you a follower of Jon Stuart on comedy central? He used a method that I call *assumptive innuendo* in which he makes a brief statement or reference; followed by a stupid-looking expression inducing the audience to assume that there is an unstated brilliance which would be otherwise obvious though not specifically identified. The audience may actually have no idea of the facts but they laugh as if they have understood and are amused although nothing original or clever has been said. Ellen DeGeneres uses this same method. It is a telling example of the methods the Left uses to manipulate the public surreptitiously. Sarcasm is really the only tool leftists have when bashing conservatives. Why was Jon Stewart on Comedy Central anyway? He used the same laugh track for two decades. Oh, and the slut who does *Politically Incorrect* (I don't care to use his name) is an unethical slime ball of global proportions. The name of his leftist TV program is a lie. How can we be expected to value anything he says when the very first thought that comes to the viewer (i.e., the name of his show) is a flagrant bold-faced lie? Are you a fan of his? If so, I suggest you do some introspective thinking.

It is the proclivity of the liberal mind-set to manage society as a group (i.e., the collective). It is the proclivity of the conservative to manage his or her life individually. It is an inescapable reality that managing a society as a group also requires mass communication (a.k.a., the media). The conservative is less likely to pursue mass communication by lack of need. This is the basis for my belief that public media are notably Left leaning by proclivity.

It strikes me as amazing that so many of the venues of our lives are oriented with a Left-leaning perspective. Consider grade schools, high schools, and colleges; network news, radio, and newspapers. Leftists even have their own publicly funded radio and TV networks, not to mention the once federally funded Democratic advocacy group, ACORN. All are Left leaning by proclivity (or design) and all are collectively directing our pop culture. Yet in the face of this, conservatism thrives. The media groups that advocate conservatism are growing but mostly are filling in a vacuum in the media culture. Conservatism thrives in the face of default widespread condemnation. There has to be a message in that fact.

I count myself as a conservative but I also am well aware that pure capitalism and strictly conservative policies will not serve our nation well. There absolutely is a need and moral obligation for "well-funded" people to help support those who can't fully support themselves. It is also true that chronically impoverished people will rise up against the wealthy if they aren't well treated by the wealthy or if they don't have a chance to share in that wealth. The problem arises when there are too many people being supported by the productive for wealth to be sustained nationally. Wealth decreasing nationally is also referred to as *recession.*

There is a very well considered principle of national economics which assumes that an over-stimulated economy can be slowed by the confiscation of public wealth through taxes. Less money in the economy will suppress inflation by reducing consumer demand. The opposite is also thought to be true in that lower taxes will stimulate a sluggish economy because consumers have more money to spend for goods and services. At this point I hope that your mind is pondering the truly profound effects of taxation and deficit spending on an economy. Our current national debt is not stimulating our economy and in fact it is producing a tremendous liability that must eventually be repaid no matter what else is true. The cash flow used to replace this debt will reduce available funds for future private and federal spending, which as mentioned can only result in an increase in taxes. The interest being paid to non-US sources of borrowed stimulus funds is also a reduction of our national wealth. And the total of our national wealth is decreasing per capita based on an intentional redistribution of wealth. More wealth is being consumed than is being created in our economy and by a profound margin. There is less total wealth to be shared. Everyone has less not just the wealthy. The poor can't afford to have less and are suffering the most. The Republican Party has desperately tried to stop massive increases in public debt and redistribution of wealth. I hope you now understand why! These simple concepts are basic knowledge to any interested observer of economics but they are not advocated in our publicly funded leftist-driven educational system. You now know why!

I also can't help but notice that liberals assume conservatives are for the most part ignorant or otherwise dim-witted. Admittedly an easy assumption given that so many principles of the current conservative community are intertwined with ancient religious philosophies that were and are woefully ignorant of modern scientific wisdom and based on absurdly incorrect assumptions. Clearly the need to explain the unknown was highly motivating and became intertwined with cultural values in the ancient world. It was the Bible (and its authors) that adopted the current cultural values of the time, not the other way around.[8]

Conservatism is not based on ignorance any more than liberalism is. It is based on a proven successful social structure that provides the most comfort for the most people. Greed is its greatest failing. But the principle of liberalism is based on greed. "Others have more than me and I am entitled to a share."

Liberals are forced by their proclivities to ignore history and its often repeated scenario of the rise and fall of cultures—cultures that evolved and prospered as free-living conservatives only to decline as wealth was confiscated by vote, suppressed by regulation, and consumed by those who had not participated in the prosperity.

It would be a monumental mark in human history if the United States could become the first culture to avoid this transition!

President Obama made this transition his goal.

These problems become more profound when the Impoverished of the world flock to the prosperous nations knowing that they will have a chance to share in *the* collective charity and wealth. It is inescapable that the principles of the "from each to each" concept of the socialest mindset, can only in our modern time include every person on the planet no matter their nation of origin. Those advocating the intake of millions of foreign nationals are not concerned with your welfare as much as they are your votes.

The point is that liberalism, by default is greedy and it supports greed by Democratic fiat. It is absurd to assume that everyone who is wealthy got that way covertly or is corrupt. Is it magnanimous to confiscate wealth from those who have labored extra long and extra hard in order to guarantee their own needs and then to distribute those confiscated funds to others who are less than diligent? Robin Hood was still a thief no matter what he did with the money and the Sheriff of Nottingham was still the corrupt government agent who taxed and controlled the people excessively. So was Robin Hood the liberal champion of the common people or the conservative antigovernment zealot?

Do liberal see themselves as providers *to* the collective or as recipients *of* the collective? Philosophically all members of the collective give and take accordingly, but most voters who support liberal politicians assume that there will be a government benefit available to them and at the expense of some corrupt capitalist. An oxymoron[9] of liberalism is that most public figures supporting liberal policies are, or will become very wealthy as a result of capitalist enterprises.

My favorite example of this is Whoopi Goldberg. How many of the poor could we feed on just her *View* salary alone yet she is frequently harshly critical of the very type of business and social structure that rewards her with, what I assume to be a very substantial income. This preaching is sanctimonious at its very roots yet it is she who condemns capitalists as corrupt! Liberalism is media popular because it is an easy sell to those who would consume the product. The product is not only shampoo. The product is also the liberal agenda. It is using capitalist methods to support a liberal agenda that condemns capitalism. I think that what I have just described is the essence of the meaning and concept of the word *corrupt*. Yes, that sounds corrupt to me! Accordingly, it is a daily experience for us to be overexposed to the capitalist-funded leftist media; a leftist media whose funding stream would collapse if it weren't for capitalism. Again, what do they really want?

"You don't know what it's like to be black." Whoopi Goldberg, as quoted from an episode of *The View.*

My thoughts?

"Yes, ma'am, I agree. I don't know what it is like to be black. I also don't know what it is like to be famous. I don't know what it is like to be wealthy. I don't know what it is like to have a national voice on a TV show every day. I don't know what it is like to have been a very successful comedian who eventually became a movie star. I have no idea what it is like to know the privilege and power that comes with fame. I have no idea what it is like to have famous friends who can share their privileges with me. I have no idea what is like to know the power and prestige that your name carries everywhere you go. Yes, Madam Goldberg, I have no idea what is like to be black!"

I feel compelled to point out that the above comments are about a woman I admired very much when we were both young. She was damn funny and damn clever and had a naturally humorous persona. These traits made her very famous and I assume, very wealthy. I never saw her as a "black/woman." I saw her as a person who added joy and humor to my life. Who changed, her or me? What has happened to her that has made her so angry? What is it she wants now that she has never had?

THE THEOLOGY OF ACQUIESCENCE, A LIBERAL PITFALL.

Why do liberals feel so compelled to appease the minority regarding religious freedom? Why are liberals so afraid to offend the few against the will of the many? Those who would demand such concessions from the majority will always see this submission to their cause as a weakness of those who submit. Aggressors, those whom we need to defend ourselves from will always be encouraged in their cause by the showing of fear and submission. History is thick with stories of people and societies who chose not to resist and were slaughtered for their grace. At what point does majority rule cease to be relevant when regarding public policy as religion is concerned? Is the democratic process subjugated by fear in the presence of a theologically sterile culture? Does anybody really think the separation of church and state should include the banning of "religious icons" in public buildings? How could the public at large possibly benefit from such a ban? Clearly the minority has taken control of the situation and with only a whimper of protest from the majority. What cowards we must appear to be in their eyes for so easily abandoning our traditions and principles. Subversives are emboldened if they know we won't fight back. Why are we so easily bullied as we condemn bullies as a pop culture talking point?

Those of us with no theological basis to our thinking have little to lose and are rightfully not concerned for the loss, however many of those whom I regard most highly have deeply based religious roots. Religion is their guidepost when other sources of wisdom or comfort have failed or are not available. How dare I not protect that resource so important to so many when the detriment to me is little or nothing? Religious freedom must also with certainty mean that I will not be required to be manipulated by other minority religions! My small community would never consider banning Christmas decorations in its school but that liberal bureaucrats require it, and those bureaucrats are manipulated by or consist of, a small demanding minority of contrarians. We have abandoned our republic when a majority does not rule in the name of an evolved high-minded culture-elitist minority that accepts all theologies as legitimate except the one that was the guidepost of the origin of our nation.

"Democracy; the right way to do the wrong thing"! Unknown

"Democracy sounds wonderful until economics and others wealth becomes a voteable issue." Unknown

LIBERALS AND CRIME

There are those who, regardless of the circumstances are simply incapable of being concerned with the difference between right and wrong. Everyone justifies the terrible things they do.[10] There are few exceptions. Those who do not justify their heinous acts are truly evil, not biblical evil but of such a careless nature regarding the welfare of others that their acts are regarded by ordinary people as evil.

I have known what others would call an evil mind. I have known it very well. I know how this mind works. I know how it thinks and reasons. In the same way that Hitler was said to behave kindly to Aryan children, his evil mind was capable of doing seemingly magnanimous things. It is well known that Hitler could behave in a friendly way to children though he might eventually order those same children to their slaughter, as needed, for his own purposes. The evil mind knows no remorse nor knows a reason to feel remorse. By default the evil mind has permission to do whatever it wants to anyone it wants whenever it wants. Such is the thinking of the truly evil mind and there are many such minds among us.

Science once defined the evil mind as sociopathic. Generally stated, this is a mind that sees itself as separate from the rest of society, an existence that regards itself as unique so that it is not bound by the rules that apply to the culture at large. Does this sound familiar to you? Does it remind you of anyone? I have not researched an exact number but a certain percentage of us are inclined by proclivity to think this way. Most of us will at one time or another use this reference point when making a decision. We are all to some degree inclined to think this way occasionally. Such thinking is normally not a problem in our daily lives but every now and then. …

Opposition to capital punishment is one of the most common earmarks to quickly determine if a person is a liberal. Libs are mostly opposed and BDLs are entirely against it. BDLs will form a human chain around an abortion clinic in the name of "choice" but they will also form the same chain around a gas chamber to protect a serial murderer's right to spend the remainder of his life in prison. Is sixty years in a living hell of a prison really more humane than a quick painless death? Who is really appeased when the murderer is saved? Who benefits? The killer? Certainly not but he might or might not believe he has benefited. Does society benefit? Not a chance! Our culture is burdened by a cost of millions to keep such people alive—resources that could be used to save innocent thousands from abject poverty. Does the victim benefit? Was his or her life worth so little that we don't dispense just punishment? What about the next victim? Dead murderers rarely commit murder again. Living murderers commonly do whether living free or in prison! It is my belief that today the truly innocent are very rarely prosecuted for a crime but, yes, prosecution of otherwise innocent criminals does and will continue to happen no matter what else is true.

Yes, ending a life can and does save lives. This seemingly oxymoronic[11] concept has centuries of human history to defend it. I could cite many examples but that seems a futile pursuit. Very high on my list of liberal absurdities is the notion that killers are less likely to kill their would-be victims if they know that they won't be subjected to capital punishment if prosecuted. Hold that thought for a moment…….. Yes, they are suggesting that criminals might be legally motivated in the heat of the moment to determine their own possible punishment for their crimes by redefining their heinous behavior from criminal assault to murder in order to get rid of witnesses and avoid prosecution for murder!

For clarity's sake, "I'll kill her so she can't testify against me!" *Yah? I was really just planning on raping this girl, but on second thought, those damn conservatives might just fry my ass if I leave a witness, so I'll just kill 'er and save myself fretting about the chair.*

The concept is an absurd scenario. Potential killers don't see themselves as getting caught, nor do they care. Do you think criminals are really so thoughtful in the course of committing a crime? Do you really want such people, the perpetrators determining how society punishes criminals? This is what BDLs advocate and even more terrifying, it is a great example of the liberal thought process. "We don't want to make bad people mad." It is also commonly true that the liberal idea of prison is not about punishment, but rehabilitation. How do you rehabilitate someone who is willing to commit random murder?

Murder takes many forms and occurs in all socioeconomic groups but it is much more common for the impoverished and accordingly the impoverished are more likely to be affected. But this is not a reason to ban capital punishment. Do I want to execute a man who catches his wife having sex with another man and then commits murder as a result? It's a common crime but I would not support execution as punishment for it. There are many scenarios where I would not advocate capital punishment for murder. I can't really deal with all of them here—and actually don't care to—but I will point out that the proclivity of the killer and the proclivity of the liberal are very different and the principles of one cannot be used to judge the actions of the other. Justice will not be done. Society will not benefit. Victims will not be appeased. Who does benefit so much that the laws of most states do not allow for capital punishment? Where does all of this political support come from? Who are those that have devoted so much of their time and energy to keep capital punishment out of our courts? The criminals themselves? No … it is BDLs. People who place concept ahead of practicality, people who have a greater social agenda and are willing to sacrifice social principles generally in order to support a specific political principle. Those who choose to impose their human will upon the rest of us contrary to basic instinct. Those minority thinkers who imagine themselves as having a special if not superior wisdom and therefore divine power and obligation to decide for the rest of us what our most important cultural standards should be.

AKA, brain dead liberals.

"Criminals thrive on the indulgence of societies understanding" Unknown!

CAPITALISM.

During the Obama presidency our nation moved toward the failed leftist political policies of Europe and Asia while those governments moved toward the successful conservative policies of American-style capitalism.

Capitalism creates wealth; socialism consumes wealth!

In a capitalist economy everyone is free to participate; in a socialist economy everyone is required to participate. It is a very distinct difference. One enslaves me and one frees me. I believe that my contribution to the socialest economy would require more of me than the benefit to me. As a capitalist I choose to suffer the consequences of my decisions and the ways in which my decisions affect my eventual wealth. I expect others to do the same. I will not blame any negative consequences of my choices on my endemic weaknesses. I will not expect anyone to compensate me for my bad choices. I understand that my personal opportunities were considerable and have given me an advantage. I am not required to compensate my culture for those advantages by any theology or principle that I know of and, I don't require that other such people compensate me. I understand that many among my culture were not granted the same advantages as I was at birth and I am sympathetic. I enjoy these advantages and am grateful that I benefit personally and can share my fortunate grace with those who I am close to. Based on these facts I offer my written observations so that we may all share my good fortune.

Government cannot invest money in infrastructure. It can only spend money for infrastructure. That is not to say that infrastructure spending can't be money well spent. It definitely can but it is commonly a vulgar waste of public resources.

Clearly government administrative jobs are necessary to maintain our culture and society. My intended criticism is that more government equals less wealth. I'll say it again: government can only consume wealth. I freely admit that consumption of wealth by government as research goes, has led to numerous prosperous scientific advances. This is the first thing a liberal would tell me when confronted by this idea. Au contraire! Actually true but not always true; actually rarely true. The economic stimulus packages intended to end the recession during the Bush and Obama administrations were at best a catastrophic failure and for reasons I have already explained. Many of the expenditures were used to fund corporate corruption by funding research and development projects; and in one case solar panels and a company that had no chance of succeeding (otherwise known as corruption). The project was not financially viable yet it was gleefully funded. Economic discretion was sacrificed in the name of salvaging the environment. Environmentalists, Left leaning by proclivity were appeased (Kumbaya!) but tremendous wealth was dissipated and human endeavor was wasted. The environment was harmed by all of the wasted industrial activity and it will be further harmed when the necessary consumed wealth is replaced. In any other context there would be criminal charges and lawsuits but politicians get a pass.

Utility is the most important concept in all of economics. I have written on the topic in "Original Wealth," and to summarize utility is the measure of the value of *anything*. Look at anything around you. It is the useful or desirable quality of the object that gives it utility. Abstract things also can have great value; for example; ideas that repress liberalism have tremendous value. Sound in the form of music can also have great value (utility), though it has no lasting physical properties. The currency in your pocket has utility in that it conveniently represents wealth although it is really just a small patch of cloth with very little utility for other purposes. Your house is stored utility in that it should shelter you for a century or more. If it is destroyed that utility is lost and therefore the value is lost!

I can offer two local examples of wasted stimulus funds. There is a paved road near my farm. The road surface was in good condition and very serviceable. It still held considerable utility and it would have normally been many years before the road was resurfaced by necessity. Enter Obama's American Recovery and Reinvestment Act which included a substantial and expensive road sign proclaiming its glory. Now the road has a brand-new asphalt surface. I like the new surface and I drive this road regularly. I liked the old surface also. Utility (wealth) was wasted when the not-yet-old surface was buried. Wages were paid to create the new surface but they were paid for something that wasn't wanted or needed. Wealth (utility) was lost if not intentionally disposed of and this wealth will need to be replaced by the natural economic process of the productive.

In this same time frame local radio stations gleefully announced the federal funding of a study that would be conducted by Iowa State University, a local icon in my area. *Ya-a-a-a-y!* But … not so fast! The funding was to study the effects of global warming on mountain forests of the west. If you are not disturbed by this scenario it might be because you don't know that forests in Iowa are primarily deciduous not coniferous as they are in Colorado or Montana and Iowa is mostly rolling hills or flat farmland. It might also surprise you to know that there is no actual definitive or conclusive scientific evidence that man-made global warming or climate change actually exists— and we are not done yet! How many aging hippie academics does it really take to determine that a temperature increase of two degrees in Oregon would have little if any effect on pine trees? And even if it did what the hell would we do about it and why?

What's more, I could send three partially educated redneck Iowans in a van with a keg of beer on a thousand-mile westward trek with a five-hundred-dollar budget and the benefits to our culture would have been identical. Twenty million dollars was the amount of the federal stipend for "research" granted to the university. A university as any other dominated by leftists who support demoncratic—er … um—Democratic candidates which now fund the careers of the voters who are most inclined to vote for Democrats (i.e., academics) and who routinely preach liberalism to the upcoming generation.

Still what are we to do with those damn conservative wealthy corrupt capitalist Republicans? The ultimate point to this conversation is that my examples of government waste are just ass-wiping money when compared to the total wealth consumed in the name of more vote-buying government social welfare. Massive national wealth was dissipated in the name of the economic stimulus package. Generations of newly created wealth will be needed to replace this wealth already consumed just to break even much less have eventual economic growth. The only other option is that all personal wealth be devalued by inflation resulting in a revaluation of the dollar to a lesser value (a.k.a., *quantitative easing*). This proclivity of the Democratic Party is endemic and it partially facilitates the socialist agenda which will always fail economically. Less wealth for all! Once again, ya-a-a-a-y for equality!

Government Jobs

The Obama administration keeps telling us that government jobs are lowering unemployment but Government jobs are not real jobs in the same way that plastic boobs are not real boobs. They look like real boobs, they feel like real boobs, and God knows they look great in a bikini, but they don't produce anything. Did I mention that they are both very expensive? Government jobs don't add to the economy, they take away from the economy. They dissipate national wealth in the same way that a woman dissipates her personal wealth when she spends her money for breast implants. It is wealth dissipated and money spent. Jobs paid for by tax money which has been taken from the economy might also have otherwise been used to create more original wealth through investment. Government jobs can only shrink the economy by the amount spent as wages. Government investment must be economically viable and profitable, otherwise it is not an investment. And government jobs that manage social welfare programs are a double dip economically (wages + stipends). It is a double dip even if all benefactors of welfare funds spend the money for essentials and not for discretionary spending. Actually the boobs might be a better social investment in that they add beauty and fascination to our day and also create an actual economic taxable revenue stream.

Socialism is an easy sell to the voting public. Which of these two choices would you make?

The sales pitch of the liberal agenda: "You will not have to work or stress yourself in any way. We will free you by giving you money at the expense of wealthy corrupt Republicans *and* we will provide you with a free vasectomy." (I could actually support free government vasectomies.)

Or, the sales pitch for the conservative mantra: "Get off your lazy ass and do something productive so that you are not dependent on me to make a living for you."

I think the first concept would sell much better to a voting public though it is obvious that a culture making this decision can only collapse under its own weight.

Liberal economist? There is no such thing as a liberal economist. You are either an economist or a liberal! The policies that guide liberalism are intrinsically contrary to a functioning healthy economy. Asking a liberal to discuss economics is like asking Satan to discuss Christianity!

I have been on a first-name basis with liberals who rigorously advocated on behalf of social programs. When those programs were approved these liberals became the highly paid program administrators. Yes, they were actually principally involved in the genesis of social programs with the primary goal of creating high-paying jobs for themselves and without regard for the efficiency or actual social value of the resulting programs. (Another example of intrinsically corrupt capitalists?) The liberals in question were not your average street liberals. They had credentials to back up their positions. They had worked their way up through the ranks of social welfare programs as employees to eventually become program administrators. As these inefficient and nonproductive programs were eventually cut as a budget issue those same people went on to the next pop culture social agenda and once again advocated for and eventually received yet another administrative political job. My exposure to these people was the result of my efforts as a volunteer for one of those socially beneficial programs.

The program I worked with *was* effective and socially beneficial but don't jump to any conclusions as to why! Summarized, it was the intrinsically inefficient bureaucratic process and its stumbling blocks that created the need for the program with which I was involved. This program was designed to circumvent bureaucracy. It was a program intended to defeat its own governmental process. I met several well-connected people with magnanimous intentions while I was involved. I also met fellow volunteers who were good people with good intentions and who were effective. No slander is intended but for the pitfalls of excessive government! On the other hand the paid government workers that I interacted with were for the most part ineffective and often afraid to take a stand for fear of professional reprisals. They were in some cases very negligent of their assignments. Such is common if not normal in social welfare programs and government in general.

THE DARK SIDE

I count myself as a conservative but I also am well aware that pure capitalism and strictly conservative policies will not serve our nation well. Again; there absolutely is a need and moral obligation for well-funded people to help support those who can't fully support themselves. The key concept here being can't. One of the great assumptive fallacies of the liberal mind-set is that there is not a great mass of people who will choose to live by the benefit of others given this as an option. I can tell you that a great many people have resolved that a life of poverty is their expected and ongoing condition and that this mind-set is generational and cultural. Not that poverty is a choice but that it is an accepted fate. Even more tragic is the harsh cultural reality that this fate can only be sustained and continued if it is supported by social charity.

We can't suddenly stop the funding stream but if we continue the stream or increase it this situation can only become more ingrained as a mind-set and will ultimately involve an ever-increasing number of people. It is a dreadful scenario in any case. The enormous increase in the number of culturally impoverished Americans in recent decades is indisputable proof of the fact that unconditional charity feeds poverty. This charity isn't solving the problem it is only making the problem grow and the general welfare of our nation is suffering accordingly. It is sickening if not heartbreaking to know that liberals don't see this or care. If you are a liberal and want to see what the enemy of your philosophy looks like, find a mirror. A war on poverty was declared under President Lyndon Johnson and with tragic consequences. Others disagree about the consequences and they will tell you that the war was a great success. The truth appears to be that poverty lessened because of sustained prosperity for our nation as a whole, (more wealth for all) and not because of social charity. For clarity and in a way liberals can understand, only a prosperous nation can afford to feed the poor. Once again the poor suffer the most from bad administrative policy. What are the tragic consequences? We now have, as a segment of our culture a social acceptance of federal charity that was otherwise harshly scorned by previous generations. When I was fifteen years old, people on welfare were considered scum. Now we have employees of government welfare programs actively recruiting benefactors! What do liberals really want?

The ethics of the political spectrum is a challenging topic. I count myself as a conservative but have to accept the harsh realities that are a part of a conservative mind-set. Yes, letting people live in need is going to happen as my political philosophy is played out. Letting the disadvantaged falter is also a reality of conservatism. These things don't go unnoticed by conservatives. It isn't a lack of compassion that fosters conservatism. The core of conservatism is about personal acceptance of the harsh realities of human survival and a personal commitment to sublimate those harsh realities without enslaving others. We accept this challenge and expect others to participate to the best of their abilities. This is actually the only truly ethical means to social survival. There are many harsh realities as a conservative perspective is concerned yet it was unfettered conservatism that created the wealth that liberals are commonly trying to confiscate. It feels a little irrational to remind you that survival of the fittest is why humans became the creatures that we are. Could we see a regression of human strengths if all are able to survive and procreate no matter what? Not likely I guess but who knows what changes to expect if a once-great capitalist culture falters and a poverty-stricken socialest culture emerges as has been historically consistent through the centuries. It is unmistakable that today, at this moment in our culture, as I am writing; the Obama administration is guiding us to that end. There are only two possible outcomes to this currently happening transition. The first possibility is that the transition will succeed and the economic giant (the United States) that led the world for 150 years will collapse and another economic (capitalist) power will fill the void. Our nation, like many before it will become another example of the European economic model that Barack Obama has envisioned for us. (This was the fundamental change that Obama promised in his 2008 campaign.) The second possibility is a conservative social revolt! This is what I believe may actually happen. It may be bloody and it will be harsh. Also I think we could actually see for the first time in American history a conservative march on Washington DC. When we (conservatives) use their (liberals') methods against them (the benefactors of liberalism), they will have no choice but to respond with force. I hope the trend toward liberalism falters and the fallacies of a liberal agenda are exposed long before any of these things happen.

I THINK I NEED TO LET YOUR MIND REST A MINUTE; SO

Apple and Microsoft functional standards for user interface in a personal electronic device:

1. Poor
2. Terrible
3. Hideous
4. Worse
5. Product is intentionally designed to frustrate the user.
6. Useless programs glorified as if they were a great and wonderful product but have no actual practical uses that are not otherwise commonly available.
7. Hideous plus a profound absence of any hint of understanding of what the casual user might actually want.
8. A flagrant violation of any accepted premise to provide a useful understanding of a product's actual capabilities.
9. A complete and utter contempt for the user combined with a disregard for the likely needs of the user.
10. A masterfully executed attempt to positively portray and sell a mostly useless array of obscure features.
11. A demonstrated hostility for any user gullible enough to actually think that most of the selling points of the programing are anything other than useless marketing gimmicks.

12. An intentional conspiracy to foster great suffering and anxiety where complex and otherwise useless programs don't include even the simplest of generalized instructions.

13. A masterful use of a tempting self-glorification of market-induced evil designed to dramatically frustrate and anger the user to the point where the user will violently destroy the device, thus requiring the purchase of a new device.

14. The fruition of a decades-long conspiracy intended to disassemble the structure of human culture by fostering a mindless obsession with intentionally difficult-to-use electronic toys.

Yes, they are succeeding!

The following are some pop culture talking points from the past. This is a partial list and is in a generalized chronological order. I suggest you attempt to meld the 2 columns as you scan those topics of interest to you.

POP CULTURE
TALKING POINTS
FROM THE PAST.

Socialism
The Cold War
Communism
Bikinis (bathing
 suits)
The Twist
The Vietnam War
Smokey the Bear
Litter
Premarital sex
Elvis
Miranda
Birth control
Bald Eagles"
The Beatles
Physical fitness
The war on hunger
The war on poverty
Radiation
The national debt
Taxes
Pollution
Acid rain
Nuclear energy
Inflation
Marijuana
Labor unions
Hippies
Smog
Feminism

A BRIEF EDITORIAL OF THE
ISSUES OF THE DAY
*Pop Culture Talking Points
For The Days Past And As I Lived It!*

Socialism and communism were very publicly scorned sociopolitical philosophies of the late 1950s with Soviet aggression as an ongoing issue. The Cuban missile crisis (1962) was still in my future.

The roads and ditches were a mess in the early 60's. Ending public littering was well received and was the beginning of environmentalism as a social cause. Our environment would no longer be taken for granted.

The bikini bathing suit was nothing less than slutty as worn by young women in the early 1960s. This controversy went on for years.

The Twist was a mindless dance craze in the early 1960s when dance crazes were a very real and very popular thing.

Believe it or not there was still a time in modern history when at least as publicly understood, people not married to each other were expected to *not* have sex!

Elvis shook in such a sexually provocative way that he was shown only from the waist up when he appeared on *The Ed Sullivan Show.* (a popular variety program of the time).

Speaking of sex, for the first time in human history (around 1970), a woman could take a simple pill and the risk of pregnancy was mostly diminished. Game on! :-)

EQUAL RIGHTS
    AMENDMENT
WATERGATE
BALANCE OF TRADE
ASBESTOS
LANDFILLS
FAT
SOIL EROSION
GUN CONTROL
WATER SHORTAGE
REINCARNATION
UNDERGROUND FUEL
    TANKS
FLOODING
SMOKING
CIVIL RIGHTS
HOMOSEXUALITY
FURNACE FILTERS
AIDS
GLOBAL WARMING
CFCs
HERPES
ANTI-SEMITISM
RUNNING OUT OF OIL
THE HOMELESS
SAVE THE WHALES
OIL SPILLS
OZONE DEPLETION
DISCRIMINATION
CHOLESTEROL
HDL/LDL
PROCESSED FOOD
POLAR BEARS"
CHILD PORNOGRAPHY
APARTHEID
PREJUDICE

President Lyndon Johnson declared a "war on hunger." It is hard to imagine how profoundly unsuccessful that war has actually been. No one could have imagined at the time that this simple magnanimous idea might foster a welfare program dependent population of chronically impoverished citizens—or that such programs would eventually encourage the immigration of illegal aliens to America.

All of the 1960s and '70's were a fog for our country. Pot (marijuana) was cheap, and everywhere, and was a very hot topic for the nightly news as was the hippie movement. The "no shirt, no shoes, no service" signs on the doors of restaurants are the result of shabby-looking hippies who were an unwelcome presence anywhere but especially in restaurants.

Antismoking fanaticism was born in the 1960s though its potentially deadly effects had long been common knowledge.

The Beatles? You had to live through the time to understand how a musical group could have fostered such a massive social awakening and with global implications.

In the mid-1960s Police questioned a Latino named Miranda after he was arrested for beating his wife. Possibly the methods of the police were on the "very insistent side"— somewhat. I recall the time well. The history-book reports of the event greatly miss the true issue which was police treatment of minorities. Equal treatment of minorities is yet another long-standing issue. This case now

Native Americans
Indian mascots
African Americans
Still running out
  of oil
Melting polar ice
  caps
Pita
Y2K
The rain forest
Evil corporations
Freon
Mercury poisoning
Murdering trees
Abortion
Bridges
Drug companies
Hate crimes
Factory farms
Organic
Teacher pay
Politically correct
Bullying
SARS virus
The Internet
Bovine spongiform
  encephalopathy
Health insurance
Sex offenders
More global
  warning
Fluorescent bulbs
Ethanol
Still running out
  of oil—again
Greenhouse gases
Climate change

known as "*Miranda*" has had a profoundly stifling effect on law enforcement which at the time was more....Direct.

In the 1970s, we were said to have only have three or four decades of available crude oil remaining worldwide. The resulting high prices led to new exploration and discoveries of vast new supplies. Environmentalism now had a new agenda and oil was it. "Save the rain forest" soon lost its leverage as a pop culture talking point.

"Save the bald eagles" was the first successful public media campaign for social change. Advocates of social control learned that the public could be manipulated through the rapidly evolving electronic medium of television. It was a match made in heaven.

There was also an unsuccessful war on poverty.

Nuclear energy and radiation became a much fear-mongered source of needed additional energy (around 1970).

The debt issues of today are profoundly greater than ever before but they are not in any way a new political issue. The national debt is a social issue as old as the Constitution.

Air pollution was a very hot topic of the 1960s and '70s, and it was really only supplanted as an environmental issue by global warming which has many more dimensions as a social issue and is therefore much more useful. Pollution generally and air pollution specifically is the reason your car is equipped with a catalytic converter. Air pollution was a common daily topic on the nightly news for two decades.

CARBON DIOXIDE
   (CO$_2$)
PEDOPHILE PRIESTS
RECYCLING
GLUTEN SENSITIVITY
PEANUT SENSITIVITY
HFC (HIGH-FRUCTOSE
   CORN SYRUP)
CHEMICAL COMPANIES
PUBLIC HEALTH CARE
GAY MARRIAGE
FRACKING
LEGALIZING MARIJUANA
HEALTH INSURANCE
   COMPANIES
ON AND ON AND ON…

The physical fitness craze began about this time; (the early 1970's). I think it actually was spawned by the Eisenhower administration and the president's' physical fitness campaign years earlier.

Acid rain was another fear mongering social issue used in the 1970s, the idea being that sulfuric acid smoke from power plants was creating acidic rain that was killing trees in Europe. This concept was also supplanted when global warming was conceived.

The Carter presidency was plagued by high economic inflation and very high interest rates.

Labor unions had gained much political power through their enormous membership and nearly fanatical loyalty to union dogma, as presented by union bosses. This was the beginning of the end of union power. Can you say, "Jimmy Hoffa"?

It is also when feminism began as a global agenda for women. There were riots! Bras were burned. The ERA (Equal Rights Amendment) was vigorously pursued for many years but never ratified. I was very much in favor of it?

Watergate, the first mass-media persecution/prosecution of a president (Nixon). The power of the media was now fully evolved and entrenched in a Left-leaning agenda.

Until modern times the balance of trade with foreign nations was a hot media issue. It only stopped being a hot issue when the news media focused on far worse problems.

Mesothelioma? Asbestos had been commonly used as a fireproof insulation material for decades but now it was found to cause cancer—maybe. It marked the expansion of the "it causes cancer" movement joining cigarettes as a much-maligned killer.

Have we run out of landfills yet?

The health craze and food mandates have not made us leaner as a society.

Silt was filling our man-made lakes and farmland would become unfertile.

Smokey the Bear was a long-standing icon for preventing forest fires. The fallacy of the campaign eventually became clear when unstoppable and devastating fires in Yellowstone National Park were much more destructive than they might have been had the forest been allowed to burn occasionally, which *is* a natural process.

Gun control is another hot topic that has been around for a long time yet nothing has been resolved.

Your shower runs slower and your toilet flushes poorly because some areas of the country have occasional water shortages. It is no matter that getting rid of excess water is an ongoing and expensive problem for much of the country, or that water is also one of the most common chemical compounds on the planet. We still *must* save water.

Openly homosexual relationships have taken a very long time to get used to! Hand-in-hand public expressions of fondness were more common then (1970s) than they are now. Those who had been known as "queers" were now free to be themselves and openly express affection for one another. The AIDS epidemic ensued.

In the 1980s, fear-mongering and anti-smoking hysteria reached a new plateau. It is the original permutation of the concept of social control through and in the interest of "public health" all enabled by an attention seeking media.

Global warming/climate change gets my vote for the greatest social control concept in history. It is true genius in that it is fungible and moldable to any unusual climatic events and actual facts are almost impossible to document or disprove. The first time I can recall hearing the concept was around 1984. It gave birth to many new pop culture talking points such as ozone depletion and (CFCs), which were both never true but were daily media fecal matter for fifteen years.

I like whales and I like knowing that they are still around and in increasing numbers. "Save the whales" had a "save the rain forest" kind of following for many years, and has been successful.

Yes, polar bears do sometimes drown at sea, but only the stupid ones. These stories were greatly overstated.

Fluorescent bulbs are another modern bullshit hoax. You have to wonder if some Chinese capitalist didn't fund a campaign to condemn incandescent bulbs and is now making a massive fortune selling more-expensive bulbs that bring poisonous mercury into our homes. LED bulbs will eventually take the place of both incandescent and fluorescent bulbs.

Fracking? Leftists hate fracking not because it is problematic for the environment but because it actually partially remedies the complaints leftists have regarding climate change.

As my observations on pop culture issues progress into current times my editorializing seems less relevant. Many of these issues are still current and we all have our own perspective as to their accuracy. I do wonder however in what way these current social issues will be regarded twenty or thirty years from now. Will we ever actually save the rain forest or end global warming? Possibly not! Possibly it is too late for planetary salvation so why bother. I hear damn little about the rain forest these days but it had a very long run as a social agenda. Has it lost importance or are there just so many other more pressing issues that we can no longer concern ourselves with saving trees? Or was it was more about getting attention and funding for those social advocacy groups that thrive through social manipulation of public opinion? Or is my thinking just overly cynical?

Clearly we as a public have a need and a right to be informed not to mention a natural curiosity about current events. But informed by whom and with what personal opinion as an influence to the reporting? I am well old enough to remember the likes of Walter Cronkite as a highly regarded purveyor of public information and to the best of my knowledge he was *never* accused of "bias." Today bias appears to be the standard for major media news programs. And what of the need for ratings? It's all about the cash flow isn't it? It is a business, right? Or is it about social agenda and political power? Possibly it simply is what it presents its self to be which is a politically neutral media response that serves our public desire to be in the know. Still, is the news media a: for-profit ratings-dependent program, a public information service or both? In either case I think the public news media have become unhealthy for the culture in that we are easily misdirected as are own character flaws are exploited while the true issues of the day are too often ignored. Ultimately it is we the consumers of media who must take responsibility for the content and we do that by assuring ourselves that the stories we are inclined to believe are indeed accurate.

The real point of this conversation is that media content is more about what you want and expect to hear rather than the actual news. More importantly you need to hone your objective skills and critical thinking skills when listening to any source of wisdom or news story. Also, there is nothing new as far as social issue hype is concerned. I want you to learn to see the media for what they are and not allow yourself to be misdirected from the truth no matter your natural political proclivity.

How can poorly educated people expect to be anything more than pawns in the face of a pop-culture, agenda-driven media?

THISPAGEINTENT
IONALLYLEFTBLA
NKTHISPAGEINTE
NTIONALYLEFTB
LANKTHISPAGEIN
TENTIONALLYLEF
TBLANKTHISPAG
EINTENTIONALLY
LEFTBLANKLEFT
BLANKTHISPAGEI
NTENTIONALLYB
LANKTHISPAGEIN
TENITALLYLYLEFT

This page was *not* intentionally left blank. It was to have contained important information that could have possibly changed your life for the better. You could have become incredibly wealthy or found a way to eat all the food you wanted to without gaining a single pound. It would also have told you how to find the man/woman of your dreams, who would have made you very happy, and you would have had lots of great sex, resulting in many wonderful children who would have become president. Also, there was to have been a lengthy explanation of how to control peoples' minds so that you could get them to do whatever you wanted. There was also extensive information that was to have been printed here that would have given you specific directions for a very brilliant way to save the planet, while having all the free energy that humans could possibly ever use. It also would have included a way to feed all the hungry children all over the world. This would have had the effect of ending all wars forever, and you would have eventually come to know the meaning of life and to be one with God. Not only that: you could/would have come to be really cool as a person, with many great friends who adored you and praised you at every opportunity. There is a little known trick that makes it possible to hit a homerun every time you go to bat, that was to have been included here, but it is also missing.

It is really very unfortunate! Isn't that just the way things go! Just about the time when everything in your life was to change for the better, a simple printing error causes a major collapse in human culture. Just imagine what kind of a world it would have been if everybody who had the good sense to read my book could have suddenly become a super person with incredibly abilities, wisdom, and grace! Instead, you are going to read every word of this book, and, yes, you will get a few laughs and learn a few things, but the really most important part is actually missing. Rumor has it that that there are only a few copies of *Proclivities* that have this error, and, unfortunately, you happened to be one of the few people who is missing out on this profoundly life-altering information. Doesn't that just really suck! I know what these things are like. While I have had my share of good fortune, I have also had many bad experiences that have left me wondering if God just hates me, or if I am not actually the devil reincarnated. I mean to say, how could so many crappy things happen to such a good person? I suspect a lot of people feel the same way. And now, a thing like this happens. Just about when everything was about to come together—just when life was about to become golden—the most important information you could have ever known just happens to disappear from the one and only copy of this book you will ever buy! I mean, this is really a bad break for you, but that is just the way it goes! Actually, there is some good news. I have been saving this for the end so that you wouldn't get too excited ahead of time. I know that you have that bad heart condition, so I wanted to walk you into this gently. I wouldn't want you to get some of the best news that you ever had, only to die of a heart attack at the last minute. So, take a few deep breaths and try to calm yourself. I need you to take this seriously, because if you should fall over dead, some asshole would likely sue me for getting you too excited, and then he (or she) would try to reap the benefits of this knowledge. It is really none of his or her business, because it was *you* who bought this book, and only you deserve the prize! Yes, I am awarding a prize to the one person who can prove to the publisher that he or she bought this book! I am not awarding this prize to any other person who might become the eventual owner. Next, is your personal winning number, so call me at ...

CLIMATE CHANGE 2

A POLITICAL CLIMATE CHANGE

"A potential end of our life style as we have known it"? A catastrophic environmental calamity? The natural punishment for human waste and social excess?

Collectively, these warnings have been an icon of pop culture talking points for nearly four decades. As far back as 1985 the phenomenon known as global warming became the popular social cause of the day. Hordes of political advocates jumped on the bandwagon as "global warming" replaced "save the rain forest" as the politically correct social issue of the time. If you were born after 1990 you might assume that global warming is a more modern-day issue. You might not be aware that the history of global warming goes back for so many years. At the time, warnings about our planet getting hotter due to man-made causes galvanized the public mind-set of our nation. Foreign nations were also more than eager to support the cause if it meant that the USA would abandon its highly polluting globally dominant role and do so in the name of saving the planet. Ultimately though, the concept just didn't work out as imagined. These warnings became a major disappointment to liberals of the era as they eventually lost their usefulness.

This attempted socially imposed mandate of universal compliance in the name of global salvation was doomed to failure as the facts played out over time. Examples of local climate extremes were said to be proof of the theory of global warming but time proved these examples to be completely unreliable. The term *global warming* as a concept had to be abandoned in favor of a more complex theory that would be more difficult to disprove. This new theory became known as "climate change." I should note that, as of this writing, the concept of climate change has seen the same challenges to its validity as global warming faced many years ago. Accordingly global warming has seen resurgence in popularity as a useful tool for social manipulators.

At the time (approximately thirty-five years ago) most of us saw these warnings as little more than a "the-sky-is-falling" mentality. Actual real evidence of global warming was nonexistent in the 1980s, yet the movement grew as the media pop culture eagerly adopted the cause. Advocates claimed it was clear that we humans needed to limit our lifestyle to a simpler more environmentally responsible way or the health of our planet would suffer. It is most everyone's social proclivity to do the right thing when the need arises. Most of us are willing to comply and conserve as necessary to "save the planet." Only a limited few will ignore the concept completely in favor of their personal comfort. Alarmists know this fact and generated a campaign condemning social waste and personal excess in the name of global salvation. Debating the issues became a national obsession. Factions evolved that remain today. Believers and nonbelievers joined their separate camps. The controversy continues to rage. Which of the two separate camps do you support? What is your belief system? It *is* about what you choose to believe. There are no indisputable facts.

What we as humans "choose" to believe defines our daily lives and behavior much more so than any actual facts. False conjecture, not "fact" is the basis of the climate change agenda. Religious beliefs have a similar genesis. Assumed facts led to the origins of both. Religion and climate change have this history in common. For now they are both faith-based beliefs. You either choose to believe or you choose not to believe. There is no hard evidence of either as fact but both groups of believers will tell you that there is much hard real evidence and that this hard real evidence is everywhere and common. I personally am agnostic on both counts.

I offer some examples of these assumed facts;

1. The faithful believe and preach their faith no matter what contrary evidence there may be.
2. When the historic set of "facts" proves to be untrue, new "facts" are substituted to replace old facts.
3. The faithful feel a compelling need to "preach the truth" so that others may benefit from their wisdom.
4. Faith requires believers to spread the word and convince others to join the cause all in the name of a better eventual reality for everyone.
5. Nonbelievers are harshly maligned and publicly condemned for their lack of faith. Careers are damaged. Heretics are vilified.
6. Believers feel good about themselves after "spreading the word" and "having made an assumed difference" though nothing has actually changed.
7. Both global warming and religion are used as a means to control your behavior. "Thou shalt not kill." "Thou shalt not emit." CO_2."

I hope to add clarity regarding at least one of the issues mentioned above, and with the best intentions for you. Let's start by getting back to the topic of the history of man-made weather issues.

All those years ago I could have not imagined that today man-made weather changes would still be a social issue. I had not given it specific thought at the time but I would have naturally assumed that the subject of global warming would most likely be a forgotten product of legacy pop culture agenda. By that I mean to suggest that global warming, as a supposed real and actual event, as a thing long discussed at all levels and venues of our culture would eventually, like all the other social crises of the day fade into yesterday's news and out of our collective thoughts. But this did not happen. Its popularity did diminish over time but ultimately it did survive to serve the future generations of alarmists. This is true because it has all the necessary components to make it a very effective social manipulation issue; thus, is still being used accordingly.

My original goal regarding a discussion of man-made influences on climate was to approach this subject as a case study in the proclivity of our culture and of humans as a whole but I just can't resist the chance to share with you what I believe to be true about global warming and make a case accordingly. I will eventually focus on the social truths of global warming (GW) and climate change (CC).

In the beginning. …

The early days of global warming were all about ozone depletion based on the interaction of Freon and the ozone layer which reflects solar radiation from the sun back out into space. I think I should remind those of you more mature and point out to those of you who are younger that all the global warming/climate change propaganda that we are cursed with to this day began with a theory that the refrigerant Freon was chemically reacting with ozone and destroying the ozone layer in the process. This was having the effect of letting too much sunlight through to the surface of the earth which would eventually lead to a catastrophic increase in atmospheric temperature.

I have listened many debatable issues and I have heard many out-right lies intended to influence the public to think that GW is or was a very real thing. But Freon was the biggest hoax of all. We were warned daily for at least fifteen years that Freon was destroying the protective ozone layer. It was said that the ozone layer was thinning and holes were forming at the poles where the ozone layer was naturally thinner. This obvious warning as to the eventual worldwide loss of the ozone layer was well headed and led to the ban of the commonly used Freon refrigerant as mentioned, but the earth wasn't saved. The Freon theory was actually a complete fabrication though it was commonly reported as fact. I have been told by a science instructor that Freon had almost no possibility of effecting ozone in our atmosphere. His argument was completely convincing when I heard it. His point was that man made Freon is a heavy dense gas in its non liquid form (R12) which would sink like a rock in the atmosphere. Ozone forms a very deep atmospheric layer but is also a very light gas. The fact that ozone is very light is the reason that it is the top layer of our atmosphere. It is literally floating on the heavier gases under it. The natural interaction of Freon and ozone is extremely unlikely if not impossible and by volume, Freon only exists as an extremely minute trace material as compared to a massive volume of ozone. These facts were never common public knowledge. False conjecture was the mantra of the day. The ozone theory was a bold-faced blatant lie told a million times and repeated globally. Freon was banned because of it! Those perpetrating the lie were never held accountable.

One would think that the banning of Freon would be the end of the story but not so. Yes, we banned Freon. Every bit of Freon that could be recovered from old cooling systems was trapped and properly disposed of and a suitable—and I should add *profitable,* substitute was created: R134a. Just the name sounds safer to me and it was. But global warming didn't go away. As luck would have it after very many years of predicting global warming, the planet finally had two consecutive years of actual warmer temperatures. The years 1998 and 1999 were indeed a little warmer than normal. Finally those who had been warning us for years and years that we needed to change our ways as a culture or die had proof of their predictions—sort of.

Another very interesting if not telling thing happened in about the same time frame as the two warmer years, and I have to ask myself (and you), how many of us actually remember the NASA space shuttle mission dedicated to the study of ozone depletion? Do you recall? Were you too young or too uninterested to be aware of the events of the day? Has no one else seen fit to educate you on the facts of this historic event? The sole purpose of the mission was to study just exactly how much damage had been done to the ozone layer based on the interaction of Freon. The public cost of this mission must have been fantastic not to mention the pollution created by the mission itself. The results of the mission should be a part of our current pop culture thoughts. Under any other circumstances this event would be a historical political case study in the nature of politics. Instead, this massive end-all scientific study is mostly unknown or forgotten and the controversy, obsolete. This mission took place in the late 1990s.

To summarize and without details the results of this mission showed overwhelmingly that GW advocates of the time were wrong and their theories were not based on fact. They were not just a little off, they were wrong and completely without merit. This is a matter of historical record and it came from NASA. As you might guess the BDLs of the day were not discouraged. They were not discouraged to the point that a certain liberal political group (whose name I have forgotten) published a very lengthy "cover letter" and staged a publicized event to reveal the contents of the NASA letter. They based their cover letter's conclusions on the NASA research verifying that indeed we were in trouble as a species based on the results of the shuttle mission and the related research. Like hogs feeding at the trough of public opinion the media widely reported on this staged press release and intentional deception intended to influence public opinion. There could be no question of our impending peril. But it wasn't long before another public document/statement regarding the facts of the NASA research was issued and the actual researchers who conducted the study at NASA issued this second letter. What did it say? As nearly as I can paraphrase: "The statements of the GW advocacy group; Do not accurately reflect the results and the conclusions of our report."

Yes, the first cover letter was a hoax! It was a complete fabrication. No truth in it at all! Politically, it was an extreme move for the NASA researchers whose funding rises or falls by public opinion to discount the fraudulent report. They earned my respect for having the integrity to put the truth ahead of personal agenda, an act considered treasonous by the average BDL. And let's not lose the point here that a liberal GW/CC organization intentionally fabricated yet another blatant lie—a lie having global implications and affecting everyone on the planet. They were caught in the act and exposed as corrupt liars by NASA. They were lying so that they might manipulate every person and every government on the planet. They used your desire to foster your own survival—the most basic of all instincts—to manipulate you for their own purposes. They were not magnanimous. They were corrupt. They were jealous of your wealth and power and drive and they don't want to have to compete with your ambition. They want you to live a simple peaceful life and this can only be true if they are able to suppress individual economic aggressiveness ! But yet again, I digress. ...

I suspect only a very small percentage of our population knows this story. Why? It received very little mainstream press coverage. It was reported by mainstream media but only in passing. This should have been international headline news. It should have been by far the biggest story of the day if not the year. Emerging Right-leaning news programs did cover this story and in detail. Unfortunately not many listened or cared and the story quickly faded from our daily lives and is now mostly forgotten.

The real significance of this story is that it likely did help bring a temporary end to the GW hoax. Subsequent statistical variations at the time were shown to be "within normal ranges"; some years were actually a bit cooler. It left a vacuum in what had become a global agenda for behavioral conformity. Clearly well-organized advocate groups inclined to such thinking couldn't walk away from two decades of what had been a very successful campaign for gaining global attention. There was now a vacuum to fill due to the failure of global warming and a new concept, "climate change," would fill that vacuum.

The real beauty of climate change is that any weather extreme can be said to be evidence of a problem. There will never be a time when extremes of weather will not take place. There will never be a time when long-term patterns of weather don't show a sudden and significant change. The opposite of the climate change agenda is what is actually true in that consistent weather is *not* normal. History documents this fact very well. It is like walking into a room backward to assume that a severe incident of weather is abnormal until you turn around and see the entire contents of the room and the related history that would normally be in front of you! It was a years-long period of unusually cool weather that led to the medieval plagues that ravaged Europe. Did humans cause the climate change of the time or were they victims of it? Also a case has been made that prior to the 1990s, the earth had seen a slight cooling period. I have no means to prove or disprove any such claims. Liberals would never let facts stop them from advocating in favor of conclusions based on a short-term anomaly. Conservatives live by a higher standard.

For now, CC and GW are almost impossible to prove or disprove convincingly. For every argument there is a contrary response. There is no reason to believe or doubt unless like the faithful mentioned above you choose to believe. I choose to doubt! For me to advocate for massive social change, to change my lifestyle, to advocate for massive social spending, to abandon common empirical evidence, I need more reason and evidence. I need a lot more and so do most clear thinking people (a.k.a., conservatives).

What would this evidence look like? I have a passing interest in physics. I casually follow advances in physics and am always curious about the current "hot" theory. Those theories are normally established and then proved in the form of a mathematical equation or disproved by the lack thereof. One such famous equation is $e = mc^2$. These types of equations are used because of one inescapable fact. In the same way that $1 + 2 = 3$ and $3 - 1 = 2$; For something to be true physically it must also be possible to be expressed as a mathematical equation; an equation that balances. All the variable factors must equal each other and balance in order for anything to be possible—according to the natural laws of physics.[12] Where is the math? Where is the inescapable fact of physics that proves that such a thing (GW or CC) is actually possible? Such an equation would prove once and for all that greenhouse gases or other factors created by man are indeed warming our planet. All debate would go away. This is the 10 million-pound elephant of climate change.

It is said that many scientists believe in global warming. Clearly, these scientists have much greater knowledge of the scientific method than I do. They know by their profession that this elephant must be by default a part of any theory or conjecture regarding climate change. Yet they are silent! To complete this book, I engaged in a quest for information on science-based facts in regard to GW and CC assuming that such information had to exist somewhere. If it didn't No one other than a fool (read: BDL) would even suggest that man-made climate change was possible. My search was brief. I admit that if I had stayed with my search I might have found relevant information but my search led me to nothing but thousands of examples of ranting extremism about the horrors of climate change. I found no empirical scientific evidence based on the scientific method that would support the notion that man-made climate change was possible!

Why are there so many negative comments about our collective future and so damn few comments about the science? Why are we listening to these non-experts and the doom they portend, when the experts are silent?

No one other than a climate scientist or a meteorologist has any reason to speak on the issue—or to be heard as an expert. Liberals have a proclivity to quote "expert" opinions as a means to forming debates where social issues are concerned. Where are these experts and why are they not public icons of pop culture in an Einstein-esque persona? As for the scientific model, this mathematical model must exist. It is the only relevant factor regarding the climate change issue and it is also the only possible representation of fact. Let me make that last statement very clear. Unless this proven-to-balance mathematical model can and does exist, man-made climate change is impossible and the CC theory was not conceived based on a scientific examination. Any meaningful conversation on man-made climate change could only start with this theory in hand. Everything else that you may be hearing is just fabricated speculation in the absence of this scientific model.

If I were a CC advocate the first thing I would do is to produce this mathematical formula. The second thing I would do is post it on bill-boards around the world. Why? To save the planet! Most of us have seen the charming little reflective model with arrows representing light beams being bounced around with more arrows pointing down than up. But this isn't math and it isn't science. Given that heat energy (radiant energy) flows in all directions all the time as much energy would flow out of the atmosphere as would flow in. Any excess of energy would be dissipated into space at a greater rate than normal dissipation because of the simple fact that there is more energy to dissipate. *And* a denser atmosphere would stop as much energy from coming in as it would from going out. There is nothing unique about carbon dioxide or any other gas molecule that reflects more energy in one direction than another. There is no such thing as a molecule of gas that functions as a one-way mirror. The concept is bizarre and ridiculous at its inception. Again, for clarification, the concept of greenhouse gas-related climate change collapses with the first scientific test for validity. The man-made climate change model is contrary to the laws of physics. Yet the unaware, uneducated, and poorly informed choose to believe! And one last thing that makes global warming impossible; a thing that everyone of modest education can understand. The greenhouse effect can only exist in an environment in which the heated air is trapped. Even a greenhouse will quickly cool if the door is opened or when the sun is blocked by clouds or goes down. Greenhouse and climate change greenhouse-gas "theories" are based on a fundamentally different concept as compared with the greenhouses that we are all familiar with. No current greenhouse gas theory has the scientific validity to affect the average temperature of our planet. Water vapor, not atmospheric gas regulates the temperature of our planet.

"Proclivities is more about why people believe than what we believe. It is intended to examine what it is that might cause us to believe in conjecture in spite of obvious contrary information. Why do so many people choose to believe in GW and CC? Why is there so little scientific effort to discredit CC and why is there no international summit on climate change that is openly public and is not politically driven or managed by those with a predetermined agenda? Why is there no global attempt to definitively settle the issue—permanently? I am not going to try to answer those questions here. The answers are addressed repeatedly throughout this writing. I hope that you have given my message/answers substantial thought and that you understand my intent. At the very least I hope you will take an objective moment to consider the possibilities.

I offer some thoughts and facts I want you to consider before you preach about man-made climate change—assuming that you still intend to do so. These are easily changed behaviors that *will* make a difference or reasons why nothing that we can do will make a difference.

1. It is theoretically possible and environmentally feasible to capture and store massive quantities of dry Ice (frozen carbon dioxide) at the bottom of deep ocean depths and reduce atmospheric carbon dioxide as a result. Why aren't we doing this? Why aren't CC advocates asking for funding to proceed with this solution to CC? Why is all their preaching directed toward individual behavior?

2. Ethanol production is touted as a means to reduce carbon dioxide emissions yet carbon dioxide gas is a by-product of fermentation. To reduce carbon dioxide emissions we should stop all fermentation or rotting of any kind. Stop producing all forms of alcohol!

3. Construction of buildings using wood sequesters carbon for the time that the building exists. Build a house made from wood!

4. Green plants are constantly converting carbon dioxide to oxygen as they sequester carbon. Stop building houses made from wood!

5. Do you have one of those lovely water fountains on a pond in your housing development? The electric motor that powers the fountain is using more energy than your house; likely a great deal more depending on the size of the water plume. If you are really about saving the planet ban them completely!

6. Garbage of all kinds in a landfill also sequesters carbon if it is not used as an energy source. Keep producing garbage to save the planet!

7. Diamond mining for gems is a profoundly high carbon emitting and polluting enterprise and it produces nothing useful. Poor-quality industrial diamonds are not rare can meet our needs for all industrial uses and do not need to be mined. No more wedding rings! No more shiny rocks of any kind except as needed for the prevention of CC. Gold has substantial industrial value but we must stop mining gold for use in jewelry and other nonindustrial purposes! Mining gold has a very massive carbon footprint per social benefit! Please turn over your jewelry and gems in the name of saving the planet. If you are truly committed, there will be no exceptions!

8. Nuclear power is by far the best way to provide for our energy needs with its very low carbon emission levels and very little pollution. Which is a greater risk: flooding seashores or death by radiation poisoning? Actually nuclear energy has a very safe track record and far better than most would believe. It has been said that nuclear energy has a lower death rate than any other energy source and there is now a safe and practical plutonium

storage facility in America that will be safe and functional for millions of years.

9. As said earlier, observing climate fluctuations and any related concern is like walking through a door backward and then describing what is in the room. You are looking in the wrong direction. What is *not* normal is climate consistency and there exists a great deal of scientific and historical evidence of short- and long-term changes in climate, some of which happened suddenly. Weather extremes are normal. Major shifts and long-term changes in local climate are normal and well documented. Casual observations of current weather patterns can never prove or disprove climate change nor prove whether or not current variations in weather are based on man-made activities.

10. Burying a human in a vault/ grave is carbon sequestration. Cremation is an extremely energy intensive process. Get a grave that is in a vault.

11. Paving a road with asphalt sequesters carbon. Asphalt is a by-product of refined oil. Deduct this massive amount from the total estimated carbon emissions based on oil production!

12. Your breath as exhaled is carbon dioxide All humans must stop breathing immediately to reduce this massive emission of Co2! All breathing animals also emit carbon dioxide.

13. It is absurd to assume that climate change can only mean that the earth's weather will be worse or that there will be an increasing number of weather-related disasters. It is irrational to assume that climate change cannot or does not include a period of much more moderate weather. To advocate otherwise is blatant fear mongering.

14. No amount of carbon dioxide sequestration can compensate for the ongoing increase in the human population and by a profound factor. Additional humans will require an ever-increasing amount of carbon-producing energy and ongoing increases globally in the form of coal-fired energy production and related carbon dioxide emissions is profoundly greater than any decrease the United States could possibly hope to manage. If it is true that

your primary mission is a healthy planet the only correct thing for you to do is to end your life immediately; better yet take a few billion people with you and don't forget to bury the bodies. You will have my gratitude for saving the planet.

15. The assumed effects of climate change will make very little or no difference to the future of our planet when we consider time on a planetary scale. Our presence here is but a blink in the planet's history and future. It is not about saving the planet. It is about saving the planet for the pleasure of humans. We are saving the planet for our own needs! Watching butterflies makes us happy but the butterflies don't care. Sharing our world with the earth's many other life forms is one of the great joys of living. It is something most everyone wants. If humans didn't exist it would not matter if the earth's other creatures existed or not.

16. We will not and cannot make any real difference long term and by long term I mean 500 million years or more. It is inevitable that this planet will live in great beauty and health hundreds of millions of years beyond the presence of humans. There could be another globally dominant life form eventually. When planet earth is destroyed the presence of humans will be less than a footnote in an unrecorded history.

I said before that climate change is much more about social control than it is about the weather. It is about uniting the group human in a common direction and as a group which is the standard social structure model of the socialest mind-set. All who advocate social policy—policy that is intended to provide for the personal needs rather than the general needs of the population—must control that population individually. We just can't have personal autonomy and self-determination for you will misbehave.

And one more thing. What is the last thing a GW/CC advocate wants? Find the answer as the first entry in "Krib Notes."

Okay, back to the main purpose and yet unanswered question: why do so many choose to believe? I don't mean the socialest agenda-driven

BDL. I mean your everyday average liberal. The girl on the street; okay, the man on the street. What is it that motivates the average liberal to be willing to accept the CC theory based on the say-so of people who are not necessarily experts? Why do so many choose to believe alarmist opinions and not CC doubters opinions when the credentials of the opinionated are, as a practical matter identical to those of the doubters? There are millions of clear-thinking people with the same credentials (none!) as the alarmists. The clear thinkers say, "It is a hoax." I should also point out that the number of conservatives who believe in CC is statistically insignificant. Why is this true? Are we conservatives just stupid? Are we just blind to the truth? Do we have an agenda and if so what would that agenda be? What could possibly be the goal of social manipulative conservatives? Liberals will tell you that it is all about the money and you should follow the money trail but without a healthy planet the stream of new wealth ends. Also, conservatives suffer from an unhealthy planet the same as liberals do. What is it we conservatives really want? Got any suggestions? I'm drawing a blank.

I personally don't have an agenda of any kind as far as CC is concerned except possibly to repress BDLs. What I do advocate is a political format that serves the most people in the best and most efficient way. There is a dramatic difference though! I don't want anything from you except that you do your best to provide for your own needs and with a background and regard for ethics. The theories I base this requirement on are long established to be profoundly successful and proved to be valid a hundred centuries ago and have proved to be successful over and over again throughout history. I will say it again for the sixth time: centralized, or socialest economies have a perfect track record of failure. None have survived long term or in a state of prosperity and the human death toll from collapsing socialest economies and the resulting revolutions and eventual wars ranks as one of the leading causes of death as human life is concerned. The normal course of a collapsing socialest government is the isolation of wealthy government bureaucrats from the general and eventually impoverished population and revolt follows poverty. Those bureaucrats are deposed and capitalism rises again. Sound familiar? It should! How well do you know your history? Are you committed to repeating it? Capitalist economies fail because created wealth becomes a votable issue and those who "have" are forced to support those who "have not," and to support those have-nots without regard for circumstances. Eventually there is a socialist revolt to "spread the wealth around."

YOU MUST UNDERSTAND.

Advocates of CC "mandates" are about social manipulation that requires everyone on the planet to reduce greenhouse gas emissions by living a lifestyle that pollutes in a minimal way and "for the greater good". ... Also, there is no point to wealth if everyone is required to live a similar and austere lifestyle based on the constraints of carbon sequestration. Climate change therefore facilitates the same outcome as "spread the wealth around" economics. No one will live in unusual luxury or in unusual poverty. It is the perfect concept to foster an egalitarian world culture voluntarily. They support the same goal. This is not a coincidence. The truth of weather changes is not a concern to the advocate of climate change. Climate change has nothing to do with the weather.

I have written a great deal about liberals versus conservative elsewhere. Differentiating the behaviors of the Left and the Right is an easy process. There is a distinct and basic ingrained difference in how the conservative and the liberal perceive the social structure. Many are extreme both for the political Left and the political Right. Many are moderate and can see both sides of an issue. Some of those moderates are clueless and compliant and are the ones who decide elections. Right-wingers want personal autonomy; left-wingers want universal compliance. Which one of these choices do *you* make?

One last thought!

I don't actually imagine an organized conspiracy of agenda-driven socialcrats. What I do imagine is an assumed and expected universal desire of social compliance that would be part of a liberal perspective which assumes that all individuals should be willingly involved and naturally participating in carbon sequestration, absent of forced mandate. This perspective is the assumed natural course of things for liberals. It is not born of malicious intent but of assumption. This particular

assumption is given no regard as to its practicality. It is not the proclivity of the socialest to analyze the validity of this default assumption or any other of the principles that define liberalism. These assumptions are magnanimous and therefore assumed to be valid by the liberal. It is the proclivity of the liberal to support the necessary plan to carry out the default natural assumption because it is perceived as the default "only natural" next thing to do. When resistance to this natural only course of action is encountered the BDL then follows the only natural next course of action, and given that liberals are not normally combative, is to fraudulently manipulate the situation to an eventual perceived common good. Decorum and veracity are sacrificed in the name of a higher cause which facilitates fabrication of facts without guilt. The final piece of the profile is the self-glorification that comes from having an assumed high-minded evolved and successful grand purpose. Yay for liberalism! And now you know what climate change and global warming is all about and what motivates it and …

Yes, you need to read that last paragraph again!

CLIMATE CHANGE 1

As I was writing my essay on the politics of climate change ("Climate Change 2"), I came across many anomalies that motivated me to explore the science and physical effects of climate change as a discussion of its facts, not just its political value, which is the point of "Climate Change 2.

There has been a lot of conjecture, both pro and con about the facts of human-influenced weather patterns and I have been hearing warnings about man-made climate change in one form or another since the mid-1980s. Most of what was said as a warning at that time has since proved to be either a complete intentional fabrication or a simple distortion and misunderstanding of the facts. Much of this false information originated from poorly informed and easily influenced activists. These activists were wealthy with intentions but poor with facts. Their bandwagon quickly filled with additional advocates while the hungry-for-content media eagerly reported the story. Thus was born the international psychosis of global warming (GW) and man-made climate change (CC).

Virtually every "fact" that I have investigated regarding man-made climate change has proved to be fungible in that conclusions based on these facts are/were subject to interpretation. It is a proclivity of activists to not only be activists but also to pursue supporting facts for their chosen agenda while ignoring contrary information.

Climate change "atheists" (i.e., nonbelievers) do the same thing but scientists don't. Scientists don't ignore contrary information when examining the facts and neither will I. I can't and don't ignore any pertinent information and we (the scientists and I) won't allow ourselves to ignore certain contrary information in favor of supporting information.

Science is about provable facts only and it requires and follows what is known as the *scientific method*. This scientific method does not allow for conjecture or wishful thinking or achieving the desired predetermined agenda-driven outcome and most importantly; only the methodical application of science and math can confirm or deny the validity of man-made climate change as a theory.

I hear accounts of "scientists," as reported by leftists who have established conclusively that man-made weather change is a proven fact. I sure would like to talk to some of these scientists. I have some damn serious questions to ask these experts. I can't come to any definitive conclusions until I have had a chance to personally examine the results of the scientific-based research and the resulting scientific conclusions. Though I have been searching, I still have not found any published work that supports the validity of man-made weather changes. I know that the scientific "papers" are out there. Thousands of people all over the world are reporting on these scientific conclusions and they have been doing so for three decades. The scientific work is out there and readily available to everyone but me. The GW advocates have access to it! Why don't I? GW advocates wouldn't be saying these things if they had not seen proof of the facts, would they? And how come this information is only available to liberals? Keeping this from me and other conservatives must be a conspiracy! They are trying to ruin my book and discredit me in the process, obviously!

I have no intention of letting leftists get away with this so I have come up with my own set of "facts." I have already established that facts need not be true to be "facts," as far as CC and the Left are concerned. I am tempted to make my own case using these same rules already established by leftists. I assume that they apply to any conversation on man-made weather change. Isn't that true? I can just make it up as long as my intentions are magnanimous, right? Or I can make whatever conclusions I want based on any weather anomaly that I find interesting. Isn't that okay? That's what GW advocates have been doing for a long time. My intentions are definitely magnanimous in that I intend to end the GW hoax. That makes it okay to lie, right? I am thinking it over. For now, let's look at a few "facts" that are true and easily established and obvious and not based on supposition.

Fact: there is no confirmed agreement that climate change is a true fact as claimed! I have had a face-to-face contact with two professional meteorologists, one of whom was an instructor at the college level. He just chuckled at the very thought that such a thing might be feasible. To him it was nothing but a senseless joke. No, there is no consensus. Remember, this person is a professional and a scientist. He refused to make the same statement publicly or to let me use his name for this writing. You will have to make your own assumptions as to why! The other person was a graduate of the same well-respected university climatology program. He said that it could never be proved or disproved though he apparently was inclined to believe CC was possible. Nevertheless, would not commit either way! This chance meeting took place at an public forum. I was not granted the time for a more comprehensive conversation yet the message of these two professional scientists/weather experts was very clear: there is no consensus. Once again, the climate change extremists fabricated a falsehood in the name of an agenda. The left has a longstanding history of this behavior; still, the faithful choose to believe.

That leads me to the next reason why we should not accept that there is provable evidence of man-made climate change. These professional scientists had no knowledge of any mathematical model (as mentioned in "Climate Change 2"). This model is still and again extremely critical for the validation of any theory yet is absent not only to me but also to these scientists who specialize in the earth's climate. When I asked about this mathematical model they each responded with a blank stare and raised eyebrows as if they had never pondered the concept. It was clear that they both well understood the meaning of its absence.

Another fact that isn't getting attention is that there are many ways to sequester carbon dioxide and other greenhouse gases, yet advocates of those solutions are almost nonexistent. Instead, leftists are all about you personally changing the way you live and these required changes affect almost every aspect of our lives. The most prominently obvious and most effective example of potentially reducing carbon emissions is the practice of fracking. Every source of energy has its potential risks to the environment and/or to the safety of the public but fracking has almost no downside and is far safer than any other conventional energy source. There will never be a completely safe energy source and it is my never humble opinion that fracking, though relatively new and rapidly expanding as an energy source, has already saved millions of "tons" of greenhouse gases from being released into the atmosphere and it will continue to do so for the next century.

It should bother me that a gas cannot be measured by the ton. BDLs have been using the ton as a unit of measure for gas for a very long time so I assume that I have the right to use the same false measurement. A vapor (gas) is is normally measured by the cubic foot because a gas is normally as light or lighter than air and air is a mixture of gases (mostly nitrogen). Therefore a gas has little or no specific gravity. This notion includes all chemically specific vapors. Natural gas is the perfect example of this and is measured and sold by the cubic foot. Natural gas is primarily composed of methane and hydrogen-based compounds.

There literally is no other solution to greenhouse gases and man-made climate change that has the same potential as fracking and natural gas. Nothing else will serve our energy needs as safely and efficiently as natural gas potentially can and for the foreseeable future. At this point CC advocates are freaking out about the fracking process that releases natural gas from subterranean rock formations. They are freaking on fracking! These BDLs, including the renowned scientist and famous widow, Yoko Ono are now publicly protesting fracking as a threat to water quality. I have already established that the last thing CC advocates want is a solution to the problem of CC. I strongly believe that this is the only reason why anyone would condemn the process of fracking. BTW, most ground or well water is commonly pumped from depths of as little as 25 feet to as much as 500 feet. Fracking takes place at depths far deeper than well water and far deeper than there is any reason to attempt to pump water. Also, well water sometimes does indeed contain flammable methane or hydrogen gas that quickly dissipates when no longer under pressure. Somehow that fact doesn't stop protests against fracking. Clearly, Yoko is not protesting fracking because of the negative effects of fracking. What does she really want?

I think I should take this conversation in a different direction. First, I ask you to do your own research in that you execute a web search on global warming and climate change. Do some real reading please. You will soon find out exactly why I am such a skeptic as to climate change. There just isn't any real science available. This real science should be commonly in print and widely distributed and it should be everywhere. Its absence is striking and inexplicable—unless it just doesn't exist. And; I don't expect you to accept my opinion as your own. I am not a climate expert or a scientist. Neither are you likely to be a scientist and neither is almost everyone who is demanding that you "fundamentally change" your life because of concerns for a pending global calamity. The preachers of climate change are not scientists and are not correctly reporting the opinions of those who are experts. Instead, there is a profound and extreme bias to advocate a false doomsday mentality based on the *possibility* of climate change. I honestly believe based on the facts; that your average scientist would see climate change as more of a curiosity rather than a calamity. In the absence of a social agenda almost no one would ever have pondered the concept of climate change based on human influenced emissions of carbon dioxide. The negative consequences of CC have been profoundly embellished. Excuse me for repeating myself again but it is an obvious and often repeated proclivity of the politically manipulative to adopt a cause by which to foster a given behavior intended to satisfy a personal agenda.

Please help yourself to any website regarding the greenhouse effect. Try to find websites that contain easy-to-understand descriptions of the effect of greenhouses and greenhouse gases and from varied perspectives. Focus on the ones you disagree with or that accurately describe the two different things. Until you understand that atmospheric green housing and man-made greenhouses are fundamentally different processes there can be no conversation between two non-expert people about the effects of climate change. The air must remain trapped as in any biosphere for a greenhouse to make a difference. The air must be artificially prevented from cooling or the air must be constantly exposed to the energy of the sun. BDLs will see such a term as the *greenhouse gas effect* and assume the theory is confirmed, which is *a* problem. Advocates see it their own way no matter the clear truth of any article. The BDLs will see such things as GW and CC as confirmed without regard for the intent of any article. A neutral perspective will see this as adding to the clarity of the greenhouse effect and hopefully, with objectivity.

The greenhouse effect is a commonly known fact and has never been doubted by any reasonable person. We all know that it can and does exist but we also know that it is always temporary. Do you remember your grade-school science class, with molecules vibrating faster as the temperature [energy] rises? The vibrating will slow and the energy will dissipate unless ongoing additional energy is added to the molecules. There is literally no scientific validity to yet another simple test of greenhouse gas-related global warming. OMG! ... on and on and on. ... And yet the faithful choose to believe!

One more thing: the much-maligned "dead zone" nitrogen that is so harmful to the Gulf of Mexico is directly extracted from the atmosphere. Yes, every breath of air you take contains 78 percent nitrogen gas which is used as the main ingredient in deadly chemical nitrogen fertilizers. This is the same sort of fear mongering that tells you that an increase of 1 or 2 percent of carbon dioxide gas in the atmosphere will be a global calamity. The "science" is absurd and the belief in it is tragic!

So let's do the math. For starters, most of the earth's atmosphere is not carbon dioxide. The percentage of the atmosphere is .035 percent. That reads as .35 hundredths of 1 percent. We are told that the percentage of atmospheric carbon dioxide may increase by as much as 2 percent, which would raise the percentage of atmospheric carbon dioxide to .0357 percent. If you are not good with decimals, that number reads as 350 thousands and 357 ten thousands respectively or an increase of 7/10,000ths of one 100th. For more clarity, if you had $700,000.00, the difference would equal less than *one* of those dollars. In my home state of Iowa this percentage would equal about three additional people in the entire state. Clearly the world is in trouble—not because of global warming or man-made climate change but because alarmists rely on your ignorance to control you. Some right-wingers suggest that lower educational proficiency will foster a more egalitarian culture and is therefore a component of the liberal agenda. What does the Left really want?

And there is more.

Global warming isn't all bad. First, it is warmer. We will use less fossil fuel if it is warmer! We will emit less carbon dioxide if the need for heating fuel is reduced.

Also, my expertise *is* in agriculture. I can expertly tell you that a small increase in global temperatures is mandatory if we are obliged to feed an ever-expanding global population. Crop-growing regions will expand northerly in the presence of GW. It is common knowledge among farmers that in recent times, cereal crops (corn, wheat, barley, etc.) are being grown further and further north which increases total global supply. Global warming is essential to provide for this need. You must do whatever you can to increase global warming *if* we are to avoid a mass starvation in the future!

Oh, and there is more.

If the polar ice caps melt which is of course impossible it is said that ocean levels will rise and flood coastal cities. Time for some more math! I am perplexed though. I have just spent a lot of time trying to congeal the rhetoric of climate change as global ice is concerned. As with the absence of the GW consensus mentioned above, there is also no consensus as to how ice's potential to melt will affect sea levels. The research and conclusions and related "facts" are all over the place meaning that there is a lot of information that says a lot of different things and says it using different "facts" as evidence. I would like to find conclusive information against the convoluted "facts" but conclusive is impossible given that the melting of the polar ice caps is also impossible. I really can think of no other reason that explains why scientifically relevant "facts" are so obscure. These things should be everywhere if CC is really about to destroy the planet. What I do find everywhere is conjecture, myth, and supposition. Again, where are the scientists and where are their "papers" that are a cultural component of the profession.

In any case I use whatever clear information I have found to discuss rising sea levels. I will tell you without apology that my numbers are not completely accurate. My math is flawed but my conclusions are based on logic and not emotion or agenda. I also am sure that my numbers are close enough to validate my opinion.

The surface area of the earth's oceans is about 138 million square miles. To raise ocean levels by 1 foot would require almost 4 billion cubic feet of water. The surface area of North Polar ice is about 1,400.000 square miles on average. North Polar ice fluctuates by area, but it is moving and is normally a thin layer. I have no average-depth numbers but for the sake of discussion I am going to use 10 feet as an average seasonal depth. Pick your own number if you don't like mine. It is true that most of this ice is below, at, or just above sea level and will have little or no effect on rising sea levels if it were to melt. The point is that to raise the ocean level by 1 foot, ice on an area the size of the North Polar ice cap would need to be 286 feet deep. There are plenty of places on earth where ice is 286 feet deep—and much deeper—but to raise the ocean level by 1 foot we need 138 million square miles at 286 feet deep. This is an area that is nearly equal to the continental United States, plus Alaska, 286 feet deep. We need this area to melt and become liquid just to raise the ocean level by 1 foot. It would take centuries to melt that much ice. Do I need to go on about this? Do I need to point out how much ice would need to melt to actually flood coastal cities? For some perspective, the diameter of the earth at sea level, from the North Atlantic ocean to the South China Sea would have to increase by 2 feet if ocean levels were to rise by 1 foot. Clearly the concept is absolutely absurd. Clearly there will never be enough melting ice on planet earth to flood coastal cities absent a cataclysmic event. No one is suggesting that this much of the earth's ice can melt or is likely or even possible. There is massive and ancient ice covering Antarctica but suggesting that it will melt enough to flood coastal cities in the next ten thousand years is nothing less than a declaration of f—ing ignorance. Again, I freely admit that my numbers are not completely accurate. They don't need to be because the truth is profoundly out of balance with leftist-extremist-brain-dead-nutcase-liberal claims of a pending calamity. Wherever this ignorant myth started; whoever first made this claim must have been speculating, and then this idea grew to become a believed fact! The claim of flooding coastline cities based on melting ice is absurdly irrational and only exists as a wet dream.

And there is more.

I would like to introduce the concept of the BDNCLEU, or the Brain-Dead Nut-Case Liberal Energy Unit! We will call it the brain-dead unit, BDU, for short. The BTU or British thermal unit has been around for a very long time and has been commonly used as a measure of the cooling power of your air conditioner. It originated as a scientific measure of the thermal dynamic properties of energy production and transfer. The BDU is a variation of this concept, in that it measures the amount of energy that a fluorescent bulb saves in your house in one year, which is about 400 watt- hours. We will use this as a comparison to other things we might do to prevent the flooding of the city of Miami.

If a fluorescent light bulb uses 25 watts per hour,— compared to an incandescent bulb which uses 60 watts per hour, the incandescent bulb will produce more light [lumens] at 60 watts than the claimed lumens produced by the fluorescent bulb at 25 watts. Do you have an old fashioned SLR camera or a light meter? You can measure the light output at home if you have such a meter. I put the ratio at about 4 to 3, meaning that every claimed lumen of the fluorescent bulb is actually only about 80 percent actual illumination.[13] Yes; the different frequency of produced light is perceived as dimmer at the same lumens, and you can do your own simple test to show this even if your test simply consists of replacing lit bulbs and visually comparing the results. But be cautious of the poisonous mercury vapor in the fluorescent bulb! Oh, and remember that the incandescent bulb also provides free heat as part of the equation. In any case, my formula translates to these simple facts: Let's assume that a basic unit of 10 BDUs = 6.5 BDUs per hour, or a savings of 3.5 BDUs per hour allowing for the free heat. Multiply 1 year at 3 hours per day average lit time, or approximately 1,100 watt-hours per year x 3.5 savings, or 1,100 x 3.5, for a savings in watts of 385 watt-hours annually, which is equal to the energy it takes to run your hairdryer for about 20 minutes.

Also the "energy saving must be properly disposed of" poisonous bulb is saving about 400 watt-hours per year rounded up (to allow for my flawed math). Therefore the BDU equals about 400 watt-hours multiplied by an electric rate of 10 cents per 1,000 kilowatt-hours, or 1,000 watts for an hour. Congratulations! By my formula you are saving about forty cents a year on electricity per each four-dollar fluorescent bulb. It is probably best that you don't include the free heat advantage in wintertime to the tune of 60 watts per hour. You probably don't want to know that your incandescent bulb is actually a much better bargain and will better save the planet if the otherwise-free winter heat is a factor.

And there is a lot more!

Do you ever use your air conditioner and your stove/oven at the same time? Both of these energy-hungry appliances can use about 20 amperes (amps) per hour and they are working against each other. That's okay though. You can just buy some light bulbs to make it back—or can you? I have been trying to make sense of a formula to convert amperes to watts but they measure different things so a direct conversion is impossible. If I use my BDU scale I can estimate that 1 amp-hour = about 480 BDUs. Your average whole-house air conditioner uses about 360 amp-hours per day or about 172,000 BDUs per day which is the equivalent of approximately 7,170 BDUs per hour. Well, you will need to use your fluorescent bulb for about one continuous year for twenty-four hours a day, seven days a week to equal an hour of running your air conditioner! You need to keep your fluorescent bulb turned off for an entire year in order to equal the energy that your air conditioner uses in one hour. And yet you continue to believe you are saving the planet by buying energy-efficient light bulbs. Running your air conditioner and stove at the same time equals two years of BDU savings if they only work against each other for an hour.

And there is a lot more!

There are 114,000 BTUs per gallon of gasoline. As stated a BDU equals about 400 watt-hours per year.

If your air conditioner is producing 8,000 BTUs and if your car gets 28 miles per gallon, that is 5,000 BTUs per mile, per minute at 60 miles per hour—or about 45 seconds of driving—which is roughly the same as two years of continuous use of savings from your fluorescent bulb as compared to an incandescent bulb. Forty-five seconds in your fuel-efficient car consumes more energy than the equivalent BDU savings for two years unless your bulb happens to be powered by natural gas or a nuclear reactor. Did your state ban incandescent bulbs? I hear it's going nationwide! What a bunch of goons! They are little more than sheep. You can't save the planet with stupid!

Of course I can't claim this statement to be accurate but I do claim that it can be used as a reasonable comparison of energy savings. A BDL will tell you that every little bit helps and the notion is hard to argue with, *BUT,* going for one Sunday drive cannot be replaced as savings of energy in a lifetime of buying fluorescent bulbs. I will mention again that conversion of power plants to natural gas in the United States has in the last few years already saved more greenhouse gas emissions than even the most psychotic brain-dead liberal leftist extremist nutcase wacko commie pinko socialist could have possibly fanaticized about just a few years ago! And it is happening as a result of free-market enterprise having nothing to do with impending doom or environmental advocacy. The problem liberals now face is that there is a legitimate and massively therapeutic treatment for greenhouse gas emissions and they are still protesting against it! Why? What is it they really want?, I say again that a solution to man-made global warming/climate change is contrary to the liberal agenda. BDLs have proved this to be true repeatedly.

I love my planet! I make my living cultivating the planet. I am very in tune with our planet as are all farmers. My grandfather farmed the same land as I do as did my father. My sons will eventually farm this land also. We are extremely invested in the earth and its potential to produce. Throughout my lifetime I have witnessed a significant increase in the productivity of my land. This is mostly the result of evolving technology. My farm is healthier and more productive than it has ever been which includes a time when it was freely roamed by buffalo and visited by the occasional American Indian. Soil erosion on my farm is dramatically less than it was when I was young. Those suggesting that our agriculture

system is "unsustainable" are living in a fantasy world. They are nothing more than manipulative fearmongers!

Potential climate change affects me and my lively-hood more than almost any other profession and it could affect my family's future generations accordingly. I am telling you that I am not concerned about man-made climate change. I know of no reason to be. What I am very concerned about is that there are those who would falsely manipulate culture for their own purposes.

[14] WHAT IS IT THEY REALLY WANT?

In case you were wondering!

Why does climate change 2 come before climate change 1? Because I wrote climate change 2 first????

THE MOST COMPELLING PROCLIVITY OF ALL
SEX AND RELATIONSHIPS

How do we explore human proclivities without examining, in great detail, the most compelling human proclivity of all: sex and relationships?

In pondering the subject of sex and relationships I find myself a little reluctant to delve into the topic. While it is a controversial and popular subject for almost everyone it can also be very embarrassing and confusing to say the least especially for the young and inexperienced. It is not my intention or desire to give details of my own proclivities as far as the sex act goes. Though tempting this is not my goal. Also it would be easy enough to talk about how horny I might get or what the sight of a hot young babe still does to me at my age. I could write about what I would enjoy doing with her if I had that extremely unlikely chance but it is not my desire or intention to write porn although I promise you I could make it very interesting. Also, as is true for many males I personally might be inclined to discuss my sexual history at some braggadocio level; but this is not a kiss-and-tell discussion by any means. I will let you assume that I am a real stud—gettin' plenty and always have. It *is* my intention to explore sexuality as more of a guide to understanding; offered to the youthful or inexperienced among us. I don't intend to discuss the easily available and widely distributed how-to's of sex but to explore the more obscure whys of sex, mating, and the resulting relationships.

At the surface the whys of sex are obvious. Like food and water sex is essential to the human existence not to mention the fact that we humans just really like it. By that I mean we *really, really* like it. By the "why" of sex I mean *why* does she do this or *why* did he do that? I do not mean in reference to the act but in reference to the preliminaries of sexual mating. I can't really explore the science of mating because I don't have much knowledge of such things. I can only explore my lifetime of personal observations and experiences. I think that I have had a little more relevant experience than the average person given that the hand life dealt me did not include a long-term committed monogamous relationship. This fact left me with opportunities that most men would envy. I can tell those men that the grass is not necessarily greener on my side of the fence. I will continue my comments by saying that, at best sexual mating is a playful and pleasurable game; at worst it is a heartbreaking personal tragedy which can lead to devastating life-altering consequences—consequences sometimes as extreme as murder and suicide. I like to have some fun with this topic but clearly it can be a very heavy subject.

So why do we like sex so much? Why are all forms of life compelled to engage in some form of reproductive behavior? Why is sexual enticement the most common form of advertising—whether it be products to enhance feminine beauty or ads to draw attention to marketed products such as cars and beer. Why is it something that the average man thinks about every three seconds? (I don't actually believe that.) What is it that makes sex so compelling? The answer is simple: basic anthropology! Over the course of human existence those more inclined by proclivity to engage in sexual activity are also much more likely to reproduce thus passing along the inclination to the next generation. The more we like it the more we do it—and the more we do it the more likely a pregnancy will result. Clearly the human need for sex is compelling at an extreme level. All life on our planet depends upon reproduction to exist and it is not just the human animal that experiences the extreme need. If you have any doubt check out some of the X-rated nature films made these days! I am still having trouble getting the image of horny kangaroos out of my mind.

A discussion of human sexuality from the perspective of my male mind is the only choice I have and is much more likely to be accurate than a discussion of the female mind given that I am male. Hopefully I can offer insight into why we men do the things we do but the truth is such a discussion will be brief. Men are very simple: we want a lot of sex and we want it with a lot of different women or, we want it exclusively with one woman who we believe to be only having sex with us. This is also a basic instinct rooted in anthropology. It also guarantees validity of our progeny. Now that we have fully explored the mind of men let's consider the other side of the sexual coin. A conversation of the sexuality of the female mind will be much more perplexing and time consuming if not impossible to break down in an understanding way! (Sorry for that wisecrack cliché girls. I just couldn't resist the opportunity.) Actually the rules that motivate sexual behavior in women are not really that much of a mystery. They do seem very confusing to men and there is some unpredictability in women as compared to men but what motivates females is at its roots very clear. For now I will stay with the male perspective.

I mentioned above that it would be wrong for to me to discuss my personal sexual experience and I will say without any fear of contradiction that most men would take the same stance. Yes, I am telling you that men rarely talk about the women they have had sexually. It is a myth that men brag about their sexual conquests. I can only remember one or two times that I actually was told by another man that he had "scored" a certain female. Yes, it is very rare! What should women take from this info? "Hey girls, it's okay to have sex with me whenever you want. I won't tell." Actually the truth is that if a guy gets a reputation to kiss and tell he is less likely to get the next "kiss," and is more likely to get shot as the result of a recent encounter with someone else's girlfriend. It is self-preservation on both sides of the equation. Going in we spread our seed, going out we stay alive. We know this by instinct. You should also conclude that we men are always scheming on how to get laid. What gets in the way of this scheming? Risk assessment! In this case not wanting to get shot down by the potential female of our desire. No one likes rejection. It is an ego thing. In the real world very few men are sexually aggressive as "hitting on" women is concerned. Movies commonly show men as aggressive jerks focused on quick sexual gratification.[15] Yes, it does happen but how many men are really so bold? We think about it but we rarely do it. I can also tell you that such aggression is rarely successful.

As I said men don't normally brag about their conquests. If a girl gets a bad reputation it likely did not come from men she has been with. It is more likely to come from the men who didn't get "it" or from the rumors of her female friends and acquaintances and not from male bragging. I think if a girl gets a bad reputation it is based on the assumptions and conjecture of those who know her. It is also based on her general behavior and demeanor. If you are seen leaving a bar with a guy it is assumed you "did" him whether you did or not. You do that more than once and you are now labeled a tramp. Be careful. Reputation can be a difficult thing to deal with especially in a small town.

We as men are faithful to one woman because we don't want to risk our access to the readily available sex we have at hand. It is the bird-in-the-hand concept though we are always thinking about the two in the bush—actually just the bush—it is part of our sexual psyche. Men cheat not out of love or the lack thereof but because we are horny which translates into our prewired instinct to spread our seed. Men don't cheat for romance; men cheat for sex. It is thought that women cheat for romance not sex. I am not sure how true this is but I do know that it is the reason why culturally, straying men are much more tolerated than straying women. For the guy it is assumed to be mostly just about sex. For the woman it is seen as a systemic violation of the social structure and related commitment. Our social structure is based on the needs of women and their children, not the naturally freewheeling and independent nature of men. Society holds men accountable for the children we randomly produce and by necessity of group survival historically but much less so in today's socialest culture.

I think it is true that men love just as deeply as women but it is accepted that a man can love a woman deeply and still want sex with another. The reverse is not accepted in women. While it will always be the quest of the male to gain access to sex, it will and must always be up to the female to decide when and with whom the sex act will actually take place. It is inescapable that only the woman can know the risk of pregnancy when considering recreational sex. Men don't get pregnant and can disappear into the night. Women do get pregnant and can't run away so easily. If you are a woman who barely knows me and we end up as a one-night stand, I have no choice but to assume that you have taken steps to avoid pregnancy. Even if I ask you about birth control beforehand (a mood killer at best) I am still dependent on your judgment. If you're a feminist and thinking that the man has just as much responsibility for birth control as the woman you are right, culturally; but as a practical matter, it is crap. If you get knocked up I will pay child support and I probably should. In the real world if I bring up the subject of birth control before I am discreetly slipping your pants down over your shapely ass, it's a sexual buzz-kill—so much so that I might just as well go home now. Not only am I being presumptuous to the extreme assuming that we are about to have sex, I might actually be suggesting that you are a bit of a tramp just by asking the question. Until the pants are off you never really know for sure where it is going. By then it's too late for a question-and-answer period.

The above notwithstanding sex and sexuality for most of us will be about the need for a "relationship," of which sex is an important part. Not having sex in a relationship is known as a friendship. I want the woman in my life to be my best friend but we aren't going to be friends for long if there isn't sex. I am not basing our relationship on sex but it is the prize—or the deal breaker—in any committed relationship. I also want the woman in my life to be someone I love and respect as a person. I will take pride in her and cherish her more if she is physically attractive and of a good and amiable character but these qualities or the lack of them might not interfere with our long-term situation. The lack of sex definitely will.

What is the most important thing a man gets from his woman? It is not sex exactly; it is validation! Female validation is at the root of almost all male behavior. It is by far the most important factor in our lives. And that validation comes from the social status we gain from our women. The more desirable the woman who validates us is, the more validation we get from her and from society at large. The more validation we get the better we feel about ourselves. When a man gives up on female validation he might become a vagabond or another sort of reclusive social derelict. Our sexuality and our consuming desire to spread our seed is so very compelling that with the failure of that goal or in the absence of that goal we men may be left without direction in life. We might drop out of society completely because our primary and primal purpose as a male has been abandoned. Some men pursue great wealth or desirable professions— doctors for example—because potential sex partners will be drawn to the highly regarded status; possibly sexy young women will be attracted which will validates us very much. There is no greater marker of success in a man's life than the women he "acquires." What else could be worth its weight in gold?

FEMININE BEAUTY

If you are a woman in a troubled marriage and your husband wants you to lose weight and you are telling him that you shouldn't have to; I agree. You are right. Also, you are under no obligation to have sex with your man at all. You are under no obligation to lose weight or to make any other systemic change to yourself. The same applies to men. Having said that the right that you *don't* have is to expect that there will be no consequences or detriment to your relationship because of your personal choices. Specifically, in this case the choice is overeating or withholding sex. There will be consequences. There are always consequences to chosen behavior both negative and positive. *Would* and *should* are killers for any relationship in the same way that liberals hold ideals ahead of practical values. It just doesn't work. Lots of things should be and would be in a perfect world. Not so much in the real world! In the real world great stock is placed on feminine beauty. Effigies to the compelling image that is the well-formed and youthful human female are everywhere in human culture. Wars have been fought and history made. Her perfect image is truly treasured by men. This simple fact puts a lot of pressure on women to look their very best and become the physical icon as such. Physical feminine beauty and its quest is an enormous industry worldwide. Women know instinctively that to attract the best of the male of the species money is not gonna do it. To get the best you have to be the best. Beautiful women are admired not only by men but also other women and even children. This quality of beauty is power and a very real power. You don't have to get rich to be a powerful woman. You don't have to be smart or talented or have any great skill. You just have to be attractive. Not fair you say? I have never known life to be fair. Fair is not a part of being human, not for anyone.

How about a little controversy.

Watch the morning talk shows and sooner or later you will hear some less-than-attractive woman (Rosie O'Donnell), (actually a different woman who is very much like her, but not her), complain that she should be judged for her other qualities. In her case not an option. I have heard other less-than-attractive women complain "I have value too! I am worthwhile and deserving also!" Probably true. Both the beautiful and the ordinary woman may be brilliant and clever. The plain woman may be a great author; she may be a great actor or singer. The average-looking woman may impress me with her wisdom or her advances to the scientific world or any number of great skills and all of these things benefit me. As a doctor she might actually save my life. So what is the difference so compelling that we men would place so much greater value on the physical beauty of a woman than the talents of a woman? It is about the *power* of beauty. The talented woman might extend my life but the beautiful woman will make my life worth living. Her presence in my life will be a daily joy and I will be validated as a man on an ongoing basis. The quality that she can bring to me is profound not only in the validation I receive but also in the social status I attain in my everyday life. When a man is in the company of a beautiful woman she brings the power of beauty with her and her mate assumes this power as his own. It is naturally assumed by others that the man is deserving. His status goes up and his life is better by default not only because he has enjoyed her beauty and her sexuality personally but because he has been recognized as worthy of that power. When I know that the end of my life is near it will be the beauty I shared not the wealth I accumulated that will be more important to me. As my time among the living passes it will be random thoughts of such a woman that will put that unlikely sly smile on my face in the aisle of a grocery store or during some other not necessarily joyful moment—or on my deathbed for that matter. The memory I will cherish for the rest of my days, the experience that my life has given me no matter what else is true in the end will be those truly precious few moments I shared with that rare beauty when her intimacy was mine and mine alone. Those moments may have been few or many and often repeated or not in life but each and every experience is like a jewel in my pocket I value highly. Not because the sex was necessarily better but because the validation was much more ... much, *much* more. I will carry the beneficial effects of that validation and the glory of those precious-jewel moments for the rest of my life. I believe such thinking to be common among men.

I also am well aware that great beauty can be a burden for a woman especially for the budding beauty of too young an age. The firm hand of wisdom is not normally a tool yet available to the puberty-stricken underage female. The absence of such beauty can also be a heavy burden for the (coming of age) girl.

Time for some actual real controversy.

ALTERNATE SEXUALITY

It is a well-known scientific fact that as we age our natural hormone levels change. Estrogen and testosterone decrease or increase with time. This is why younger people marry as heterosexuals but eventually adopt a gay lifestyle as they age. This is not an uncommon thing. We likely all know someone who meets this description. They married when young and produced children. As time passed their gender-specific hormone levels decreased (or increased) for one or both partners to the point that homosexual tendencies made a conventional marriage unworkable. The reason is not only that the naturally gay person was trying to live a conventional lifestyle but is due to the eventual and gradual changes in hormones. I am convinced that this is the common reason for the situation in that the person eventually just had to accept that he or she was gay and "come out" publicly. The hard question is; what if this scenario could be reversed? What if these natural changes don't have to happen? What decisions would be made if the homosexual question could stop being a question? As a culture we have access to artificial hormones that can reverse these trends but we don't we use them. Yes, it is true that a straight man, when given a drug that reduces testosterone will develop gay tendencies. A straight man can become gay and a gay man can be turned straight when given testosterone. The same is true for women. If you give a gay masculine woman enough estrogen you will not only create an emotional wreck, but you will also create a truly feminine woman. It is all about the hormones.

I am betting you have never heard this before. I am betting you never thought about the fact that gay does not have to be gay! Homosexuality has been about gay rights and gay acceptance and gay is not a mental health issue. No, gay is not a mental health disorder any more than straight is a mental health disorder. Homosexual tendencies can be a psychological disorder—sexual assignment disorder for example—but are not by default a mental health issue. Again, why don't we use these therapies to help the homosexuals? The wording of my last sentence is the answer. As straight man I don't consider myself needing "help" with my sexuality any more than a gay man would. The same would be true for a lesbian. "I am what I am" and for a gay person such is a much more pertinent issue. We are what we are. I don't want to be gay. I assume gays don't want to be straight. There is another issue that I should point out as pointed out to me by the health-care professional who enlightened me. It is a matter of medical ethics. A gay person is not ill by any medical definition. No treatment is warranted medically. No prescription can be written ethically that would not be contrary to standard medical practice. Homosexuality is not a health issue. Still the question of whether or not any gay person would seek a medical option if given the chance is one that I raise but I will end the thought there.

I do have to ask why so many of the world-renowned successful artistic and creative types are also gay? I don't have any proof of the assumptions of my question but it does appear to be true that many gays, by proclivity are the highly expressive and creative among us especially as men go. The gay community also has a history of high profile if not radical and demanding behavior. Historically the gay movement has demanded acceptance but too often in a way that alienates the gay community from the straight community. I can't assume that radical behavior is a proclivity of homosexuality because I have known gays who are anything but radical. I think the need for public acceptance must be so highly motivating that those affected are driven to extremes and too often, highly questionable extremes.

GAY MARRIAGE IN IOWA

Nationally, there were only a handful of states that recognized gay marriage at the time when Iowa became one of those states. The rest of the nation might have looked to our state as an example of a "progressive" state with modern views of society and an acceptance of evolved thinking given that we had chosen to support gay marriage as an equality-for-gays issue. Not so! Iowa was not progressive in its decision; Iowa was vulnerable. Iowans were victims. Our first-in-the-nation status as elections and primaries go has drawn the attention of many political activists. Those same activists have come here to advocate liberal politics. Some have made Iowa their home or maintain an ongoing presence here. Iowa is a very middle-of-the-road state historically, as politics are concerned. We are for the most part a pragmatic people and we concern ourselves with being "the right kind of person" and "doing the right thing" as part of our lifestyle. Integrity is important to most of us and we use it as our daily guidepost. This is apparently not true for liberal activists. The gay-marriage advocates pursued an ends-justify-the means" strategy but they do not see themselves as subversive. It was an agenda so important to a few social manipulators that principles became secondary to personal advantage. Gay marriage became possible in Iowa because of a unanimous Iowa Supreme Court ruling declaring that gays were being discriminated against if they could not get married legally. It was a discrimination issue entirely. The population of the state at large is against gay marriage and our legislature passed laws accurately reflecting the will of the people.

How then could the Court have ruled unanimously in favor of gay marriage? Doesn't the court reflect the will of the citizens of the state? Doesn't it ultimately have an intrinsic responsibility to do so? Shouldn't the court reflect the will of its people? In this case the answer is an emphatic *no!* How is it possible that all six judges of the Iowa Supreme Court agreed to the same legal principle? When were six randomly chosen people ever able to unanimously agree on anything? The answer is that they were *not* randomly chosen. Liberal activists, liberal governors and a liberal bar association stacked the deck. This stacking took place over a long period of time. I am not suggesting a conspiracy in favor of gay marriage. I am suggesting that a surreptitious loosely organized group of extremists advocated their policies and did so in a state where the people tend to be trusting; and these liberal extremists managed to get six liberal judges on the bench at the same time.

If you followed this story you will know that three of these judges are no longer on the bench. They were "excused" from their positions based on the majority will of the state's citizens. Another of these judges was not excused in a subsequent election under the same standards and also was not granted the same honors as granted by leftist institutions to the three former justices. Keep in mind that these honors were granted to people who stood in direct defiance to the will of the people they theoretically serve. Their position of power was gained based on an agenda and not on judicial qualifications generally.

Personally, my observation is that no gay has ever been denied a marriage license in the state of Iowa. I am sure that this is true except where other issues were a factor. Gays have always gotten married in Iowa the same as anyone else as long as gender opposites were involved. It can only be discrimination if you have already assumed that same-sex marriage is appropriate and should be legal. Think about that for a moment. The decision comes *before* the argument, not after. It is not discrimination if you have already assumed that same-sex marriage is not appropriate and should not be allowed. There literally is no valid claim of discrimination by homosexuals. Gays can and always have gotten married in Iowa. The court ruled by the first assumption; an assumption that has never been

validated or determined positively by any court or legislative body. The deck was stacked and law was never an issue.

Historically, marriage was about the public and social approval of the couple's right to engage in sex and the resulting procreation. This approval came with several obligations attached, most notably sexual exclusiveness and a lifetime commitment. I assume that culturally most of us know this by instinct if not by extremely obvious example. Given this notion, public acceptance of gay marriage is not about rights but acceptance itself; public acceptance has always been an issue for anyone who through no choice of their own was different. As stated, I have or had gay friends and for the most part I have no reason to care about their sexual proclivities. I may or may not like them as people and I would hold them to the same standards that would lead me to like or dislike any person. I hope they like me also. A chasm forms between the homosexual community and me when my approval is demanded and that approval requires a cultural realignment for two-thirds of the people on the planet. I have no right to control what two consenting adults choose to do in private sexually. Two chicks "getting it on" is a sexual hot button for most guys and I am no exception. Two men having sex is naturally repulsive to me. It is not because of cultural training and it is not out of an ingrained threat to my heterosexuality, or a secret desire to give it a try. It is an ingrained instinct which is much more than a proclivity and most likely due to centuries of anthropology. Gay men are less likely to breed and the result is less male proclivity toward homosexuality in our species. Gays not reproducing because they are no longer expected to marry out of their gender may actually, over a long period of time lead to a decrease in the number of gays as a percentage of the population.

Gays are demanding full rights as married couples which includes unrestricted access to all the social benefits of a committed long-term relationship. Liberals are more than quick to jump on the bandwagon of social acceptance with an "anything goes" mentality—as long as the Christian religion is not part of the deal. Going back for as many centuries as you may care to speculate, religious social bodies have been the sanctioning authority as sexual intercourse is concerned. Marriage is and has always been the moment when two people assumed the right to engage in sexual activity as much as any other members of the the community. It also meant that a father would allow the male of his daughter's choice, and no other to "screw" his little girl. Big deal for a father! Big, big, deal. This sanctioning became a sacred moment in cultures all over the globe and throughout history. Ceremony and tradition grew and this event became a celebrated moment in the life of nearly everyone.

Today there are still billions of people around the planet who hold these traditions sacred and connect these traditions inextricably to their religions. The two things are one and the same. I am not religious but I will honor those who are without prejudice regarding the marital union.[16] I will not condemn or validate their religion based on my own opinions but I will grant a specific grace to those who do believe. This thinking is not an option for gays though. What gays need and want is social acceptance and validation just like everyone else—but at what price to billions of the otherwise faithful. What gays require is an incredible philosophical realignment and on a global scale. Public acceptance of homosexuality requires nothing less than a complete abandonment of the social guideposts of the religious so that 3 percent of the population can have a more positive self-image and have a few more automatic legal rights. Rights that often offer very fleeting real-world benefits. It is about demanding acceptance and validation without concern for the consequences to others. I will personally grant that validation but I will not respond to the demands that others should be forced to grant this same validation against their will. In this permutation demanding gays are actually the "bad guys." They are the same bad guys that condemn others for being unaccepting.

STRAIGHT TALK

I mentioned previously that we have rights in our relationships but can't reasonably expect to express those rights without the related consequences, good or bad. I did a little relationship counseling once upon a time. I have no professional credentials; nor do I care to. The work I did was as a volunteer and it was not extensive. However, my eyes were opened wide to some interesting issues regarding sex. The issue was using sex, mostly the lack thereof to control the male. This is a relationship killer. It is beyond reason for a woman to expect to be getting what she wants from her man if she is not available sexually. Let's face it girls. Your man will be grumpy if he is not getting a little physical lovin'. If you are forcing him to live a sexless life when you and he and would otherwise be sexually active you cannot expect an amiable relationship. You are not likely to get what you want from that relationship. Also; I would never suggest that a woman should put out on demand for her man. This is also a relationship killer. The romantic motivations of a woman need to be recognized. She will resent her man if they are not.

Guys, your lady needs to feel good about you before she will feel good about sex with you. She needs to approve of her sex partner, psychologically, mentally, and emotionally. And if you are tempted to satisfy your sexual urges elsewhere there will be a price to pay well beyond the cost of getting a new female friend drunk—or the cost of a hooker. What to do? What to do? You have no choice guys! It is just the nature of things where your lady is concerned.

FEUDING COUPLES

Another thing I learned from my counseling experiences is that the primary issue in troubled relationships is an underlying need for control, power, and autonomy. More specifically it is about winning which results in control and power. Winning and being right becomes the dominant issue in your daily interactions. Winning against your partner! Winning to the detriment of the partner with whom you share your days and nights! I hope it seems a bit silly when worded this way. This is a cycle and it is a cycle that needs to be broken. *YOU* can break the cycle if you have learned this concept and it works better if your partner is not aware of your contrived change in thinking. Both partners can't break the cycle at the same time. It cannot take the form of a mutual agreement. If you could make a mutual agreement—and you keep your mutual agreement—you would not be feuding in the first place. It must be one or the other partner who takes a proactive stance for the betterment of the relationship. How then do *you* break the cycle? How then do you re-cycle your relationship? You don't need to get your partner motivated to want to break the cycle. The cycle can end by default. I am skipping ahead a bit but it will always come down to stepping outside your relationship mentally and emotionally and make one critical decision: do you or do you not want this relationship to continue assuming that it can be made a peaceful (if not sexual) experience? If the answer is yes—and it normally is—you need to adopt the concept of what I will call *objectifying your partner.* By this I mean not seeing him or her in terms of what you expect them to be personally but rather seeing him or her objectively as he or she truly is! The assumption here is that you have unrealistic expectations about what your partners' capabilities are. When you see your partner realistically and objectively for what he or she truly is you will stop fighting with them. You will no longer have a reason to fight. You will stop trying to change your partner. You will also take control of the relationship because your partner will stop hating you. This mindset will lead to an automatic change in the way you interact with your partner and will actually give *you* the power in your relationship. Your reason for debate will end. Accept your partner for what he or she is or get out of the relationship. Again, people normally stay in the relationship when faced with this decision. I have seen this work repeatedly and it works best when only one person in the relationship understands this concept. Stop personalizing and start objectifying.

OKAY, THAT'S ENOUGH SERIOUS STUFF!

The greatest sexual power is not the naturally hot eighteen-year-old but the more mature thirtyish woman who is well maintained and has the moxie and character that come with experience. This woman can be very intimidating to the less bold among us as men but she is really the greatest prize and the most rare. This is the woman we men admire from a distance. We tend not to approach her knowing it is likely that we will be ignored completely if not flatly "invalidated" as a man.

I have been known to wander several aisles out of my way while shopping just to get a closer look at such a woman. I can only guess as to what she might be thinking as she ignores me but I do know that most women are flattered to be admired physically. I think they know or assume at some level that I have strayed from my normal course in life to check it out. It is I think, natural for an attractive woman to display an aloof demeanor as a defense mechanism against any unwelcome interaction given that her opportunities for male interaction are very common. However, on one occasion past I did just as I described previously when I sighted one of those rare slightly mature and powerful beauties. I may have actually strayed twice or more just to take in the sight of this iconic image. Her natural grace and inherent charm enhanced the vision. This time was different though; this time I was afforded a knowing smile as a subtle brief acknowledgement of my admiration and my resulting uncontrollable grin was indirectly returned. Satisfied that there was nothing left to be gained I continued my shopping and eventually went to the checkout to pay for my purchases. I was pleased when I glanced around and saw her coming my way and I was thrilled when she came into the line behind me and there was no doubt that her presence in my line was contrived. Desperately grabbing for whatever composure I could find I coolly responded when she smiled at me again and actually spoke to me. The encounter was brief as was the conversation but it was flirtatious and with more of those knowing smiles. I was so inspired by this meeting that I eventually wrote something of a sonnet to this now illusive goddess. It seems a bit silly in retrospect, and I won't include it here but possibly I will put it on my website if I get enough requests. This chick was flaming hot and way out of my league, sexy as hell by default and not by dress or overt intention. This encounter was nothing but a brief game and I thank her for letting me play! I will not forget her.

Have you ever noticed that it is almost impossible not to smile at someone you are attracted to?

THE SEXUALITY OF WOMEN;-

FROM A MANS POINT OF VIEW;

Clearly, I can only guess as to the motivations that drive a woman sexually. I am not talking about reproduction or obligation but the mind-set of a woman when she just wants to get laid. I know for sure that a lot of women really like sex and some want it frequently. An injustice of the human sexual experience is that as young men we want a lot of sex and are capable of doubles if not triples when highly motivated but this is also the age when "old enough" girls are for the most part reluctant to engage in sex. I think this is a self-protective reaction on the part of these females because so many of the men around her might be looking at her in "that way" and these women/girls become anxious and confused as a result. I think an attractive young female learns very early to take a defensive stance sexually. This defensive stance may be interpreted as a lack of interest in sex by the male, or it may actually result in a lack of interest by the female given the stress and uncertainty. Also the risk of pregnancy must surely weigh heavily on the sexual urges of the young female. Fortunately for us guys there is still that urge if not desire to find out what all the excitement is about for most young women. It is very clear that some young females have a very high interest in sex and are frequently willing. The aforementioned travesty is the fact that as women age they commonly develop a much higher sexual proclivity. As men age we tend to lose interest in sex. We still want it but the extreme motivation of our youth fades. Many things in life just don't seem fair. I can live with this inequity but it is not fair. It's not fair for either gender. It occurs to me that if this travesty were corrected somehow people might look forward to their mature years with much greater anticipation.

I understand why it is that some mature women are on the hunt for younger guys. The reasons are obvious. I can't help but see this behavior as a little pathetic at some level. I am not judging! It is just how it feels. Mature men hunt for younger females but this is standard accepted behavior and I feel good about it. We hunt for the younger female for most of the same reasons mature females hunt for younger men. They look better, they will be more pleasing, and we will feel more validated. The older woman is also more likely to get herself more thoroughly f—ed as a result of her quest than she might from a man her age; this being the main difference.

As I have said previously, the carrot at the end of the relationship

stick for men is the ongoing sexual contact. There are many other aspects of any relationship that I could explore but I am much too lazy for
that and these topics would not be interesting. Again, my motivation
is that I can hopefully offer useful insights during those stressful times
that are a part of every romantic situation—whether it be a marriage, a
friend with benefits, or the undefined civil union that is becoming more
common culturally.

EQUILIBRIUM

"Don't marry a woman who will have sex with you on the first date."
It isn't about whether she is a tramp or not a tramp. It's about the equilibrium of a couple. Any woman can be promiscuous (or not),mostly
depending on the man she is with. (BTW, all men are naturally whores
when it comes to sex.) A woman might "do" a guy she is really hot for
hoping that they will become a couple and knowing that he will likely
be coming back for more sex. The same woman might never have sex on
the first date with a guy she is not all that sure about or she may delay
sex for months thinking that she will dissipate any rumor in her guy's
mind that she might be a bit "easy." It is also true that unless the chick
is really hot the guy will likely think her a tramp if the pants come off
to soon and he will likely not call back if he is looking for a serious relationship. The other unfortunate truth and common scenario is that the
male ego is consistent to the point where if the hot chick—or any girl
for that matter—goes horizontal with him right out of the gate he will
likely assume himself to be such a stud that every girl is just naturally
vulnerable to his charms and wants his seed. Hopefully these comments
will add further clarity to the young and often-vulnerable female who is
still unclear as to how the game is played.

The actual point to my comments is the equilibrium mentioned
earlier. The dating and mating process is about finding that equilibrium. Equilibrium is not about sexual compatibility or common values
or similar interests. It is about balance and equality of both desirability
and cultural value; it is not necessarily about personal values. It is about
your status as a human that needs to be equal to that of your mate. It is

about genetics; it is about education; it is about background; it is about your personal culture and your experiences.

Those who know me would tell you that it is odd that I should write about relationships. I have had two unsuccessful marriages. It is easy enough for me to find friends or relatives who would condemn my X-wives for their qualities and blame them for the resulting failed marriages. I suspect the same would be true in that I am/was the problem. I think it is normal to blame the other person when a marriage fails or at least, to point out the other's failings. We all justify the questionable decisions we make no matter what the subject or circumstance and especially when the social expectation is to maintain the marriage no matter what. Getting involved in other people's relationships as a counselor gave me a very different perspective on this same subject. I heard condemning statements similar to statements I had made regarding my own marriages coming from others people's mouths and I couldn't help but be struck by how utterly useless and unimportant these comments sounded. I think this natural condemnation of the "other" bitch or asshole—is to keep people from thinking it was I/me who was at fault. . As far as my own situation was concerned it took me a long while to realize that for the most part people really don't give a damn who was at fault or what travesty was committed. Blaming serves no purpose.

It was just two two good people who couldn't get along! Does this sound familiar to you? It is total bullshit. In my limited experience and more importantly in my obsessive observation as the years have passed I have never seen this statement to be true. What is commonly true is that one partner is guilty of outrageous behavior not conducive to a successful long-term relationship (assuming that the situation mentioned earlier in "Feuding Couples" is not the primary concern). And this is true not only with unsuccessful marriages but with unsuccessful marriages as well.

If you watch the daytime talk shows you will hear highly renowned therapists and counselors say that money problems are the number 1 cause of divorce. (If you watch daytime TV, you'll have a lot of misconceptions.) I didn't deal with any couple for which excessive spending was the primary problem. Financial matters were at most a secondary issue. There was always a much more compelling issue. When spending is an issue blaming money problems falls into the category of "justifying"—as in, "I did this because"—which is used to hide the real issues. The real and unstated issue is that some people who become dissatisfied with their relationships will behave in ways that ultimately degrade the relationship and alienate themselves from their partners. The aberrant behavior is the result of dissatisfaction not the other way around. I saw this commonly if not normally. In other words, excessive spending is how this contrived alienation is sometimes expressed. If you really value your partner you will not put the relationship at risk over money and your partner would never dare do this either if your marriage were a high priority. Dissatisfaction is also used as a justification for cheating. If you are a counselor who disagrees with this notion you are likely not doing well. You should reconsider your career. You are also not likely making marriages better. The standard model of marriage therapy and its effectiveness is terribly diluted by professional sanctioning bodies primarily concerned with doing no harm. As I learned this "standard model," I was appalled at how absurdly shallow and unproductive it was likely to be. If you had marriage counseling did it help you?

Here is another myth "It is the philandering husband who was at fault." Actually women are statistically only slightly less guilty. Don't believe me? Ask yourself this one question: Who are all these guys screwing? It can't just be one or a very few promiscuous females. I guarantee there are many outlets for such activity and many of them have husbands. The most common complaint: "he was controlling"! This was like a catchphrase for every dissatisfied wife I dealt with. True, men can be very controlling and harshly so at times, so can women. A man who is the primary breadwinner in a marriage probably thinks he has a right to be in control. The same is true for the women. I had to "control" my amusement on one occasion when I heard a complaining woman say she liked a "Take-charge kind of guy." The problem was that her take-charge husband eventually turned out to be a controlling asshole. Now there's a surprise! When she found she couldn't be submissive to his domineering will the marriage was doomed. Control is a huge and very contentious issue in marriage. My observations are that it is necessary for one or the other partner to dominate the marriage and for one partner to be submissive. "Equal" is a fantasy as far as marriage goes. Female-dominated relationships tend to be more successful but the why of this thought is an unpleasant reality for men.[17]

I mentioned earlier that what I normally saw as a counselor was that one or the other partner was behaving in a completely unacceptable way or had unreasonable expectations in the marriage. Clearly infidelity was a common problem and completely unacceptable for most couples though the perpetrator commonly made excuses for this indiscretion and often blamed the partner. Lack of commitment is the most common reason why marriages end but it is rarely seen as such. The aberrant behavior would not exist if the misbehaving partner were committed to the relationship. Most successful couples will tell you that commitment was what made the difference. Lots of people get married but later regret it. The aberrant behavior mentioned comes after the person decides to get out of the marriage not before. This mind-set is often counterproductive given that the described behavior usually draws the still hopeful and about-to-be-dumped partner desperately closer.

A LITTLE OFF THE SUBJECT

The courts have evolved toward a neutral perspective regarding parental rights in recent years. This was rarely true in past decades. When no-fault divorce became standard across the nation in the 1960s the lack of fault left women squarely in control of divorce because they knew that they would almost always get custody of the children or get alimony where no children were involved. Women filed for divorce in droves; actually, at a rate of 9 to 1 in my jurisdiction as compared to men and especially where minor children were involved. Why? Like it or not, believe it or not, an extreme financial and control imbalance was created and it favored women profoundly. There are and were many hardships for divorcing women but the legal inequity was a heavy finger on the scale when divorce was considered. The power and control were seductive as marriages faltered. The personal motivation to make a marriage work was often little or none for the wife/mother. If you doubt me think about it this way. A custodial mother could get that asshole out of the house, confiscate a substantial portion of his salary, take control of his children, and get a fresh romance. She felt she had little to lose and much to gain. Most fathers care very much for their children but lose interest when negotiating with that "bitch" becomes a hopeless issue. I have seen noncustodial mothers react in a similar way when custody was granted to the father. The situation of custodial/noncustodial parentage creates a hostage-ransom mentality as control of the children is concerned. The fantasy of a non-adversarial relationship for divorced parents is often just that, a fantasy and is likely true only when the male takes a submissive posture or is absent from the relationship.

The cultural stigma of not having custody can be devastating to a mom but much less so for a dad. It became common knowledge in my state that judges were ignoring the state laws regarding custody as a means to avoid publicly castigating the mother. Except in extreme cases of abuse or neglect mothers were nearly always granted custody in spite of laws to the contrary. Gender and related behavioral patterns were the only compelling issue. Inescapably these facts led to many divorces that otherwise might have been resolved out of court. I have talked to women during candid moments at social events (drunk at a bar), as they proudly proclaimed the glory of these facts. It was a devastating situation to marriage as a cultural institution. Divorce became more common and more publicly accepted. My local court officers (i.e., judges) openly admitted that they didn't have time to have a lengthy hearing for every divorce. This led to an ever-increasing number of divorces to be heard as the outcomes were predetermined. Subsequently; Judges had even less time to hear each case. The law of unintended consequences prevailed and with dreadful results for families as an adversarial relationship was the inevitable result of divorce.

Today custody is not guaranteed by default and the rate of divorce petitions filed has fallen dramatically and continues to fall. You may hear the network morning news programs confirming this "unexplained coincidences as these female market oriented programs advocate in favor of women's needs. This is a case study in human nature and proclivity in that when any group takes an advantage over another group by fiat tyranny results. In this instance our culture and our children have suffered. It is also a case study in that "Paybacks are hell." For centuries fathers were omnipotent where families were concerned. Women had few if any options when living in a bad marriage situation. Resentment and hostility evolved and grew over a long period of time. Again, paybacks are hell. The social pendulum swung too far in both directions.

AND NOW FOR SOMETHING COMPLETELY DIFFERENT

OK; It's time for what you really want. It is time to discuss the stuff that has kept you reading this crap up to this point. It is the raunchy stuff... The sexually offensive vulgar and crude. I shall not disappoint!

Yes, it's a man's world, but we are willing to trade it for sex!

X-wives? yes, I have two. I keep a spare just in case something really bad should happen to one of them!

I am not saying my X-wife was dumb, but she took an IQ test and failed, so she had her head examined. They didn't find anything!

THE 20 RULES FOR RELATIONSHIPS

1. A man's boobs should never be bigger than his woman's, nor her ass bigger than his.
2. A woman should never ask what a man is thinking. It is better that she does not know what he is thinking.
3. A man should never express a positive comment about another woman no matter who that woman is.
4. A woman needs to pretend she sees her man as a hero, no matter how incompetent he is.
5. The woman is always right when the man is horny. Wait for it.
6. Men thrive on sex like they thrive on food and beer. A woman cannot expect to have a healthy relationship with a partner she is not screwing.

7. If your lady is denying you sex it is probably because of something she is not getting that she feels she needs; a new house for example.

8. If you are a woman using sex to control your man he will hate you for it.

9. If you are a man using sex to control your woman—well, good luck with that!

10. Men should never demand sex from a mate who will not willingly participate. He should get her drunk first!

11. Every man has a kinky, mildly perverted side that should be recognized by his mate.

12. Every woman needs a kinky, mildly perverted side which should be expressed to her mate.

13. Gay and lesbian couples are still breaking ground and defining the rules for posterity. I will get back to you as information is made available to me.

14. A man should expect to have to kiss his woman's ass now and then, especially if it is nice.

15. Keeping your weight low will avoid injury to the male partner, when the woman is on top.

16. Women need girl time because men don't really want to hear about your personal issues.

17. Men need guy time because being around a woman constantly is unnatural.

18. Men need to show compassion and concern for the emotional needs of women. It is critical for men to learn to fake this concern.

19. When a man commits to a woman, it does not automatically include the right for the woman to complain.

20. Women believe they have the right to act irrationally if they choose to. When a man sees this behavior, it is best to just go along with it.

21. Women expect men to lie to them now and then. A woman won't respect her man if he doesn't lie to her.

22. If your woman is talking on and on, pretend to be listening and don't interrupt.
23. If your man is willingly talking to you about your relationship, get him to a doctor. He has a brain tumor.
24. A woman experiencing frequent headaches can be cured with a dozen roses.

And the most important rule of all:

25. Never, *never* confess to any sexual indiscretion. Do your partner a favor and take this secret to your grave!

She had the wisdom and common decency to meet me at the door naked or leaving a note with a trail of lit candles leading to her bedroom. Smart girl! No games equals high-quality relationship. Why pretend that something we both wanted to happen could be an optional thing before the evening was to end or came after some predetermined conditional events?

I can honestly say that I have never been unfaithful to any of the women in my life, but there *is* still time.

Ya know!

Inflation has been tough for strippers. The dollar I would donate to the G-string in the 1970s just doesn't go as far as it did back in those days and five dollars for a booby slap just seems a little overpriced! I can think of no better reason to bring back the two-dollar bill. Strippers could double their income overnight which would help with income inequality. Women just need to make a living wage. Also, the more money strippers make, the more strippers there will be. Again, it's a win-win. Maria Shriver should advocate for the more frequent use of the two-dollar bill as an income-equality issue.

Recently I heard one of those highly regarded sexologists (what a great job!) say that bright-red lipstick on women lips serves the purpose of imitating the female labia major (a.k.a., the vulva or layers of skin surrounding the entrance to the vagina); therefore the lipstick serves to entice men sexually. Sounds like fun but; as a young male I was damn enticed by the concept of the female sex organ long before I ever had any idea of what that organ actually looked like. Red lipstick bares no resemblance to the organs that I eventually came to know. Did this sexologist actually make a living doing research that led to this conclusion? If so, what facts led the researcher to arrive at this conclusion? I can't help but point out that "bright red" in the area of the vagina is usually not good news for a guy wanting sex.[18]

THE SEXUALLY PROMISCUOUS FEMALE

I was recently involved in a conversation condemning sexually promiscuous females. The others involved in the conversation were young adult males. Their comments were harshly critical of a certain few young(ish) "female friends" who were quick to remove their pants in the presence of a sexual opportunity. My first thought was *Yay for you, you lucky jerks!* Second thought: *Why the hell are you complaining?* Personally I thank God for promiscuous women. I have known such females that I was actually very fond of as people and I have known some chaste women who were just bitches that I wouldn't have anything to do with. Three cheers for the promiscuous female! Yay, yay, ya-a-a-a-a-a-ay! It is an ongoing joy for me to have my memory sparked by some random event that reminds me of the precious moments I shared with that person who was "less than resistant" to my sexual desires. What great and treasured memories! Having been single for much of my life, yet still wanting feminine companionship to share my days, and nights with … well, let's just say that my closest and most important friends have always been women. Some were not so close. Some I barely knew but each is precious to me including those who broke my heart or were "without sexual integrity." Each is a sparkling star in the night of my memories. If only there were more!

As far as the complainers are concerned: yes, she must be a tramp if she chose to share herself with you! You should be grateful rather than condemning her for the pleasures she provided. BTW if she was quick to the sheets or the back seat with you what made you think you were so special that she would only do that with you? If you had a chance to "jump the fence" where she was concerned wouldn't you have done the same damn thing eagerly? Your mistake is assuming that you were special because she bopped you. Enjoy such a girl! Be thrilled by her and grateful for what she did for you but don't count on her any more than she could count you!

The previous conversation clearly opens up a lot of controversy about youthful sex. It is also clearly true that nothing much has changed since I was young. Media ranting are occasionally focused on the tragedy of sex at much too young an age. My experience as a young man was that the average girl became sexually "available" at around the age of sixteen. Rumors were and still are common that some much younger girls have dived into the sexual pool and have done so very frequently. I hear stories of twelve-year-olds being sexually active but I assume this is not the average child. Again, nothing much has changed. Clearly a child of that age should not be having sexual intercourse but I also know that sexual exploration normally begins much earlier in life and is an ongoing thing from early childhood in most cases. For the most part the parents never know. Sexual interest is a powerful and lifelong proclivity but sexual intercourse is an entirely different matter where the young are concerned. Disease and pregnancy are the primary issues. Plus, no father wants to think of his precious "little girl" being hosed by some creep of a guy.

The lucky bastard!!

Every now and then, there comes a pop culture news story regarding sexual activity between an older female and a younger male which is portrayed as some sort of tragedy. Recently, much was made of a "sexual assault" by a very attractive twenty-something female schoolteacher upon a seventeen-year-old male student. This now former schoolteacher was also a former NFL cheerleader. (If only I could get her phone number.) Was a crime really committed? If you remember this story you will know that it was headline news and stayed in the news for several weeks. This boy gained considerable attention as a "victim" of this terrible "child molester."

The problem I have is that this "boy" probably spent a month trying to get the smile off of his face after this terrible crime took place. If I know seventeen-year-old boys; (and I used to be one) he was probably talked into repeating this crime over and over and over again because he actually believed he was enjoying it. She no doubt brainwashed him into thinking that sex with a beautiful more mature woman was something he would actually want with her sly womanly ways. If only I could have stopped this crime and protected this child. I would have gladly taken his place to protect him from this vamp. The woman involved claimed the story was not true and was the result result of a jealous girlfriend spreading a rumor.

SOME MORE THOUGHTS!

No, this boy was not a victim; he was a damn hero. He was no doubt a hero to his friends probably even to his dad. I think that all of the other boys in the school were wishing the same crime would happen to them. This (boy) only became a victim when the press turned it into a headline story. No doubt the backlash from this media blitz left him traumatized and irreparably socially harmed. His only saving grace is that he got to have sex with this mega babe. The actual molesters here are those who refused to distinguish between a very lucky moment for this young man and the terrible crime it might have been if the gender roles were reversed. We just can't have a double standard where student/adults sex is concerned. If the teacher were a male and the student a female then let the legal process take its course. I am of the mind that we as a culture should stand in defense of any young female as older men are concerned and the teacher–student relationship is sacred in its absoluteness. Is the same true for the male almost-adult child??? No f—ing way. This kid lived a fantasy come true until the media got their hands on this story. If the accused criminal proves to be innocent then the true perpetrators of a crime are the media. And in truth a double standard is the natural scheme of things. Seventeen-year-old boys don't need protection from older women; they need access *to* older women. Clearly there is a line that can't be crossed. Where that line should be is not a stand I will take. Eighteen has always been the historical cultural standard for a young women when sexual activity became a personal choice; however, it is absurd that a seventeen-year-old *male* needs to be protected from an older women sexually.

I was a young man during the sexual revolution of the 1960s and

'70s, and I can tell you that I was thrilled to be a part of it. ¡Viva la *revolución!* At the time the pill, (birth control pill) changed the game completely. For the first time in history couples could engage in sex with the very diminished risk of pregnancy that had plagued previous generations. The door was now open to random sexual activity. Again, *ya-a-a-a-ay!* And the feminist movement was the icing on the cake. Women were burning their bras in opposition to the historic sexual repression their mothers had known. From my point of view, shedding of bras was very good news especially where young women in T-shirts were concerned. The sight of those perky precious mounds gently float-ing under form-fitting shirts, headlights blazing, yes, nip-ups made me a very big fan of the bra-burning concept.[19] Let's also not forget that the miniskirt was another fashion hit of the time. It is when the term "bea-ver" was coined, in that the very exposed silky bare thighs of the young lady resembled the protruding teeth of a beaver. Oh! And "hot pants." Let's also not forget hot pants. For those of you too young to remember, the still-famous style of the shorts of the Dallas Cowboy cheerleaders was born of that time. Clearly hot pants were the best fashion concept ever conceived (followed closely by the push-up bra.) Bikini bathing suits were also getting smaller and smaller. It was a great time to be a horny young man. What ever happened to "designer jeans"?

Sexuality was now on the mind of the nation, but had things really changed? My father told me at the time that my generation was not the first to discover sex. My understanding is that many "had to" marriages still took place when he was a young man as had always been the practice when a girl mysteriously became pregnant. Now we have abortion on demand and no more unwanted children. There was truly a cultural shift in thinking and an increased public acceptance of a more sexually pro-miscuous lifestyle. There have always been girls who "would" and girls who "would not" but now the discrimination against girls who "would" was greatly diminished. It became culturally okay to marry a woman who was known to not be a virgin. It was my self-imposed mission at the time to personally guarantee that the young ladies I dated were not virgins. When considering a potential spouse virginity was not an issue for me. It was desirable but not mandatory. The joke of the time was "What's the definition of a virgin?" An ugly third-grader! It is hard to imagine today that in the 1960s there was still an underlying expectation of female virginity prior to marriage. I think that virgin brides were just as rare then as they are today but it wasn't publicly accepted. Living together out of wedlock became common in the 1970s. My regressive rural culture tolerated this sin but there was always an underlying unacceptability of the situation. It seems that today such conversations are as obsolete as the era. It can be said that gay marriage makes a mockery of the institution of marriage but clearly the sexual revolution I lived through had a far greater impact.

THE EXTREMES SEXUAL OBSESSION

I have experienced the extremes of sexual desire as females are concerned. At times in my life I could not imagine why we don't have a national effigy to the glory of the female pubis that is the focus of all that matters in human existence and the source of all life renewed. At other times I have known the same thing to be nothing more than a disease-infested stinking rotten hellhole where no man should tread. How is it possible that the same thing could inspire such extremes of emotions, both contempt and unmitigated obsession? I must have sex—if it doesn't kill me. Even if it *does* kill me. Possibly I should have it till I am just ill!

HOW TO HAVE SEX

In a tree, in a car, in a boat, in a bar—anywhere you are! Have it here, have it there, have it everywhere, here and far! I like the missionary position. This is your basic full-frontal mount. It is the most passionate and the man can participate in the communication so important to women, *and* enjoy himself at the same time. Said to be the "proper way," as advocated by Christian missionaries.

We love our canine friends. They offer a good example of a very popular and erotic sexual experience. I don't normally imitate animals but in this case I recommend it.

A somewhat perverted and vulgar much elder uncle of a friend once told me, "give a woman a pillow; if she puts it under her ass she is smart." He was right! A great variation of this thought involves the same mid-body location of the pillow except that the female is facedown. I definitely recommend this concept. All the favorite female body parts are in play and easily accessed. It is easy to find something to do with your hands and don't ignore the back of her neck. Do this right (vaginally of course) and you can depend on a repeat visit from your new best friend!

Woman on top gives her a chance to set the pace and get everything she wants before he unloads. The guy can entertain himself with those lovely mounds if he gets bored. This one's for the girls and is best for satisfying her needs! It can get a little painful for the guy if she moves up too far and comes down suddenly so keep track of her movements and anticipate.

I gotta tell ya most of the rest of what you have seen in those culturally enlightening porn videos is more about show than pleasure. You will likely find most of those kinky variations lacking in a goal-oriented "outcum" due to the lack of appropriate friction. Stick with the basics but don't be afraid to experiment. If you have more suggestions of something special that I am missing give me a call or e-mail me.

Drunk sex has never shown much promise for me personally. Buzzed sex is best but sober sex is the most meaningful. It's all good.

Loose Lips Don't Get Results!

Oral sex? Don't talk about it, just do it. Receiving for me has never been successful though several self-described experts have tried. Bummer! But there is something special about having a woman bring herself before you in the ultimate submissive posture. It is as if you are now the king of the world and all that you desire is at hand. I recommend that you give and take at the same time with the guy on his back and the girl on top facing the opposite direction. Apparently, two people entangled in this position resemble the number sixty-nine (69). You guys need to know that the part of your body you most cherish is repeated in miniature on a woman. I recommend that you find it with your lips and think of it as a straw; and, don't ignore the most famous nearby opening. Hang on tight! It could be a rough ride. This is by far the most likely way to rock her world if she is not easily orgasmic. I highly recommend that you make sure that she ends her night happily! The most important thing here girls is freshness. We cherish your intimacy but cleanliness and your next orgasm are one and the same.

A dirty mind is a terrible thing to waste.

So ya wanna be sexy!

Every now and then I see a female who doesn't necessarily fit the exact mold of sexy and yet she has some vague quality that makes her very compelling sexually. My personal weakness is toward quirky. I am also compelled by apparent high intellect; so much the better when they are in the same person. I very much prefer petite and anything that looks fat is an undesirable option for most men. A modest level of physical fitness is always a plus. I think my tastes are more or less standard except that I have no choice but to avoid tall given that I am not tall, though I find tall chicks can be very hot. There is the old cliché that women want tall, dark, and handsome; well, one out of three ain't bad. Yes, I am dark! I have always envied tall men in that women would be compelled above all else to choose them as a mate. A tall guy can be a complete jerk and a woman will put up with it. No charm necessary no wealth no class; it doesn't matter as long as he is tall. I don't condemn women for the choices based on natural selection. Taller men have a survival advantage over shorter men and women are naturally inspired. Men are naturally inspired by beauty. All men. I feel bad for the chick who just isn't going to make it as a babe. Natural selection is very coldhearted. There isn't much demand for unattractive women. They learn it young and many give up on beauty. We are all more likely to respond to physical perfection no matter the circumstance, even when mating is not a goal. Physically attractive males are also attention getters. Who wants to see a less-than-attractive male as a TV commentator? And there are some real female hotties giving me my local news.

Not too long ago my sons and I visited one of those restaurants that feature cultured young ladies dressed in very appropriately skimpy outfits, cleavage wonderfully enhanced. The young lady who waited on us was a visual gem. *Mmmhhh!* Flirting with these girls is easy for me as a mature man because there is no risk. Even if I piss her off she is still dependent on the fact that I am paying the bill and the eventual tip. The twentyish boys were not so bold. (Actually very intimidated.) Also younger guys are commonly exposed to young good-looking babes. I am not. For me the experience is much more rare and therefore more relevant. These girls don't find the older guys a threat and so are normally very responsive. It's all good. This particular hottie made a few silly mistakes with our service and was very apologetic. She actually expressed a desire to be smarter and not making mistakes. My response to her? "You gotta be kidding." Paraphrased: "I know a lot of smart chicks. They are common and everywhere. I meet them every day. No big deal. A girl who is smokin' hot is not something I see every day and so much the better in that she is wearing that outfit and makes it look so-o-o good." The message was: "You have very real value as a person. You don't need to be anything you are not." There was a noticeable change in her demeanor and posture as she looked at me over her shoulder walking away and with a look of thoughtful appreciation for my comments. It made me feel good also.

It is true that smart women are common and I benefit from their skills and talents as mentioned elsewhere. I can't help but mention that most of the smart chicks out there wished that they looked like her. Life would be so much easier for them if they didn't have to rely on their skills to get what they want. Being attractive opens a lot of doors for a woman and there is no reason at all *not* to step through those doors as far as I am concerned except that other less physically desirable women will condemn their contemporaries for doing so. As a man, I would encourage attractive young women to use their sexuality at every opportunity. It is the natural scheme of things. You are making a mistake if you don't take advantage of your natural gifts although it does require a cautious self-discipline.

"Young women here! Get your fine young women here! Get 'em while they're hot!"

Beauty is a shared thing. What is the point of beauty if no one is exposed to it? What is the point of being beautiful if no one admires you? Only shared beauty has meaning. I encourage women to undress when in my presence, based on this concept.

If you are a woman and want to victimize a man, the best way to do it is with your breasts! He will fall for it every time!

Don't make this complicated. OMG! Dating and mating can be a terrible experience for many people and especially the young. Don't fret the failures. Eventually it won't matter at all. Life is a marathon and relationships come and go. Invest in yourself first and the rest will come naturally and over time.

I can't believe that you spent your time reading this all the way through!

WORDS THAT START WITH *N*

I have no idea how many words in the English language start with the letter *n*. Thousands I suppose. Possibly as many as ten thousand! Some of these words are really very useful for a political writer like me: *nonsense, nutcase, nincompoop,* and *narcissist* to name a few. Narcissist sounds fancy and smart and it is a little hard to say. I like it. It refers to someone who is self-absorbed. Other n-words can have great impact and powerfully convey an intended meaning. Some are obscure and rarely if ever used in common conversation, for example *neap.* The word refers to certain tidal movements. (I pulled it randomly out of my dictionary otherwise I have never heard the word.) The letter *n* can also harbinger of tremendous negativity. I am referring to the prefix *non* which makes the word it precedes something that is not, something that isn't, Great power for a three-letter word!

By now you are thinking of the really bad word that starts with *n*. You are thinking of the word that has become the most vulgar and offensive word in American conversation. I will not and cannot use the word here. I dare not type it, I dare not say it. I should never think it. In the event that this writing should see the light of day—I would be labeled a racist just for referring to it much less actually using the word; and my entire body of work would be condemned as racist as would be true for any non-black writer using the term.

If friends were to say the word to me I wouldn't repeat it back to them. I am compelled to respond with the more politically correct *black* or *African American*. The real root word of the word is *Negro*. This is not a slang or racist term. It is a scientific/anthropological term. It is a reference to the Negro or Negroid race. Science and anthropology distinguish three races as human: Caucasian, Mongol, and Negro. in Spanish *negro* means "black". The term *African American* is incorrect and I don't normally use it. It can only refer to someone that is both African and American. Almost all of those known as African Americans have never been to Africa. Also masses of native Africans are actually Caucasian and millions more are descendants of what was once known as the mongoloid race. Yet some "Negroes" demand the term "African American" from we Caucasians and to avoid angering blacks and we whites are happy to comply mostly out of fear of pissing off Blacks. We whites don't want blacks to hate us. We don't you to be be angry with us! We want to get along with each other as races.

We fear you black America. Obama said that he knows what it is like to walk across the street and hear car doors lock as he comes near. (Actually sounds a bit paranoid.) The truth is, there is a damn good reason for our fear. We whites know that life is tougher for you. Your life may be more dangerous and more crime ridden. We know that discrimination makes it more difficult for you to succeed as a productive part of American society and therefore you are more likely to be a bit desperate. It is natural that we should fear you. You likely have a lot less to lose than we honkeys do. You live a life more on the edge. You are compelled to show *attitude,* threatening, intimidating attitude as a self-defense issue! You need to act tough on the streets of the potentially dangerous communities that you may live in. It is a necessity of survival. Also, you resent us whites. You seem to still be hostile toward whites because of the history of black slavery in America although no living whites—or living blacks—had anything to do with slavery. Neither did our grandparents or likely their grandparents. And many of you resent us because we are white and life is easier for us because we are more likely to be given the benefit of the doubt from society.

SLAVERY

Slavery was and is horrible injustice and an ancient injustice as old as recorded history. A war was fought in America with the greatest death toll ever in any war up to that point in time— and the primary goal of that war was to end or continue slavery depending on which side won the war. White America made a tremendous sacrifice to end slavery and can do nothing more to right this injustice. Only blacks can make the rift of slavery between white and black go away and for black and white to be truly equal socially, there can be no residual animosity from either side.

I personally have never done anything to the detriment of any person of color. To the contrary! I have invested a great deal of my time on a personal level to the aid of two black families. It is also true that a great deal of my money in the form of taxes has been directly given to minorities and on an ongoing basis Whites live with a sense of contempt from many blacks. We whites are sometimes publicly condemned by black leaders even though we are doing everything we can to make your opportunities more universal. Still, many black leaders who are also supposedly men of God publicly condemn White America in far too many cases. No true Christian of any race could ever make such a statement without being condemned to hell by the God of that faith. And in the face of all these ongoing issues as presented by black advocates whites are still frequently and commonly condemned as racist. It is true that most whites know that these accusations are made with the purpose of political manipulation. Liberals are easily manipulated where race is concerned and the black culture knows that it will benefit from white racist accusations no matter the truth. When all these things are considered possibly there is a good reason for white contempt of the current African American pop culture. This contempt is not directed at black individuals generally but at the pop culture of high-profile advocates of racial issues! These advocates are more accurately described as social agitators who manipulate us all by convincing blacks that they should be angry about slavery by whites 140 years after the fact and that blacks should be compensated today for a long-ago injustice.

RACISM?

Racism is fun. That's why it is so popular. It is a natural thing to assume ourselves better than the next guy or town or country—or anything that sets us apart or makes us different from one another. We are different as races. We whites sometimes see blacks as peculiar and vice versa. On average we think differently. We have different priorities, different ways. And we whites often perceive blacks as being unworthy. Not because we choose to but because of stereotypes fortified by the demand for more grace on our part in spite of blacks' apparent hostility for whites. "Get up and do it yourself." Why should I help the ungrateful? We whites resent your demands black America and every time one of your highly regarded spokespeople starts condemning whites publicly the animosity only grows. (Obama's preacher Reverend Wright as an example.) And there is plenty of reason for blacks to hate and fear whites. Random beatings and hangings are still fresh news in the minds of many black Americans. Many racist whites react with violent thoughts and actions toward blacks and oftentimes for no more reason than our own legacy contempt for those we imagine to be less than we are combined with a desire to indulge in a sense of self-imposed superiority. White racism is still extreme in parts of our country and is an ongoing danger to blacks. Until that isn't true, we whites will always have ourselves to hold accountable for racial strife, after all we are the majority.

Most of the whites I encounter would never use the n-word in everyday conversation. It is rare for me to actually hear that word spoken by whites. Most of what I will call "somewhat racist" whites agree that there is a difference between a "you know what" and a black person meaning that a small minority is seen as a n—. We whites have no reason to be afraid or feel threatened by most black people and for the most part we don't care what color your skin is. But if your pants are hanging below your waist or your underwear is showing or your "shorts" are nearly dragging the ground we then have no choice but to believe that you are likely living a life of sloth. You likely don't have a job—or want one—and you are likely engaged in criminal behavior as a lifestyle. And yes, whites do the exact same unacceptable things and garner the exact same contempt

without regard for race. Whites are held similarly and equally accountable in the mind of most whites given the issues I have mentioned.

By proclivity blacks might be more animated than whites. We whites
don't like this behavior and we sense falseness when blacks behave this
way. Blacks tend to be more braggadocios than whites. We whites don't
like this either. I understand the counterculture appeal of rap music
but I have said elsewhere that I consider rap to be the personification of
the essence of human sloth expressed in lyric and rhyme. The ranting
and primitive rhythms offend me and I am embarrassed for those who
would enjoy them. Most of the blacks I meet seem to be good and decent
people and yet my somewhat negative pop culture stereotype is that of
the threatening, apparently hostile anti social derelict that I should stay
clear of. That stereotype needs to change and for the benefit of both
races! But how do we change a systemic and natural mistrust for each
other as races?

Blacks and whites technically speak the same language but we com-
municate very differently. "Say wha-a-a-at," spoken with great animation
as compared to a stone faced gaze, eyes rolled when faced with obvious
BS.[20] The term *Ebonics* was coined around 2000 as a name for a separate
language reflecting black American Culture. Slang terms and the desire
to be "not white" gave way to a speech style that reflected the thinking of
American blacks. Whites who wanted to accept black speech sometimes
imitate this speech style as a sign of acceptance of black American ways.
Blacks hold whites in such contempt that "acting white" has been harshly
condemned by some blacks. It is treasonous to behave like a white person
in the eyes of some blacks. Again some whites do choose to "act black."
I am not sure why. I could speculate that it is a simple admiration of
the stereotype street culture as a compelling lifestyle. I don't know why
anyone would intentionally want that. I can see no advantage to this
behavior as a lifestyle. I think very few people would willingly accept a
life of poverty and idleness that held little in the way of hope for a more
prosperous meaningful future.

We whites really do want to get along! We want universally acceptable behavior and we are willing to adapt if blacks are. (willing) One

more thing that every black American needs to know without question is that there is absolutely nothing to be gained for whites to imprison blacks other than to suppress criminal behavior. It is a known fact that blacks are held in prison at a much higher rate than whites but it is not because of skin color. Those particular blacks have been found to be criminals. We imprison these blacks at tremendous social cost to law-abiding citizens both white and black. It is a massive social drain on any economy and this is money spent in the name of public safety. It is absurdly expensive to keep prisoners in prison no matter their race. Nobody wants to spend this money except for the need to suppress crime. Other factually contrary assumptions by blacks can only lead to contempt from whites.

THINGS PRO-BLACK ACTIVISTS MUST STOP SAYING!

1. "We deserve reparations." (Fact: not ever gonna happen!)
2. "Too many blacks are going to jail as compared to whites." (Fact: black judges are sending blacks to jail at a higher rate than white judges; it is also true that whites are more likely to be prosecuted and jailed though they have with fewer prior convictions.) Yes. it is whites who are not being treated fairly.
3. "We are being discriminated against in America based on nothing but color." (Fact: there is no higher status that can be awarded to any American other than to be elected president. This could not have happened without a majority white vote.)
4. "MLK's dream never came true and is still a dream!" (Fact: We in America have seen a massive improvement in the social opportunities for blacks (or any group needing public grace). Yet there have never before been so many blacks living in poverty. Whites are not responsible for that fact. There are no whites who want to keep blacks living in poverty. More than anything else we want you to have a good job or own a business and be self-supporting and prosperous.)

POSSIBLE SOLUTIONS

Solutions are like diamonds, they are very hard to find!

The breakdown of the traditional family structure has had a negative effect on all of American culture but much more so for non-white minorities. These traditional standards are by far the most effective way of avoiding any cause or form of poverty. Advocating the strengths of the family structure must be a part of any long-term solution. If you were or are a child born to an impoverished single mother the eventuality of a life of poverty is almost a certainty. Every child born that cannot be supported by his or her parents is another reason for a deeply troubled life, regardless of race.

We need to have an honest conversation between blacks and whites, one that deliberately avoids spineless liberalism and any politically motivated false accusations and hidden agendas and states out loud; the hard ugly truths.

Poverty is not racial; it is cultural. There are many millions of wealthy successful blacks living in comfort everywhere in America. How in the hell can a cultural rebirth take place if blacks don't actively take control of the transformation? White America is more than willing to help but it can't be done for you!

Gang violence is not just a black issue. Such violence is common for all races and again, it is also mostly a cultural issue. Gang violence is killing more blacks than anything or anyone else and black-on-black murder is the number 1 cause of death for black males under the age of forty. I have no idea how to stop this but welfare programs guarantee that such a thing will continue to be possible. The crime-ridden community can't exist without public funding.

These issues are a social conundrum. I fear that there is no social solution that can be managed effectively. If there is to be a better future for race relations among whites and blacks and a better life for minorities in general it will start with a modern and dynamic and black leader; another MLK if you choose to imagine. This leader will more than anything else advocate that blacks take control of their own destiny and pursue a course that leads the individual to take responsibility for his or her personal future as is frequently advocated by conservatives. Clearly such an idea will not be well received given the long-term cultural condition.

At some point, whites are going to need to be recognized for the tremendous social cost afforded by whites in order to give minority races a better opportunity in America. This will encourage peace among the races. Yes, whites historically enslaved blacks. I personally took no part in that slavery nor do I benefit and I can not be held accountable, nor can any living white can be held accountable!

We whites are for the most part are very compelled to live in peace with blacks.

It is not about race, it is about culture. Blacks have been at a disadvantage in this country for a very long time. It will take a very long time for that to change. Much progress has been made! Again, for the most part we whites don't really care what color your skin is! We care about who you are as a person. We care about your personal integrity. We care about your willingness to stand on your own two feet and proactively create your own best opportunities. When I see that you are making a diligent personal effort is when I will offer you my unconditional support.

It is the most basic notion of human existence that we each live by our own design and are not compelled to live in servitude to others—except as own choices would commit us.

PHILOSOPHY RELIGION;
THEY ARE ONE, AND THE SAME

I believe that there is an ultra natural component to the universe, which is an ongoing part of our existence. I also imagine a separate transcendent reality that is not part of our normal perceptions. I believe that there is an undefined nonphysical "existence" that transcends time and location and that we may at times be able to perceive said existence. I believe it is possible that the idea of a simultaneous coexistence in the same time and space is a real thing. It is likely that our conscious mind is defeating access to any ongoing connection to these alternate realities except when our normal conscious state is repressed or altered.

THE MONO GOD THEORY

There is symmetry throughout the cosmos. It is an immutable consistency that compels all components of the cosmos to be the same. Not the same in form or composition, but the same in nature. This sameness is universal as all that exists is concerned. All that exists includes matter and thought and energy. Not that all thoughts and energy are the same, but the same in nature, and this sameness is universal in all of nature and all that exists, wherever it exists. All that exists is bound by all else that exists to adhere to this sameness. Living sentient thought is not excluded. Wherever sentient thought exists, nature requires it to be consistent with the cosmos. The cosmos defines the limits and nature of thought, wherever it exists. Thought can be simple or complex but all simple or complex thought is the same in nature wherever it exists or whenever it exists. Thought is critical to what it means to be sentient and its existence. Sentient beings rely on the consistency of universal thinking. Thinking and a spiritual undefined presence are one and the same. This absolute is the nature of God. It is what we pray to, whether simple or complex of thought.

I believe that it may be possible that thought (not just human thought) can affect the cosmos. It may be true that thought defines the cosmos. It may be true that the concept of prayer is not as useless as many people assume it to be.

Unrecorded human history almost certainly included a belief in a mysterious controlling entity that could condemn or grace people at will, and by approval or disapproval. The randomness of life and a notion that this randomness was being controlled by some unseen entity is the genesis of the God concept. If you prefer a different phrase, the original conceived notion of God. It is the moment when the animal man became the being, Human.

In those times our species had evolved to an agrarian economy that gave us the freedom to ponder issues beyond those of our daily survival given that a steady supply of food was now a likely truth. Humans were free to ponder the "something spiritual" because we now had more power and control over own destiny. As a species we were able to assume the likelihood at some level, of long-term survival. We were also free to think at a more esoteric level and we imagined what might be the source of the unseen power that was all around us, the power that is now known as Mother Nature (the consistency). The so very mysterious forces of nature were beyond what humans understood at that time. Imaginary nonhuman ultra natural beings in our own image were conceived as an explanation. History has shown us that these perceived beings oftentimes took various forms and/or were imagined as multiple entities having different powers. Today the various gods of the past have evolved to the one God concept in that a single entity is commonly believed to hold autonomy over all. The pitfalls and ravages of nature were assumed to be controlled by this entity. This assumption resulted in a fear of this imagined being, and led to the concept of an absolute servitude to this single controlling entity and in the name of personal salvation. This concept eventually evolved to a notion of an afterlife of pleasure or punishment based on an individual's level of compliance and servitude to this unseen entity. This is still a widely held belief today.

The clinical summary of religious history is not necessarily intended to refute the existence of God or condemn religion. Personally my thinking style is clinical and analytical. I can only see God from a practical scientific and analytical perspective and as I described. I cannot accept the idea that a human-like spiritual entity exists in a non-physical place and oversees our daily existence. I consider such thinking to be an idea completely without merit although I do recognize and condone the notion that a great many people find comfort and hope in this belief. I see no reason to object.

For my entire life someone else has been telling me about God and always from a fear-mongering concept. In other words I was and am still told that if I live as a nonbeliever I will burn. Not just burn now but burn forever. By that they mean scorching searing skin eternally. On the other hand as told, I could exist in eternal pleasure if I followed their belief system and lived a simple sin-free life but there was a catch though: I had to die first. Not sure of this afterlife concept I have decided to enjoy myself now just in case I had been misled. I can always repent later.

I fit into the Christian religious model. I was raised in a Christian culture and community. We were not a religious family but the local church *was* a part of my upbringing. The principles of Christianity were the normal mind-set for my community and my friends. We knew of other religions but ours was a default normal religious perspective and we saw it as universal and global.

It strikes me as odd that today religion and conservative thinking are considered one and the same. Leftist pundits take pleasure in pigeonholing the religious community as archaic and simple of mind. The religious community is a favorite target to malign by implication if not by the direct condemnation of contrary thinkers. It is true that some high-profile religious leaders are indeed conservative but my personal observation is that this is a stereotype and it is a stereotype fostered by people who condemn stereotyping: (AKA liberals). My personal observation is that a great majority of the people I know who are strongly religious are also left leaning by proclivity. For the most part I would pigeonhole these somewhat liberal religious people as apolitical. They are not politically motivated but an observation of their political thinking is indisputably left leaning. It is left leaning and consistent with the leftist teaching of the Christ icon that is the focus of their religious beliefs.

I see Christ as having been a liberal. I think what made Christ so significant to so many is that during his time in history his culture was in a state of transformation to a more knowledgeable understanding—a cosmic intellectual upgrade as humanity was concerned. Christ was born to a Middle Eastern culture. It is the same culture that is a harbinger of regional strife and political discourse with global effect to this day. What made Jesus different was his absolute conviction to his extremely liberal social-structure concept. His Roman invaders had conservative ideas that they imposed on a conservative culture. Jesus stood in defiance of that conservatism and was crucified for his contempt. His saving grace culturally was his completely compliant if not adamant servitude to the God concept that dominated his culture at that time. His prosecutors gave him a chance to survive but Jesus chose not to do so. This self-sacrificing act grew as legend and 200 years later the worship of Christ became the dominant Roman religion. Yes, in case you don't know, the very culture that crucified Christ was also the culture that fostered the genesis of the elevation of Jesus to the Son of God icon.

JESUS WAS A LIBERAL..

Think about it. Free health care (raising the dead), feeding the hungry (with three loaves of bread and some fish), soft on crime (who will cast the first stone?), and pacifism; (turn the other cheek). Also, let's not forget that he didn't think people should have to repay their loans (forgive us our debts). There was even considerable speculation about who his real father was. (an absence of social morality.). Was it God or Joseph? These principles reflect the essence of what it means to be a liberal, actually *mandatory* for BDLs.

THE TEN COMMANDMENTS

A review of the Ten Commandments as written by Moses, abbreviated and editorialized for clarity:

1. "No other God, etc." (I have described God as a single concept (*see* above.)
2. "No, to the Lord's name in vain." (My dictionary summarizes *vain* as a lack of respect for God. Respect for others people's faith seems a reasonable thing to ask.)
3. "Chill out on Sunday." (I like this one!)
4. "Don't piss off your parents." (This is clearly a notion conceived by a parent, but I am okay with it.)
5. "No murder." (No killing, subject to translation. This is the worst of human misdeeds in my opinion!)
6. "No adultery."(cheating. Sexual contact with a person who is not your wife covers the idea fairly well. I think a lot of people are in trouble with this requirement.)
7. "No stealing." (Sounds right to me.)
8. "No bearing false witness." (This likely had implications beyond what we would express as "don't lie." It is most likely to be accurately translated as meaning, "don't falsely condemn someone as a criminal.")
9. "No coveting thy neighbors' wife." (Haven't we already covered this with number 6? I suspect a modern translation would sound more like, "Don't be going after my wife asshole!")
10. "No coveting." (again?!) neighbor's property, and also subject to modern interpretation. The original list included the neighbor's home, servants, and ass. Why does the ass thing get mentioned as a timeless unimpeachable commandment?) It just doesn't seam to fit with the other commandants.

I assume these rules to have been written by men not God, or is it okay with God for my neighbor's wife to covet me? I think God would have been gender neutral on this one. I think human males would not have been neutral and this is also why God is never portrayed as feminine. Please don't be offended by my irreverent summary of what is known as God's law. I know these notions to be sacred to many Christians and Jews; having recognized that, I can clearly see that God, in my concept of God includes a sense of irony.

By what principle do I define right and wrong you may ask given that I consider the Ten Commandments "vague"? Fairly simple really: the above principles as written by Moses were seen by him as a common man's guide to acceptable social behavior. There is nothing profound in these notions. Any man of an educated status living in that time might have written them. The concepts honor God as required by God and are otherwise just good common sense in the name of social tranquillity. The survival of any social community requires laws that guide behavior and standards of conduct that will avoid social chaos. Religion does not own these principles. These principles represent what is necessary by logic. Most of humanity is not Christian yet lives by similar constraints. Many Christians are not devoted to the religion as regular churchgoers but still adhere to the social norms of Christian teaching. It is not because of their religion but because of an understanding that it is simply the right thing to do and that we will all benefit and survive longer if we comply. If I am caught with my neighbor's wife I could get shot. If I steal I could get the hell beat out of me or be sent to jail in our modern times, (or both). Those who have chosen not to comply with these accepted cultural standards are those who occupy our prisons.

In my local radio market there is a talk-show host who regularly refers to the dilemma of social compliance and an afterlife reward/punishment system based on heaven and hell. He is normally fairly sensible if not wise but he has a dreadful blind spot regarding morality and decent behavior. He cannot imagine a reason to behave with grace except for the wrath or reward of the afterlife. This suggests to me that as a person he is intrinsically corrupt. He is a criminal at heart, a killer and a thief. He has no natural understanding of the reasons for a peaceful coexistence. It also establishes him as a social threat. If his religious principles should fail him he knows of no reason not to kill me of his own whim. Only the threat of eternal fire motivates his social compliance. He is a religious man and occasionally refers to his faith during his program but this reference is not pervasive. I don't actually assume that he is dangerous to my community. I do assume that he is unknowingly conflicted about his own religious beliefs. He makes what I consider to be absurd statements regarding social behavior and the need of a religion based compliance model. He has no choice but to ignore this dilemma. He must either discount his chosen faith or admit to a natural understanding of social compliance based on his own best interest and the best interest of those he encounters daily. I think his conscious mind has blocked this contradiction. His Christian faith serves him yet simultaneously represses his otherwise free mind. This is the greatest downfall of any religion. Having listened to this man over a long period of time I know that he is capable of very clear thought though in this case, he is repressed by this self-imposed barrier. I also know that he was raised in a union household. He freely admits this but I would know it without his admission. He talks of a "living wage" and other semi-socialist union dogma in direct conflict with his religion.

THEOLOGICAL SIMILARITIES; THEOLOGICAL DIFFERENCES!

Socialism and the socialest model of society require by default an absence of religion. Both socialism and religion require submission to a greater good leading to a more grand and glorious end. They both conspire to control my thinking and behavior in order to achieve this goal; they are locked in a polar conflict for power over me. I shall submit to neither!

The Obama administration is/was clearly very liberal; possibly the most liberal of our nation's history. Many regard him as a socialist including me. Right wing extremists have condemned the presidency as conducting a war on religion. Obama says he is a Christian. He is known to attend a Christian church. It is likely true that our nation is not yet ready to elect a non-religious leader and preferably Christian based. Barack knows this. You may draw whatever conclusions you like as to his religious sincerity but a war on religion appears absurd to me. What is not absurd to me is that socialism and religion are naturally conflicting theologies. Their coexistence as cultural guideposts can only result in ongoing conflict. In the tyranny of the USSR religion was repressed. The same repression will always be necessary in any socialist state. This is why liberals frequently malign Christianity. It is a threat to their natural proclivity to instill a one-and-all, from each-to each politic.

An afterlife reward/punishment system that is based on heaven or hell flies directly in the face of a political system where everyone is assumed as equal no matter his or her personal behavior. Christianity requires us to believe that we are not all equal and this inequality is based on the personal choices we make. This is the driving functional principle of all religion, and this inequality is based on the likelihood that we might or might not eventually qualify to go to heaven. An absence of universal behavioral standards is the reason socialist societies fail.

At the time of this writing socialist health care and birth control issues are in conflict with the Catholic Church. If the church is as conservative as leftists assume it is other conflicts will continue to rise. The church does not condemn wealth. Socialism does. Karl Marx described socialism as a transitional state between the overthrow of capitalism and the realization of communism. We as a nation are being pushed in that direction.

Clearly President Obama with his ridiculously wasteful economic stimulus package had no working understanding of economics and its complexities or just doesn't care. The church does care. The church advocates and facilitates charity. Socialists require charity by the fiat of the voting public. The voting public benefits from public confiscation of others' wealth. Under different circumstances this scenario would be regarded as organized crime. The church uses guilt-based tactics to acquire funds but contribution is still optional. Corruption of the mainstream church is rare and giving to the needy is subject to situational need. Benefactors are held accountable by the presence of the givers. Not so with government. Corruption and waste are normal in government distributions and everyone is eligible no matter the circumstance. The church exercises discretion and judgment, socialism does not. In a social welfare system anyone can benefit from publicly mandated charity no matter how corrupt or slothful he or she may be. The church is therefore the more ethical and honorable option.

THE CATHOLIC CHURCH

The child sex-abuse scandal that disgraced the Catholic Church a few years ago wasn't exactly news to me. As an adolescent I knew that it was not a good idea to find yourself alone with a Catholic priest. My Catholic friends at the time often joked about the sexual nature of priests and that was forty-five years ago. For the most part young males dealt with this issue on their own terms. At the time we (young males) did not dare openly expose any sexual advances from adults especially if those advances came from a priest. In this case it was not the church that was corrupt but some of its representatives—and possibly *a lot* of its representatives. Sodomizing a child is not church policy. It is the policy of some homosexual priests. Straight men and straight priests are not sexually attracted to male children. I intend to point the finger of blame away from the church generally and point it toward those who conspired to put themselves in positions of power, which would make it easy for them to exploit young males.

When this scandal first surfaced I was exposed to a story regarding a convention/gathering of would-be priests. This gathering as described was nothing less than a drunken gay sexual convention in black. Without knowing if or how much the story was exaggerated I have very good reason to believe that something very similar to this story actually did happen. There was considerable detail in the story that gave it credibility. I have no mission to protect the church but it is my mission to scorn those who felt justified because of the burden of a genetic anomaly to bastardize an otherwise innocent institution—an institution that has a lot to answer for yes, but *is* in service to humanity. If I were gay I would definitely want to distance myself socially and politically from people who would do such things. Has the gay community taken a public stand of condemnation against this proclivity? If so I missed it. Also I have to wonder how much of the Catholic Church's history has been influenced by homosexuality. It naturally connects that the no-wives policy would be a part of this proclivity. Men who are not naturally interested in sex with women and are more attracted to other men would be more likely to advocate for such a thing. I don't intend to impose any conclusions here but you gotta admit that it makes sense. I know that the concept of celibacy is one of servitude and absolute conviction above all else. I get the concept and respect its theoretical intent but again, I will raise the question of its genesis keeping in mind that sodomy is a well-used and harshly condemned concept as referenced in the Christian theology.

THE PAST AND THE FUTURE!

Religion and its power is fading in modern times. Greater knowledge of the realities of nature has left little room for speculation about the answers to what were once life's profound mysteries. The Church's historical answers to these questions have become less and less plausible if not completely absurd. Yet the church still has a role in modern culture no matter the level of human scientific understanding. The ceremonial church-sponsored burying of the dead is and will likely continue to be important to our culture. The church has also traditionally sanctioned by ceremony the right for a couple to procreate (a.k.a., marriage). I will also note that as acceptance of gay marriage evolves socially it will be interesting to follow the church's opinion and participation. There are women and men today functioning as leaders in service to the Lord who are preforming wedding ceremonies for same-sex couples. I am told the Christian Bible specifically forbids homosexual behavior. The power of the church is weakened by the deeds of those who would defy the principles of the church by which they were sanctioned.

Historically the churches that were built during the westward settlement of our nation more than 150 years ago had a role in guiding small communities similar to the one in which I live. Most of those churches still exist but are anything but strong and no longer have a leadership role in our small-town culture. I consider the current participants of religious services as holdouts of a former time and archaic mind-set. Some of the local churches have failed financially, others are poorly attended yet financially stable. My countryside is dotted with long-dead towns and still-standing churches that were established when the church was seen as the moral center of the community and essential to the administration of the moral principles of the people. Many of the towns no longer exist at all but for the church that stands as a quaint reminder to a bygone era. They still serve the area and most importantly, maintain the accompanying cemeteries where our ancestors are buried. I expect to occupy a spot in one of those cemeteries eventually. As my mid-western stomping grounds were claimed by early settlers I imagine an almost squatter's rights competition among the varying denominations of churches to stake out their religious territory.

Our nation was established based on religious principles. References to God and religious freedom cannot be separated from our history. We were and continue to be a Christian-oriented nation. The eventual fading of those Christian constraints is inevitable. Our cultural guidepost is no longer the teaching of priests and other ministers of God but of our media and its enormous daily presence.

Religion has a presence in the media both corrupt and honorable. Some of the televangelists we see on TV are anything but godly and are actually contributing to the obsolescence of religion. The god-awful (literally) supposed messengers of the word of God have repeatedly disgraced themselves and Christianity in general. They are truly evil by the religious definition of the term. Conversely, I have recently seen an upsurge in public demonstrations of religion at public social events and other demonstrations held in the presence of grace and positive regard by the otherwise nonreligious community, but more importantly held in direct defiance of the leftist agenda.

I will speculate as to what is to become of the still-important contribution of religion in America. A literal belief in the Bible is almost certain to become a historic memory as the centuries pass. Other religions will almost certainly follow this same fate. The Muslim religion that has long been a fierce threat to global peace will also almost certainly fade as a harshly provocative theology-wrought religion. It will fail by self-condemnation or self-destruction. Peaceful Muslims may distance themselves from their legacy religion given the terrible behavior of the minority of Muslim extremists who claim to be "of Allah."

The more you know of the history of Christianity, the less of a Christian you will be.

WHY DO THEY HATE US!

The Christian concept of righteousness should be and is seen as a threat to other religions. Imagine for a moment that you are not of the Christian faith. Imagine that you are a deeply devoted practitioner of a conflicting religion. As part of a conflicting religion you may turn your spiritual self around and see a Christian and ask yourself, How devoted *really* is this person to spreading the word of his God? Does he or she really intend to preach to me in the hope of replacing my faith with theirs? Is it the real intention to spread the word of God to the point where all of those of my faith are converted to Christianity? Those damn infidels! How dare they try to replace my religion with theirs! No matter what it takes Christians must be stopped! But how do we stop them? They have a centuries-old history of "spreading the word" to all corners of the world. "These people will try to convince me that I will burn in an eternal fire if I don't believe the way they tell me to believe. If that weren't bad enough they tell us that even if we die for Allah, in war, we will not get a fleet of virgins to deflower! Such lies! Where will it all end?"

As a Christian, you must also be well versed on the history of the Crusades. Yes, we Christian faithful slaughtered Muslim children by the thousands Many centuries ago. Our history has a component that is as brutal and savage as that of the Muslim!

In these contexts we Christians may be seen as corrupt. We may be seen as the bad guys. We are the murdering hoard. We know that this is not true but we need to understand why others might see us a such. It is not hard to understand why when the hypothetical conversation presented as above, that they consider us a threat. They see us as those who would bring an end their religion if we could. We stand as a conviction of our religion to spread "The" word" to all so that they may also be saved. Our Christian faith requires this of us.

But what of righteousness? What of the notion that we of the Christian faith are the only just religion? What other reason could there be to spread the word of God which is intended to give a chance for salvation to all? But isn't that self-righteous? I personally believe that it is desperately self-righteous. Isn't self-righteousness one of the sins specifically condemned by the Christian church? Could it be that spreading the word of God is contrary to the word of God? For the most part we Christians honor the faith of others and are very accepting of others beliefs. We know this to be true but do they know it? Do they believe it? It is true that most of us regard those of the Muslim faith as generally peaceful except for an extreme few yet we assume it is they (the Muslims) who harbor ill will toward us and without just cause. Why do they hate us? Why do they kill us? We should at least consider the fact that crusading Christians campaigned to exterminate by slaughter the Muslim religion some 400 years ago and these Crusades lasted for almost a century. The point being that we are not without sin. Having said that; It is my deeply considered opinion that a Jihad is actually very rarely the desire of the average Muslim. What I believe to be true is that there are a few extremely radical and naturally violent Muslims who use Jihad as an excuse to participate in terror and violent murder. I believe that desperate and culturally regressed people who have little to live for are attracted to Jihad as an outlet to compensate for the anxiety of a futile and meaningless existence. I believe that those among us that I have previously described, as "sociopaths" will be drawn to the Jihad as an outlet for their perceived right and desire to kill anyone that they should choose kill. Such people will join the cause of Jihad with no true intended goal of fighting a war in the name of Allah. Such like-minded people will congregate from around the world to participate in murder with out penalty. Week minded and ignorant participants are easily recruited in the name of Jihad given the extreme comradeship and an organized wealthy terrorist group power trip

It *is* true that media (mostly movies) frequently typecast religious types as ranting theological dullards. What could be the point of this portrayal? Is this an intended editorial against Christians? The other extreme of the stereotype is the secretive conspiring priest type inclined toward underhanded manipulation. Why are these stereotypes so popular? I have never been exposed to either of these characters in my daily experience. Religious people tend to be naïve and those indulging in piety are prone to indulge in the notion that their lifestyle is completely without "negatives". And there is a piety. But isn't that the point of religion. Isn't it intended to offer comfort to the harsh realities of life? Doesn't it exists to mitigate concern about the ultimate concern which is death? The assumed morality of religion is mostly riddled with non-compliance but it does offer moral guideposts. Yes, the religious are just as likely to ignore those guideposts as anyone else. I think the moral mandate also adds another level of excitement and intrigue to violations of that mandate.

As I ponder the future of humanity and the religious component there of; I can't help but think that, in particular the religion of Christianity is doomed. But Christianity isn't doomed for its faults, it is doomed for its qualities. It is doomed for its sensibilities. It is doomed for its practicality. It and other religions are doomed because its following isn't mandatory. Some religions demand compliance. We cannot expect that an established religion whose standard is absolute compliance, will fade away anytime soon. After two or three thousand years those religions likely will likely continue to thrive into the future. I imagine the Following of Allah will suffer from its extremist following but will none-the-less thrive. More moderate thinkers will distance themselves from the Muslim community over time and as the Muslim death rate climbs. I think that deep down inside most Muslims know that there is no horde of virgins waiting for them after death. Eventually Muslim women will also turn away from the servile mandates of the males of the Muslim faith.

QUANTUM
(THE MATHEMATICAL VALUE OF MASS AS IT RELATES TO QUANTITY.)

There is no such thing as *pure energy*. Believing in pure energy is the same as believing in God yet one belief is scorned by science and one is widely accepted. Neither will ever be proved. All energy is kinetic. There are no exceptions. All energy transfer is friction. There are no exceptions. Light is a stream of particles in which pulses give color to vision. Light has mass and is deflected by gravity given sufficient mass to overcome its speed and energy relative to its mass. But light is only a small part of what comprises the spectrum of particle waves. Its relevance is greatly valued as evidence of warps of space-time but that is because light is easily observed. Where is the reference to other frequencies of particle waves and their detectable anomalies? *Space-time* is a concept which suggests that intense gravitational fields can actually warp the fabric of space and time. I would like to hear an explanation of what the nature of this fabric actually is. As described this dip ignores the more than three-dimensional quality of space-time that must exist. I have seen this so-called warp represented as a circular dip and funnel shaped and capable of consuming objects as they follow a circular plunge to whatever is at the bottom—apparently a passage to another time and place, but time has no matter, no mass or energy. Time is a concept and nothing more. Only your *perception* of time can be changed. Time does not exist physically. We cannot travel *in* or change something that does not exist physically.

What am I missing here? The standard model of particle physics

mathematically prove this previous theory of warps of space and time to be a fact? How can time be altered if time is actually only a human concept, an idea that measures predictable changes in matter as observable by humans. Time has no other quality. We can measure time as it passes. We use the sun as our measuring stick. The rotation of the sun may someday change but time will change at the same rate as compared to other predictable changes of other matter and as *relative* to each other (a.k.a., *relativity*). The theory of relativity requires that photons have no mass but, energized electrical power lines cast a fuzzy shadow which could only be true if massless photons are affected by and can influence an electromagnetic field which can't be true if they are massless. I guess I am just not smart enough to understand.

I hope I can live long enough to know that *gravity* has been defined. The not scientifically accepted statements I made in the first paragraph will be known to be true at that time. The currently accepted principles of physics do not allow for gravity yet it is absolutely the most relevant quality of the physical universe. What are these great minds missing? What simple fact is interfering with their logic? I think it has more to do with ego than logic. Some suggest that gravity is actually the result of the intervention of matter from another unknown dimension of the universe—another concept similar to belief in God.

The Higgs boson is said to have been confirmed and isolated by the CERN Large Hadron Collider (LHC). The LHC was not built in the United States because rational American physicists saw the fallacy of the project's assumptions. It is assumed that the structure of the sought-after particle is a particle that is responsible for all mass (i.e., an autonomous solid particle thought to be the basic building block of all matter. By all appearances the Higgs Boson—if such a particle is confirmed to meet the expected specifications—might only be a fragment of known particles. At some point the basic structural component of matter must be something that resembles pure energy. But that notion assumes matter that has no physical material and means that the scientific experts have no idea what motivates gravity. You can make yourself more famous than Albert Einstein[21] if you can solve this puzzle.

I wonder if it could be true that not all mass *is* actually energy. The concept of pure energy has been around for some time but I never had much faith in the notion. Possibly it is the syntax of the statement that is wrong. The notion that matter and energy *are* the same thing could possibly be more accurately expressed (as in the *big bang theory)*, where all matter was pure energy up until the time of the actual event. It is much more likely true that all matter can be expressed in only one form as the mind can conceive and the mind can conceive energy or mass and nothing more; and mass is actually structured by the amount of continuous motion of energy present. Gravity is still the unknown mechanism of the universe but it could only be the result of an autonomous moving and undefined mass and that mass exists beyond the constraints of what the human mind knows or is the result of mass not in our observable universe and most likely the result of the unknown actions of dark matter. Or it might be the result of a residual energy of common matter not measurable as the mass of the object; which might be responsible for the big bang: the more energy the more measurable mass.

I have heard that some physicists now describe protons and electrons as more like sparks than particles rotating in orbit around a nucleus. The first moment I heard this idea, I assumed it was true. The power of fusion would become a reality based on the concept. The idea supports the facts of fission very well. It wasn't long before such thoughts were disproven or abandoned. I hope I live long enough to know that someone has brought all these principles together to form a theory. Pop culture physics has reached a plateau. Inconsistencies exist mathematically. Current equations don't balance. The four defined forces of energy (electro magnetism, the two nuclear forces controlling atoms and radioactivity; and gravity) are in conflict with each other and cannot work together as described. Einstein invested years trying to evolve the *unified field theory*. He was not successful. The time is near when the current track of physics research will be abandoned and physicists will retrace their steps. A new direction will evolve where research is concerned. The course of research set by Einstein will falter. Personally I lack the wisdom, knowledge, and intellectual power to imagine what the answers will be but I am excited by the prospects. I likely will never know the next major breakthrough in physics. If I could come back a hundred years after my death the first question I would ask is, has gravity been defined?

Wormholes and time travel are nothing but fantasies designed to entertain the imagination. Time is linear and does not exist physically. As stated previously, time is only a human concept that we use to measure changes in matter. The fantasy is based on a perception of time given that we might travel faster than the speed of light as visually perceived which our mind translates into images of past events relative to our current thoughts in regard to a timeline which is another means of expressing the idea of relativity. In physics the past and the future are both right now! Time cannot be circumvented beyond perception. No one is suggesting otherwise in spite of what you are seeing on the Science Channel. There is a little hype on these TV shows just to keep it interesting. My writing is also meant to be interesting and as close to true as my level of understand currently is. My comments should not be taken as fact, just so you'll know!

I see and regard those great minds. I see many (not personally) that don't adjust well to common life among the rest of us. History shows that many of the most intellectually talented people have lived lives of torturous discontent. Great artists and musicians of the past are commonly said to have led troubled and tormented lives. Is this a side effect of intellect? Is there just so much more to know by the greatest minds that making it relevant to everyday life is just too disconcerting? Many of members of the genius category do live great and happy lives. Many are profoundly successful and contribute greatly to society. Others die lying in a ditch poor and drunk. The challenges of great intellect must be tremendous. I suggest it is like taming the wildest and fastest horse or the most powerful car. It requires a firm foundation of preprogrammed facts mixed with an innate guidance and natural proclivity for mental toughness. I think all great achievers must possess a necessary intellect whether they be athletes or politicians or race-car drivers for that matter.

It is impossible for me to know what they know for their ability to know is much greater than mine.

It is impossible for me to imagine what they can imagine for their ability to imagine is much greater than mine.

I can only write about what I see and understand and only write about what my own intellectual limits can comprehend. I can observe and analyze but I can't really know! The simple among us must suffer terribly not by confusion of excess information but by confusion of a lack of understood information. I think that I am not a dumb person. I think that I am a person who understands more than some but less than others. I am somewhere in the middle. I have no great talents or abilities, just minor ones. At times my mind is occupied completely by the mysteries of life and physics and the presence of what we perceive to be the universe.[22]

I once had the pleasure to share my life with a person whose intellectual capacity was clearly well beyond mine. I didn't like that she had that advantage over me. I admired her for it but resented her talents at the same time. What did she see, what did she know that I didn't know? She was troubled at times and made mistakes in simple logic that would be embarrassing for most people. I think she made the common mistake of fallacy in that she assumed that other lesser minds understood thinking at the same level that she did. It is a fallacy of intellect to not set itself apart where understanding is concerned. Psychologists call this issue *projection* in that we assume others are thinking the same things we are thinking and in the same way we are thinking them. She assumed that others understood as she did and as I knew her she humbly never assumed that her natural talents made her special.

Mechanical Engineering?

As a child I found that I was very interested in how things worked both generally and specifically. I was the child looking under the washing machine to see just exactly was going on under there. As I got older my curiosity grew to more complex and powerful machines. Growing up on a farm machines were a common part of my day. I was actually a lot more interested in go-carts and motorcycles than I was in tractors or combines. These various machines had gas motors in common and I wanted to know more about them. Taking them apart and trying to put

them back together again and in working order was a normal afternoon for my brothers and me when I was twelve. I bought my first motorcycle at the age of fourteen and sold it for a profit when I was sixteen. The socialest part of my spirit was forever repressed.

In those times most of my neighborhood friends also had small Japanese motorcycles. It was a common sight on a summer day to see a menacing gang of fifteen-year-olds on Honda 90s' terrorizing the neighborhood. We were the original biker gang cruising the gravel roads. No, none of us had a driver's license but that didn't stop us from putting hundreds of miles on our little Hondas.

I remember trying to overhaul my neighbor's failed Honda motor pretending that I knew what I was doing. I had about half enough knowledge necessary to make the repair which was not enough. Eventually my knowledge base did grow to the point where I could actually fix a motor of this sort. An epiphany struck me at some point during those times. I remember thinking that as I was attempting to disassemble a motorcycle engine and doubting my skill and knowledge I came to an inescapable conclusion: Human minds made this motor, my human mind can fix it! Surely I can figure out what they did to design it and surely I can use that information to get it running again. This otherwise unimportant event was important in that I recognized that while I was not smart enough to have designed this motor, with all of its hidden engineering, I *was* smart enough to understand those mysteries given that engineers had solved these mysteries before me and had used that knowledge to build this engine. I have carried this concept of the subject of higher wisdom and knowledge in that those capable will teach me things that I could never know without their cognitive talents. We are all dependent on such minds for the comforts of our age and the tools of the time.

RECIPES

Every book should have recipes.

CHILI

Yes, an American favorite and a cold-weather staple of the American diet. I went to Mexico on vacation a few years back. It was one of those all-inclusive resorts that offer unlimited drinks, food, and bad manners. Sure you could have all the food you could eat but when the offerings were put out for the taking you'd better make your move because whatever meat, seafood, and other good stuff might be available was gone in the first ten minutes. The booze flowed freely (into a plastic cup), but where was the umbrella and fruit? Try as I might I was only able to drink a half dozen or so of these lackluster drinks at any one time. I soon lost my taste for them. Was it not about the booze? Was it really about the ego-boosting ceremonial luxury of having some subservient waiter bringing my then wife and me an elaborate and very overpriced alcoholic treat? I had always thought I was not vulnerable to such things!

One afternoon while hanging around the pool a Latino fella parked a food cart in the vicinity of our lounge chairs. I quickly investigated his offerings knowing that the early bird concept was likely still in play. He had chili! Not really what I was expecting but okay. I'll bite. I came to call this "Mexican chili." This stuff was delicious. What made it remarkable was its simplicity. It was just diced tomatoes with their natural juice, ground beef, black beans, refried beans, and a few jalapeños thrown on top. The beef in it was especially delicious. It reminded me of the way beef tasted when I was a child. We Americans pride ourselves on having the best of everything so how is it that this beef tasted so much better than our US beef? As a farmer I know that it is likely a result of the breed of the cattle involved and we no longer produce that breed in the United States.

When I came home from my vacation one of the first things I did was to attempt to duplicate this chili. I was successful. The elaborate legacy chili I had been making for decades is now just a memory. My point is that simple was better, quicker and much easier. It doesn't take an elaborate scheme to get the desired results. If you try this recipe, as described above I can almost guarantee that you will also abandon your exotic and elaborate recipe in favor of a less-managed process.

EGGS

Never, never, never whip eggs. *Never!* The taste of eggs is destroyed by oxidation when whipped then cooked. Do you like the floor mat–like omelets served at Denny's? I don't. Instead, gently fold and blend your eggs with your desired added ingredients as they are cooking. Remove them from heat when there is no longer any noticeable liquid. One taste and you will never whip eggs again! You should use this method as the base to making your omelet with the ingredients gently mixed through-out rather than folded in a pocket. The less complex and more practical way of cooking eggs yields better results.

BEEF STEW

If it were not important to follow these directions carefully I would not have gone to all of the trouble of writing them.

Diced beef; actually cut into small chunks of various shapes and sizes and not the cheap stuff but preferably sirloin and with most of the fat trimmed off: about 1.5 pounds and Also not just tossed into your mix but fried in your pot until the juice evaporates and the beef is noticeably seared. Add a medley of chopped vegies; I use potatoes, carrots, sweet corn (homegrown if you have it), a good pile of diced onions, peas, and celery. Salt is also important but should be added carefully (and to taste).

Water added to the amount of your preferred density but keep in mind that this stew will thicken a little as it is cooked. Lots of freshly ground black pepper and a little pearled barley; include three bay leaves, and let it all simmer till the veggies are cooked soft.

This recipe is also just basic cooking. It has many ingredients but they are tried-and-true components that add up to a basic and useful product. You will find yourself wondering why I think this mix is special. You will also find yourself wanting a second serving. This mix is neither exotic nor elaborate as a plan, but it works well together. It is a mix of compatible things. It is a recipe for success.

PRIME RIB ROAST, CHARCOAL GRILLED

You gotta do this if you think of yourself as an outdoor chef. About four pounds of prime rib, large end works best. Have it tied tight with string. Coat the meat heavily with *"Blackened Steak"* seasoning. The real trick here is to cook and sear the outside hot and quickly. What you *don't* want here is roast beef so the need to monitor it constantly is imperative. Use your meat thermometer and keep the center rare. I put the meat directly on the grill and rotate it frequently so that all sides are seared. Keep in mind that the center will cook a bit after you remove it from the charcoal. This is absolutely my favorite way to serve high-value cuts of beef. Again, it is a simple plan that if done correctly will yield great results.

I always recommend that anyone preparing a meal or a particular dish do a little experimenting with variations on any recipe. This is how all the really good things we love to eat were discovered and developed. Humans learned to cook meat long after the habit of eating meat became a common experience. What if no one ever accidently got meat hot in a fire? I love a steak but I don't know how much of it I would eat if it were raw. Another thing to remember is that if your experimental recipe is unsuccessful and doesn't work together, simply feed it to leftists. They are very well accustomed to accepting things that are unsuccessful. They might actually advocate that everyone in society eat your creation in spite of the fact that your ingredients are not compatible and don't work well together. I know that this sounds unlikely but I must point out that this is a normal behavior for leftists given that they commonly advocate failed programs long after any chance of a successful outcome is feasible.

Disaster

To get a really good disaster you need to carefully manipulate a situation intended to create something wonderful and new and based on an intended result but without first carefully understanding the unintended or unforeseen possibilities. For example, we might build a building along a beautiful coastline only to have it destroyed by hurricanes or be forever vulnerable to hurricanes. Clearly the person or group who built the building didn't allow for the obvious risks of the location. Bad recipe. We might also try to create a social situation that is carefully planned with all the best intentions but if those components/ingredients that are the body of the plan don't work well together they will not produce the desired results. It could quickly become a political and social disaster. (Obamacare!)

Here is another disaster that is possible though I admit is very unlikely. Just imagine what terrible things would happen—theoretically of course—if a fraternity of individuals somehow managed to get themselves in a position of power which also put them in control of a portion of everyone's money. This fraternity would actually have the power to confiscate money from individuals and use it to foster their own personal self-serving agenda. ... Once they had this power they would then use the confiscated funds to maintain control of the funds by distributing a large portion of these funds back to the people in a way that would garner favoritism. This favoritism would leave the fraternity in a position to confiscate an ever-increasing volume of funds and at the will of the people they were theoretically serving.

What makes this hypothetical scenario really tragic is that the people are getting back less money from the fraternity than is being given to the fraternity. Of course this fraternity must skim a percentage of the funds to fund itself. This would be very personally beneficial for the members of the fraternity given that they had control over enormous amounts of money and the small percentage being skimmed would not be thought of as important. It also stands to reason that the fraternity would grow and keep growing given the enormous profitability, and the people are supporting the existence of this fraternity because the people believe that they are gaining wealth through the fraternity which would further foster its own growth. In truth the fraternity is incredibly expensive to maintain because the members are spending others people's money and have no reason to care about cost or efficiency or effectiveness. Things just couldn't get any worse—or could they? Actually, yes they could. The fraternity could conspire against the people by engaging in massive borrowing of funds in the name of the people. The borrowed funds are then given in part to ever more people so that the people can continue to get something for what is perceived as nothing; thus fostering more goodwill toward the fraternity even though this scheme must fail eventually.

It is hard to imagine that any group of people could be so terribly self-serving if not evil. I realize the absurdity of my theoretical scenario. Still, I think it is actually possible! Also you have to ask yourself why would the people be so damn gullible as to allow such a thing to happen? Are they stupid or are they just terribly ignorant? Possibly they are just greedy. Some of the dependents may actually be willing to accept the stipend as their only source of income. They would come to realize that going to work every day would only improve their life marginally. They would now be completely dependent on the fraternity and will vote in favor of it no matter what else is true. Of course they are now no longer able to generate funds to fund the fraternity which will then as stated, need to borrow more funds to replace the funds that are no longer available from the people.

The fraternity is now condemned to borrow an endlessly increasing amount of funds in order to maintain the loyalty of the people. Plus, everyone that has become dependent is consuming wealth though not replacing it with anything of value by his or her labors. Now the economy is inextricably lessened by wealth dissipation of the unproductive recipients. Also, the ability to ever repay this debt becomes less likely day by day. The only possible outcome of this conspiracy is the collapse of the participating economy.

As you may have observed by now, I am trying to create a not-particularly-clever analogy. Could this scenario be the same reason why political programs are so grossly inefficient or not effective at all and yet they go on and on? Our politicians don't really care how the money is spent and they are well rewarded for their management (glory, power, and control), so they keep doing it. Could this be the reason that the suburbs of Washington, DC are becoming some of the wealthiest communities in America?

The only worse thing that could happen in the above scenario is the person put in control of all of these things as the head of the fraternity, profoundly advocates the principles of the fraternity and intends to make such behavior permanent and standard. Eventually, so much future wealth would be consumed that these future economies would suffer because the newly gained national wealth would not be enough to replace the previously and already spent wealth.

Of course there are people out there who are horrified at this situation but their warnings go unheeded because so many people are benefiting from the extreme spending. You could use my analogy that compares this to your being broke from your personal overspending, so you now only use your personal credit card to buy whatever the hell you want and the *limit keeps going up.* Eventually the credit card issuers are going to want their money repaid and they are going to want it when you no longer have enough income or assets to meet your expanding debt. When you don't have the money to pay the debt; they will then own you and all property that was previously yours. Countries in Europe have faltered financially because of this scenario and yet in America today, we are following this exact course! The unintended consequences of social spending will not only leave the nation unable to pay its debts, it will leave the nation unable to help impoverished people and these impoverished people will suffer greatly when the federal stipend that they have come to depend upon is no longer an option.

Remember, that the people who took your money to support the fraternity (government) will not suffer or be held accountable because they were given public permission to commit this tragedy. The poor will be hurt the most and they will have no choice but to continue supporting fraternity spending. Financially well-off citizens will not suffer because they never became dependent on government and will continue to thrive. The poor will be the most damaged. They are the true victims of this scheme though they supported it. Even if this scheme were continued to the last available dollar the poor would suffer the most once there is no longer enough national wealth to carry the weight of the needy. This scenario is the only eventual possible outcome for our nation. I really believe we have already gone too far to recover as a nation economically. A nation that was once so very wealthy that we could afford to support many millions of nonworking, nonproductive citizens without incurring debt.

Anyone proposing the previous scenario as an all at once suggestion for running a nation would be considered a lunatic and laughed out of the room for his foolishness. The recipe is clearly absurdly unworkable when proposed as a single all-at-once formula.

The ingredients are not compatible. The various components do not complement each other. It is a mixture of strong influences that are in conflict with the original goal of satisfying a need. Clearly the ingredients of this political stew would be better utilized if they functioned separately. Each has its intrinsic value and can function on its own successfully. As a mix, these otherwise separate components can only lose their relevant qualities.

Why do we as a culture try so hard to blend not necessarily compatible ingredients and then expect beneficial positive results? When we try to create things and situations that don't work well together naturally we fail to reap the rewards and efficiency of an unforced naturally occurring outcome.

Things that naturally work well together are better if left to their natural processes. Use quality and practical ingredients and you will get good, efficient, and reasonable results. Government is intrinsically incapable of doing this. I hope it is clear that this recipe is an exact description of the desired agenda of leftist politics.

KRIB NOTES

If you bothered to read the opening to this book, you will know that this section contains my notes on possible content as I was writing Proclivities. Krib Notes is mostly just random thoughts or trashed content that did not make it to the main body of text.

First Entry!!!!!

"A solution to climate change!"

The 1960s and '70s were about something beyond the obvious—the "more" of human experience; the next level up of human understanding. Today's culture—and rap music specifically—is about the lowest of thinking; a regression of human evolution intellectually. It is the essence of human sloth and ignorance expressed in lyric and rhyme.

The primary purpose of government is to collectively subjugate the effects of life's natural cruelties; the problem is, we cannot legislate away these cruelties. Harsh cruel reality is a part of life, in the same way that joy and pleasure are a part of life.

BDLs think that they are being sensitive by not using such terms as

Indian to describe Native Americans. What they are actually being is weak and fearful as far another culture goes. My local Native Americans tell me that they prefer the term *American Indian*. With this knowledge you are now politically incorrect if you use the term "Native American."

It is very telling that the "trained to pretend to be someone they are not"[23] Hollywood actors and liberal extremists are frequently one and the same.

An example of how liberals think and how their politics work?????? Liberals like to vilify corporations as evil and making too much money! The solution? Raise taxes on corporations, what else! Of course, this encourages corporations to shut down or relocate to avoid paying taxes which means that corporations need a tax break to save jobs. This leads to liberals vilifying corporations again as they complain about corporate welfare in the form of tax breaks. All of this is about manipulating your vote; it has nothing to do with real world economics. *Are you voting for these people?!*

Socialism is a weight-loss program: there will be less food for all! There are far fewer fat people living in socialest cultures.

The conquerors of history have always operated under the assumption that the resources of all lands should be shared equally, as do liberals.

When the public pays health care costs, the public can control how you live.

Hyphenated Woman? Really? Can't you just pick one last name and stay with it?!

It's a natural human tendency to protect and provide for children at all costs. That means any child, and men are every bit as involved in this mission as women are.

Voting anonymously gives every voter a chance to vote on behalf of his or her own personal agenda and needs and without regard for the greater good, which is the political opposite of democracy.

Thirty years ago, I was told that the world was getting hotter because the atmosphere was thinning (*ozone depletion*). Now I am being told that the world is getting hotter because the atmosphere is thickening (*carbon dioxide emissions*). I hope these people make up their damn minds real soon!

Now it's smokefree.gov! These f—ers don't have the slightest comprehension of why people smoke. They are spending the nation's money and gaining nothing! I see them as fools. Rectally/cranially inverted to the point where they can actually see through the holes in their belly buttons, if they turn their heads just a little.

What do you mean when you say "everything happens for a reason"? Are you referring to divine intervention or a preprogramed course of events in your life? Or do you mean that everything you do eventually affects everything that eventually happens. In either case, what can be the divine reason for bad things? How can the horribly tragic loss of a cherished loved one be reasonable or have happened for a predetermined reason?

A life based on pleasure is an empty life. Today's pleasures are tomorrow's disappointments. You will always need to achieve that next level of high to keep the pleasure coming. A much better life is one based on joy generally; the joy of simple pleasures. The hug of a child; the sense of accomplishment; the knowledge that you have done the right thing; the joy of giving; the joy of shared love. And on and on. … Satisfaction with life cannot come from hedonistic pleasure. How do I know? I have spent my life trying to prove it could be done—unsuccessfully.

Marijuana is not a harmless drug. How do I know? Do you really have to ask? I came of age in the 1970s. … Pot takes away aggression. We need to be aggressive to be prosperous, to thrive. Long-term use of marijuana causes memory issues later in life. There is no such thing as harmless inhaled smoke. Marijuana will give you a life of nothing. You will eventually use the drug until it is all you really want to do. You will learn to be satisfied with very little else. Any potential benefit to the cultural condition will be diminished by the recreational use of any drug. Dopers frequently miss out on the really great things that life offers.

If I were a hard-core socialist, I would create a national program of marijuana production and distribution. It would be free to everyone. Potheads would tend the fields and experiment with and evaluate new varieties. Burnouts would manage distribution. I would go global. Eventually most of the world's people would become so passive that I would be able to easily control them. People would not resist social control at all. A simple quiet life would become the status quo. Successful socialism would finally be realized. People would drive slow and save gas. Economic activity would collapse and the industrial cultural world would regress. Carbon emissions would plummet. The planet would be saved. Of course, I would need to maintain a population of fully functional administrators. Infrastructure would need to be maintained. Quality of life would be diminish for everyone, but the planet would be saved. Kumbaya!

Obama: "Hope and Change" or "Hopeless Change"?

ASU, I like it! American Socialist Union. It's USA backward. It is an anagram and a great new name for our nation! It even has an offensive connotation in that it can sound like "ass U." It is only a matter of time until the name accurately describes the United States of America.

Anyone educating you is likely to share his or her personal beliefs and thinking. We assume that our teachers' thinking is accurate and universal by default until we are exposed to a contrary set of facts or use our own objective influences.

"You didn't do that alone" is an Obama notion which, at its roots is the ultimate expression of what it means to be a socialist. The notion is born of the worldview that we are one group. That we people are a single thing. Anything that is done is done because the group facilitated that accomplishment. We are not individuals thriving on our own. We are a combined entity. All we do individually is a result of all else that was done by the group. We do not exist autonomously. He made a mistake as president when he preached the above concept. "You didn't do that alone." It is of course, an absurd statement. In fact that this nation exists as it is because you *did* do that alone and on your own initiative. Our individual enterprise option as citizens is a legendary fact of our nation and it is the reason why our economy is the most dominant and wealthiest to ever exist. Our economy is unique in that most of the wealth is not in the hands of a ruling or privileged class but widely distributed among the citizens. Many live in poverty but never have so many lived in relative wealth. The fact that yes I did do that is the reason why so many of us *do* live in some state of wealth. But Obama simply doesn't perceive the difference. It isn't that he doesn't believe the difference. It is that he can't know the difference. His proclivity is that of a socialist. He measures every political concept from the perspective of a socialist.

He will only see that it was a group effort that created *THE* wealth and he can only see that the wealth exists collectively and is not the property of any one individual. And we should "spread THE wealth around."[24] In other words stimulus money is only the normal and socially just way that things should be. The wealth belongs to everyone equally, no matter its origin.

The concept is innate to Obama as a person not born of this culture and who has absorbed the notion of the European economic model of a "not wealthy and living modestly main body of citizens" led by a ruling body; in this case, led by him or by like-minded people. In his mind and from the European perspective, wealth and social aggression are considered tawdry if not intrinsically corrupt.

It takes a self-aggrandizing arrogance to pursue this sort of work. (Writing). It is very tedious. In moments of introspection I realize that very few people actually care what I think!

I want to feed every child of course I do but the random and mass breeding must end or there will be an endless stream of new and desperately needy children. It isn't one child that needs to be saved. It is an entire community of humans that needs to be saved. But I have to ask to what end? The horrible truth is that more surviving children just puts more pressure on the desperately scarce resources and the next child born will have even less of what is needed for survival. It is a horrible injustice that the more we feed starvation, the more starvation we will have and our prosperous selves cannot change that fact. No matter how much of our resources we contribute the starving populations will eventually grow and require an ever-increasing supply of donated resources. The solution can only be local self-sustaining production of food. When you contribute, contribute to a solution.

At any given time, there are more pertinent on thoughts on my mind than the issue of freedom.

Freedom. What it means to the rest of the world is very different from what it means to Americans. You may hear that we Americans take our freedom for granted but what does that really mean? The last time I heard that statement I casually brushed it off as most people would. At any given moment I have many more-pressing issues on my mind than whether or not I am free. It is not rare for media outlets to feature conversations regarding our freedom and our apathetic attitude toward our it—again with very little impact on my thinking other than that "ain't nobody takin my freedom away." It is simply not a part of my thinking that such a thing is even possible. We, as a country and citizenry really do take freedom for granted and we know it will never be an issue that any foreign power will come to our nation and repress us. Our borders are secure and our military is and long has long been the dominant human force where nations are concerned. We are not threatened by a foreign power. Our freedom can only be lost from within. Only our own politics can threaten our freedom. How much government control are you personally willing to tolerate? How much of your personal autonomy are you willing to sacrifice in the name of national social equality? How much of your private wealth accumulated by your own efforts are you willing to sacrifice in the name of a political principle? Does knowing that this political principle has a profoundly high failure rate historically, make any difference to you? Or is it all about believing that you will personally prosper if the government provides for your needs?

It is the default assumption of the alarmists that we citizens of the planet, generally, are just not bright enough to discern the need; therefore, we should rely on their expert opinions and change the way we live accordingly. They know that most people will not question their motives—and their "facts" —which, in effect, isolates the alarmists from public condemnation.

Middle ground. Life will always be lived in the political middle. The problem is, the middle keeps shifting!

As of this writing, all the basic necessities of life are free in America. Food, shelter, and health care all can be had for the asking. If you are willing to live with only the basics, there is no longer any reason to have a job. Don't ya just love Obamanomics!

If you are really about the collective society you will do what ever is necessary to foster that society. You will demand less from it than you give to it. This is the only way a "liberal" society can sustain itself. I am calling for a conservative revolution that requires liberal pundits to live daily life by their own principles and this includes Hollywood actors and MSNBC commentators.

There is no such thing as *government money.* By proclivity, economists (both academics and professionals) don't study economics from the standpoint of conservative economics. There is no reason for economists to study conservative economics. The economics of conservatism are a given like sunshine and rain and they are very well documented. There is little mystery in conservative economics. It just *is.* Conservative economics is easy to understand and doesn't require manipulation only restraint in order to suppress inflation. It is a fair statement that many of the most notable economists of the previous times were primarily concerned with validating an economic principle that supported collectivist economic systems. Yes, the primary goal was to validate socialism. And Nobel Prizes were awarded.

More and more I am becoming disenchanted with those among us who are less than committed to an elevated social achievement. I am trying to carefully describe those who just aren't really trying. Those who don't give a shit about being something, or someone, who will not draw the scorn or contempt of the community at large. I mean to include the slothful, the obese, the dirty, the drugged, the drunk, and the sloppy. Is this just because I am an arrogant prick or is it because I have done okay and will never be a drag on our society? I have lost my sympathy for the less than successful. I know that there are many of us who just are not especially capable. Such people may really be trying, possibly harder than I am, but they just don't have the potential or aren't smart enough or are not of a healthy mind. Let's call them "Walmart people."

I assume you have seen the Internet photos showing a 300-pound women in a G-string going through the checkout lines at Walmart. (Excuse me while I barf.) The real problem I have here, is that I *am* a Walmart person. I shop at my local Walmart on a regular basis. I don't feel uncomfortable or threatened there and I can go dressed as I am. I don't feel superior to the average customer because I *am* the average customer. I actually think it might be a good place to score an easy if not desperate, chick. And you can buy a TV at Walmart for a really good price. I am well aware that there are many in our culture who would hold me in contempt for being someone who *wants* a TV. Cultured, educated people see TV as a harbinger of cultural debauchery. Only a fool would spend his or her life watching a stupid sitcom or a senseless crime drama. But I do have a TV, actually more than one. Clearly, I am a Walmart person and shop with those who have "it's my money, and I want it now" money.

Most of us, including me, have no choice but to accept that many others among us would look down their noses at we common people. I am one of those people who is really a "nothing" as far as humanity goes. I will never have any real impact on society. I will never be famous or have a book published or marry an NFL cheerleader. I am a farmer and proud of that fact, but I am still just a farmer. I actually don't mean to suggest that I resent those people who would consider me as less than they are. The simple truth is that many people have invested themselves in life profoundly more than I have and most of them deserve the rewards of their efforts. They are also in many cases, just simply far more capable than I am and I cannot expect to achieve at their level nor do I deserve their wealth and glory. For example, medical doctors may invest a full decade of their time before they can become actual practicing doctors working and earning on their own. It is also true that not all such people are culturally valuable. Liberals extremists for example; they can be highly educated, have great skill, be highly ambitious and very academically successful, yet still be a detriment to our culture. Is there a point to this? Yes, not all greatness should be honored; not all sloth should be condemned. The 300-pound Walmart woman has no means to understand how extreme her persona is. If she did she would change. Liberal extremists also just don't understand how extreme and unaware they can be. At this level, they are one and the same person. Be gracious to the lesser and cautious of honoring the greater.

Awareness. I am aware that you are aware of awareness. Okay! So we can stop talking about "creating awareness." Please!

Falling behind in education as a nation is not an education issue; it is a cultural issue. It is not about needing more money and/or more teachers for education. It is not about higher teacher salaries. It is about students showing up at school with a need and desire to learn. It is about masses of citizens who have no or very little family structure or parental guidance. It is about a lack of motivation of the student to take the personal responsibility to become educated for his or her own personal benefit. It is about the individual need and desire to get the education that will facilitate his or her eventual self-sufficient lifestyle.

In high school I was one of those students who was not at all motivated to get an education. I was the poster child of the person I described above. I have expertise on this subject. I lived it. No one can tell me that motivation is not the issue. All the hype about teacher pay is just pure bovine fecal matter. I think the quality of the teacher has become more of an issue as discipline in schools has collapsed. Teachers now spend their time and skills trying to manage BS leftist agendas. It takes a lot of skill to effectively manage such a profoundly corrupt and unworkable social structure and teachers are also required to spend time teaching actual knowledge.

Had my parents forced the issue I would have been much more than a "barely getting by" student. Funding could not have changed this fact.

And who are the most vocal among us that advocate for more—more money, more teachers, and more classrooms? The teachers themselves and their unions, that's who! I will never accept that a community can create a social entity (your town, your school), and then those who are hired to serve that entity, administrators/teachers) have a default "right" to determine the compensation for this service. This is yet another example of leftism that is corrupt at every level. Creating a public service entity and then demanding compensation for the entity which you created is known as *social tyranny*. If we want to improve the results of education—and I do—only changing the desires and motivations of those being educated will make the difference.

There is an unintended consequence of trying to improve education in America The goal for education has become satisfying proficiency testing standards and gaining the resulting prestige of wages and advanced educational degrees and additional funding for the schools. The real need of education is passing along the knowledge and wisdom of all who have come before us. Has this goal become secondary? For the most part I will blame top-down leftist administrators for their proclivity to advocate a political agenda and also to place the financial rewards of their personal careers as a motivating priority to servicing the needs of the community. Those financial rewards can only be the result of higher student test scores and this is because the administrators have created the system that facilitates this cause. Again, what we really need as a culture—and civilization and species— is to give our future generations the best chance to thrive not only by knowledge but also wisdom. The advantages of fostering wisdom have become secondary to a self-serving autocratic agenda.

Insane. My definition of insane is "any behavior that is inconsistent with the propagation of the individual and community." Does that sound insane to you?

Al Franken is a wonderful example of what it means to be insane but not clinically insane. He condemns corporations as "Not people"—as if there were a major contingent of politicrats claiming that corporations are actually people and most likely, rich Republicans.[25] Clearly Mr. Franken has made a statement that is profoundly obvious and actually very simple and true. But the implications of the statement are intended to engender a much larger notion or thought that has actually not been stated. (The perfect example of babaloney by the way. Like taking candy from a baby he makes a comment that is undisputable and will not be challenged as a concept. Of course it is true that a corporation is *not* a person. Most everyone knows this but at another level, corporations are made up of people and owned and designed by people and employ many, many millions of people. Both statements are true but Al knows that most of his listeners will assume that he has made a wonderfully clever and true statement that is the end of any argument or discussion about corporations. It is clearly absurd and ignorant if not insane thinking—no matter what else is true—if we take this statement as a factual declaration. But we understand it to be a ploy and it then becomes a plausible statement with no assumption of insanity. What is really disturbing to me is that he is using this false ploy to manipulate social thinking. Yet those of you in Minnesota elected him; or did you? His first election was a very close count as I recall! Just what level of deception is he capable of?

The real ploy is that the less than astute among us will embrace this opportunity to support a notion that assumes others (Republicans) are not as wise as "me, we, us." We (Democrats) who assume this "truth" as our own are obviously smarter than the conservatives and Al becomes more politically powerful as a result because he is obviously much wiser than those who think corporations are people! (conservatives). Yet nothing whatsoever has been accomplished politically or socially other than to foster his personal political image! I freely admit that deep down inside I personally am a scumbag; however, Al's social manipulation to foster personal self-glorification is an act profoundly beneath any act that I would ever consider participating in—or would ever imagine in the first place for that matter. This concept is just too profoundly corrupt for me to consider it as an option under any circumstances. It is disturbing and ethically beneath me, an admitted lowlife. Is he delusional? Is he evil? What are his motives? Do you assume that he is magnanimous? I will remind you that making this statement has accomplished nothing. No actual benefit came to you or me or anyone else, nor can any benefit come from this "social policy." Do you feel better about him when he says corporations are not people? Do you like the idea that he might be using a ploy to manipulate your thinking, all for his personal gain? It is clear that nothing else useful can come from this statement. Such manipulations are deeply corrupt and based on an "ends justify the means" mentality and behavior. Such people commonly manipulate you in this way for their own personal gain!

If you think you are going to lose weight by eating something—a special food or a diet as sold on TV—I got bad news for you. It's only *not* eating something that causes weight loss! You need to *not* eat in order to lose weight. If you think you can lose weight without being hungry, I got more bad news for you! Being hungry is the only "weigh" to lose weight. It will always be about personal self-control!

If you are selling a weight-loss program, it doesn't matter if it doesn't work. In any case, the seller no longer has a potential customer. If customers lose weight, they no longer need you. If customers don't lose weight, they no longer want you! There is no scenario in which a weight-loss program needs to be effective to be sellable. You may safely assume that any weight-loss program you buy into is a fraud! Why? There is only one way to lose weight. Calories in calories out. No exceptions! You prefer to believe that there are exceptions and convincing you so is how the weight-loss industry sustains itself.

After the 2012 election I observed a phenomenon in pop culture politics where the media are repeating stories of what Democrats think Republicans need to do to win more elections. Yes, it is true: demoncrats are telling Republicans how to be better Democrats, and the willing media are currently thick with this story. Republicans are now expected to follow the advice of Democrats, as media types would have it. Even former joint chief of staff Colin Powel has joined the fray by publicly stating that the Republican Party should follow the lead of the Democratic Party as far as our public policy is concerned so that we can win more elections. Pause with that thought for a moment please! … Yes, a famous former Republican, a man of very high regard in the US government has chosen to abandon the principles of the party that brought him to prominence in favor of the political emotions of the moment and consistent with the politics generally common to those of his birth. It must indeed be a powerful force to which he has succumbed. So powerful that he would freely abandon his historic political perspective. I also have to point out here that the Left-leaning (by proclivity) media have taken frequent opportunities to show us Republicans the error of our ways, and they use political traitors to the party as examples. It is not a common news story but one that the leftist media have advocated in that we (Republicans) should follow the lead of Democrats!

And also—OMG! —the media expect us to abandon our political philosophy so that we can win elections based on a contrary political viewpoint. Contrary to what we actually believe in and what we believe is the best for our nation so that we can win elections so that we can put our people in power and they will then advocate social policy contrary to the platform on which they were elected. This is *not* the thinking of Republicans, It is the methodology of demoncrats who are now advising conservatives to do the same. (And yet they condemn Republicans as corrupt!)

I advocate social needs through capitalism. Demoncrats advocate capital needs through socialism!

Government can't work at all unless it is grossly inefficient. Checks and balances are a must to prevent graft. Checks and balances are expensive as are regulations, administration, compliance, legislation, and enforcement. Private enterprise is not burdened with any of these costs. By default all government programs dissipate national wealth. No, these are not beneficial jobs. Government jobs are a cost to the nation, not a benefit for the nation. Yes, taxes are paid but they are taxes paid from the national treasury to the national treasury at a fraction of the original amount.

Supporting yourself at all costs is the natural scheme of things. Whatever it takes is the only standard within the culture's recognized laws. Politicians like to use the term "hardworking" in their rhetoric. First thing I want to know is, what about the *not* "hardworking" people? It ain't hard to find people who are f—ing lazy. Should these people expect to be afforded a comfortable living at the expense as the rest of society? I don't think I owe lazy people a damn thing and yet they get the same welfare benefits as hardworking down-on-their-luck "folks." The hardworking moniker is a ploy used by politicians because it flatters the listener. And none of the listeners say to themselves, "Gee, I guess I really am kind of a bum! He isn't talking about me when he (Obama) says 'hardworking.'"

It is inescapable that there are many among us who will simply choose to accept—or are resigned to accept a social charity minimal wealth living. We have, as a component of our society a subculture that expects nothing more of itself.

Regarding your existence!

If you ever ask yourself, *why?*—and if you are any kind of decent human being you eventually will or already have—. The only transcending answer that I have been able to come up with is this: It is all we got it is all there is so there is no reason not to play along; what else are you going to do that makes any sense or can have a meaningful outcome? The futility of what we see around us is all we have. It is all we are going to have till we die. You *are* going to die. Can you imagine how useless and senseless life would be if we knew we weren't ever going to die … not ever? Same old thing forever day in and day out for a thousand centuries. About three days after you absorbed *that* knowledge you would be looking for ways to kill yourself. No matter what the perceived advantage, life would eventually fail to have meaning. No amount of glory or wealth or fame would have value if you knew that life was forever. There is nothing that could not be achieved for everyone given enough time.

America has long been in the habit of giving racially disadvantaged Americans a measure of grace where tolerable behavior is concerned. By that I mean that certain races are held to a lower standard in terms of society's expectations, generally speaking. What is on average expected of white America is not necessarily expected of minority races. It is just assumed that because of discrimination and social disadvantage, those of a certain culture will not be held to the same accountability. I have made an observation that possibly the same is true of Barack Obama. In recent months a long list of controversies that would have led a white male Republican president to be jailed are only casually mentioned in the media—except as mentioned in *conservative* media, which are apparently compelled to obsessively attack Mr. Obama.

Wealth represents life. All wealth is an accumulation of those who have lived before this moment which includes you. Money is used to represent and easily transfer wealth. Wealth is accumulated to provide personal security into the future which increases the likelihood of survival. Money is what you get in exchange for your life, your time, and your trouble. Money is how you are personally valued. If you are valued highly you get lots of money. If you have no education, no skills, no ambition, you will get very little money or you will be supported by someone else, or you will steal or become a drug dealer etc. Most old people have lots of money! They have been accumulating wealth throughout their lives. They *should be* rich. They deserve to be rich and they will need that accumulated wealth when they are no longer able to earn a living. Being old is expensive. Most of those people you hear referred to as "the rich" are actually older people. Most of those older people started out with very little personal wealth.

The next time someone uses condemning references to wealth and "the rich" and their quest for money you will know how to respond!

This is a true story that you do-gooder libs ain't gonna like!

A good friend of mine, a truck driver whose services as a truck driver were donated by her company for a food drive, shared this story with me. She was very indignant about the actual results of the food drive.

She was present at the collection point of the food drive and participated in the eventual loading of the truck, which she was then expected to drive to the food bank. The satisfied food-drive organizers believed that they had fulfilled their mission to help feed the members of an impoverished Latino community. After a brief ceremony the crowd of self-satisfied organizers walked away believing that their efforts had made the world a better place. What they didn't do was, *follow the truck!* My friend described an event in which the supposedly responsible recipients of the donated food led her to an entirely different location other than the local food bank as she had expected. Those who had assumed responsibility for the truck's contents soon secured the truck and opened its doors. Almost immediately an informal auction began to sell the donated food to a gathering crowd. Some of those present eventually took possession of large quantities of the donated food with the obvious intent of resale. The intent of the food drive was to give free food to needy citizens. Instead, a few corrupt profiteers bastardized this otherwise magnanimous event. The community as a whole was not served. If anything, those who stole the food will eventually commit this crime again and will be joking with each other about how gullible the food drive organizers are/were.

This kumbaya moment for the volunteers and organizers of the food drive was in reality, a hoax. It was not a hoax by the organizers but a hoax by the intended and mistrusted beneficiaries. I don't know how common this story is but I know that it did happen. In a culture where food stamps and SNAP cards (sure, cards!) are traded as currency and at less than face value. What can we really do to help impoverished communities? I want to help them have a better life but it doesn't appear to me that this community had character enough to live a better life. I think that there is a default assumed right among needy people that the rules of conduct can be "bent" in the name of exceptional need. "we should not be condemned for breaking the rules because we are disadvantaged" We who are not impoverished are willing to donate our personal time and wealth to aid those disadvantaged, *but* charity can never be unconditional if it is going to benefit the intended in a long-term meaningful way. Without conditional charity all we have done—and all we will continue to do—is to foster a dependent class of chronically impoverished people. The above story is the perfect example of why this happens.

I want you to step outside your personal box for a few moments, as far as the media are concerned. Imagine yourself as part of a media outlet, or pretend that you are the manager responsible for a mass media organization. Media include TV news programs of all perspectives, newspapers, magazines, radio, billboards, various Internet sites and platforms—actually, anything that includes a message or is trying to sell something to you or to inform you at the expense of an advertiser. As the manager, what is the first thing you will need? The answer is, *content!* You need something to say a picture or an image to show; anything to convey a message. You not only need content now you need it day after day hour after hour. If you suddenly found yourself in this position I think the first thing you would do is panic! In a hurried moment you would put anything out just to satisfy the need to convey content. How far would you go outside the lines just to get anything out there? Imagine what is happening at your local TV news station two hours before airtime. Those attractive people you see and trust to tell the unbiased truth are busy writing "content." A half-hour show needs at least twenty minutes of content—any content! And what do you use as content on a very slow news day? Anything thing you've got!

My point is this: there is a default assumption of expertise and validity where media outlets are concerned. "These people wouldn't be on

TV if they didn't know what they were talking about or didn't believe in the notion what they are saying was important." But in fact, the previous statement has no truth to it at all. The most important thing for anyone to know about media is that the media can't exist without funding. Media will always be about the cash flow. They must have a sellable product and in truth liberal media types are often naturally clueless people. They are the type of people who are naturally "out of the know", as far as facts go. This proclivity is what attracts them to media. They find the transfer of information more fascinating than the average person. We are all attracted to things that are mysterious to us. By far the most important quality of your local newscaster is *physical appearance*; next would be *articulation* (the ability to speak understandably). Being a naturally knowledgeable person is never part of the equation. As for content; liberalism sells. Liberalism sells to the not-knowledgeable people in the same way that useless products are sold with infomercials. Only the clueless will buy it.

I could just as likely been born to a starving and extremely impoverished family in sub-Saharan Africa—or could I? If that were true, I would not have become me. I could only have been me if born to a rural farm culture in the American Midwest. Yes, I was born to opportunities but my proclivity and ability was to take advantage of those opportunities while others of similar opportunity chose not to do so. The point is: Don't give me a guilt trip about how fortunate I am. I didn't choose this life. It chose me, and I have paid my dues.

You are reading this book because of a million random circumstances that led me to spend countless hours writing it, and also; during those occasional moments when you ponder life, you chose to read my book in the hope that you might find something useful or entertaining. I hope you are not disappointed.

"But hark. What light through yonder window breaks? It is the east and Juliet is the sun" (Shakes Spear).

Modern translation: "The sun is coming up and shining through that window. The sun reminds me of Juliet 'cuz that bitch is hot!"

You may have noticed that, at least metaphorically, I like throwing rocks at liberal ideas.

"Sometimes I guess there just aren't enough rocks" (Forrest Gump).

You can automatically eliminate any proposed social program that uses the word *should* as part of the rhetoric pundits are advocating for its passing. Only programs in which the standard is *must* should have any chance of becoming social policy or law.

Your pro-leftist vote requires involuntary servitude to the slothful. If you have a job, you are supporting the slothful, lazy, and drugged; no exceptions!

If you are food insecure, here are the likely reasons:

1. You are a bum!
2. You have a mental or physical defect (challenge) that makes it difficult to maintain a job. I am sympathetic to this need.
3. Obamanomics have been so incredibly successful that finding a job has become hopeless.
4. You are lazy.
5. You have chosen not to find a job because unemployment benefits and other federal programs have left you with very little reason to look for work.
6. You and your children don't know who their father is.

7. You cannot find your local food bank.
8. You are a druggie and too burned out to find your food bank or mission shelter.
9. You are not interested in finding a job.
10. You are willing to accept a food-insecure lifestyle.
11. You can't find the welfare office because you are too stoned!
12. Your birth control failed.
13. Your mother's birth control failed.
14. You thrive on the sympathy and political attention you get from leftists.
15. Your father has never had a job.
16. You don't spend your money on food.
17. The city administrators burned your homeless camp, and now you don't have a home!
18. You got so caught up promoting liberal politics that you didn't have time to go to work.
19. Housing is free; food is free; federal benefits just keep coming. Suppose *you* tell me why you are food insecure.
20. And the main reason why you are food insecure? Politics!

Virtually everything you eat is *processed food!* Pulling a carrot out of the ground and washing it before you eat it is a proscess! Peeling the carrot is a process. Cooking it is a process. Slicing it is a process. Salting it is a process. Adding butter or margarine is a process. When you peel or cook a carrot, it loses some of its nutritional value! When the leftist extremist brain-dead nutcase liberals condemn "processed food," what is it they are really are trying to say? What is it they want? A person would need to be fond of the taste of dirt in order to avoid a "process," at least in the most minimal way. During every process mentioned above, the pure healthiness of the carrot is lost! Why are alarmists warning us about processed food? What do they hope to gain?

As an expert on food production, I will assure you that the organic food, which you are paying extra to get, is a scam. Again, it is fear-mongering, in that if you are sensitive to a molecule that is present as measured in parts per million, you have far greater health problems that will adversely affect your life—profoundly more so than any trace residual farm chemical or fertilizer or GMO (genetically modified organism). We farmers are commonly exposed to these chemicals in harmless quantities that are millions of times greater than any possibility of exposure for a person eating the food produced. I have never known a farmer who was harmed by the normal use of, and normal exposure to, agricultural chemicals or fertilizers. There exists no known case in which a GMO has been linked to harming any human being. Such harm does not exist at all, nor is it possible. A drug company can make a mistake and produce and eventually market a drug that later is found to be problematic. The food industry cannot get away with this sort of mistake, and must live by a higher standard. If ever there were even one illness attributed to GMOs, those who have invested massive wealth in those GMOs would be instantly deprived of that wealth. I hate Monsanto as an "evil corporation" poster child, but this company would never assume the risk. Never!

THE BIG CLOSE

Is that all there is? Is that all ya got?

When I started this writing I had an aggrandized notion that my writing would somehow influence the world and there would be glory and wealth and fame; not so much now; Now that it is done.

It has been an interesting journey. I think my new adopted proclivity will be to never try this again.

If I did write another book it will be a lot easier. After 80,000 words or so, I have actually learned to type. I am also learning to spell, thanks to spell-check. This makes typing even faster but here's a surprise. I don't really care about spelling. Correct spelling of this convoluted mess we call the English language is a damn joke. Somebody needs to get off their ass and revise the spelling of English words. This *should* be a new government program so that all English words are spelled, fonetically. We would all be a lot better off. Correct spelling is for people who are anal-retentive. Believe it or not, I have actually begun to critique others' spelling and find myself being a bit prickish about others' mistakes in spelling and syntax—one of which I just made. I call these mistakes my writing "*style*". My editor is not amused!

When I look back on what I have done I can see that my underlying motive was to scrape away multiple layers of extreme cultural bovine fecal matter and replace it with pragmatic logical knowledge. Unfortunately pragmatic and logical knowledge doesn't have as much public appeal to the average person as does finely crafted BS, which is in constant flow from our pop-culture advertisement-driven media.

I would like to think that you have been entertained by reading

Proclivities. Entertainment was the main component of my original intended goal. I hope I have also brought you a unique perspective and mindset and have helped you to evolve your understanding of the nature of pop culture issues, no matter the era. I also hope that I have cleared up some of the personal misunderstandings that are part of your and everyone else's default grooved-in mind-set. We all need to have our assumptions challenged now and then.

A close friend who had been reviewing my work asked me recently, "Where does this stuff come from?" referring to my apparently warped thinking processes, and as if there is some unnatural mental force at work. I couldn't give her an answer! I still haven't thought of one. The truth of the situation might not be good news for me.

I am getting a little older. I have a lot of history behind me that gives me expertise on living. I hope that I have given a little useful insight to those who wanted it, and possibly a little wisdom to those who needed it.

Postscript: I forgot to mention that half the proceeds from the sales of this book will go to my children after I die. They will use the money to buy fast cars, most likely very expensive cars with turbo chargers. I will have spent the rest of the money on my tropical island. I have been out looking for recruits for my free college. I almost got arrested in the process! I need to be more careful in what I say to good-looking young women. I would like to give a portion of the proceeds from this book to some charity but I don't trust those people any more than I trust liberal politicians. Does the director of a charity feeding children really need to make 500 grand a year? It would seem that organizers of charities aren't very chartable since they won't do it for a very modest wage. Here's a new law you libs can pass. Every advertisement for a charity *should* be required to divulge the percentage of contributions that actually go to help the described beneficiaries. This should be part of the advertisement. There should be a prison just for people for who advertise these things and then only distribute a small percentage of the proceeds to the needy. Of course, that won't work or can't be done because half the Republicans and all the liberals would eventually go to prison. Public flogging did have its just cause. There was purity in it. There was no ACLU or leftist extremist brain-dead nutcase liberal claiming the killer was actually a victim. No agenda, only punishment, swift and sure and then you could go about your business. Punishment is obsolete as a concept. It once fostered discouragement from repeating bad behavior. Today, it is all about rehabilitation just in case the scumbag had ADHD or was suffering from hemorrhoids. Discouraging crime is definitely a concept that had its time. Now days it is much more important not to offend any one of the millions people who have come to be easily offended. Has there always been this hypersensitivity culturally or have we just become hypersensitive to hypersensitivity?

All BS aside, thank you for reading what I wrote. Thank you for giving me your time. Make sure you kids know you love them! Hug your dog! Pay your bills! Lose weight!

Most important of all I hope I have given you an example of the process of critical thinking. I hope you have become more objective and critical of your own social opinions. I have been very blunt and have taken some risks on your behalf. There is a lot at stake for our mutual future. Never before has the general public been exposed to so much available information as our media provide. I think that this readily available information should make things a lot more difficult for politicians and other self serving scam artists to exploit the public, but the opposite is actually true. Don't take anyone else's word for "it," and that includes mine! Winning and being right means that we all do the right thing and understand what that right thing is, and why.

GLOSSARY

Yes, this is a glossary. I don't care if you don't approve of my way of displaying a "glossary"

BDL (Brain-Dead Liberal): A chronic delusional condition in which the victim advocates senseless political agendas, without regard for feasibility. Potentially contagious. Untreatable.

Babaloney: A deceptive statement having no basis in fact, designed to engender an emotional response favoring a particular social issue. Frequently used by liberal activists.

F-ing: *F-you-see-kay-i-n-g*; as in, I want you to know this s—t; also, the act of sexual intercourse.

S—t: shit.

DFs: Dumb f—ks.

Asshole: The location at which fecal matter is ejected from your rectum. Also, a person, normally male, who creates the same sensation, through personal interaction, as if you were ejecting hot sauce out your ass.

WTF (What the F—k): Expletive; normally used when a statement is heard that makes no sense at all, such as when liberals activists are talking. It can also be the vocal emanation resulting from an observation of something visually absurd.

Fondologist: A woman who was blessed with every advantage by birth that any person could possibly hope for, yet is still complaining. She is famous not because of her talents, but because she was born in the spotlight and has played it for all it's worth. Her fame was surreptitiously garnered. This type of person is a master of diabolical behavior, with the skill to present herself as a cultural victim, though she has committed acts of social and national disgrace. She is a user by nature, and feels justified in her behavior and attitude, given the perceived misdeeds imposed upon her (i.e., "father issues").

Kumbaya: A mindless feeling of personal satisfaction, accomplishment, and well-being, no matter the actual truth. Psychologists describe this feeling as a *psychotic ecstasy.*

CC (Climate Change): An absurd and disproven assumption based on a theory that the release of fossilized carbon dioxide energy is detrimental to the health of the planet.

GW (Global Warming): The greatest hoax in human history, as perpetrated by leftist extremists; GW was eventually documented by NASA to be a complete fabrication.

Demoncrats: Those who present themselves as the salvation of the disadvantaged and impoverished, though they are primarily concerned with wealth, power, and control.

(ENDNOTES)

1   "Sara Pelosi" might actually be phony name for some famous but undefined politician who has better lawyers than I do

2   **Oxymoron:** If you tend to measure your life in terms of absolutes; —and if you believe that there are universal truths and that these truths are one way or the other, always; —you will linger in intellectual and philosophical darkness. Congratulations! If you think any one event or thought is always true, or always wrong, you will be always wrong.

"Lowlifes"

3   **BFF** means "best friends forever." Good luck with that one! Okay, so I am being sarcastic. I would like to think the best-friends-forever concept could work for any and all women. Guys don't say this crap. A long-term friendship is a blessing for anyone, *but,* the last time you said it, what were you really thinking? It sounds so damn disingenuous as a concept. True best friends forever would not feel a need to make such a proclamation! Again, good luck with this one! No sarcasm intended.

4   **Control the controlling!** In the same way that a man assumes the power of a woman's beauty, his wife assumes the power of the controlling male and may imagine that she now has or will gain that power by controlling the controller.

5   Darrin Stevens is/was a character name in *Bewitched,* a sitcom from the 1960s. Played by Dick York

"Original Wealth"

6   During a public campaign event in 2008, an unemployed plumber named Joe declared Barack Obama to be a socialist. This individual, who came to be known simply as "Joe the Plumber," was right!

"BACKGROUND THINKING"

7   Libs and Christians both have the same mind-set where satisfaction with life is concerned. A vacuous smile is born of this same mind-set, in that liberalism and Christianity give a person a fantasy reality to exist "in." Pragmatic harsh realities cease to be an issue in the face of a self-induced dream world substitute for reality. Meanwhile, realistic conservatives go about the business of making the world function and carrying out the business of our daily existence. Liberals amuse themselves with delusions of fostering a mutually and voluntary universal compliance and a mono group function of society. This keeps them out of the way; but, liberal programs foster poverty and crime and lawlessness and political corruption. These slothful behaviors find fertile soil in which to spread roots. This can only happen because the libs are naturally assuming criminals and the socially corrupt just need a better environment so that they can live a more homogenous life. They just need a chance! The Christians, meanwhile, are still praying. Prayer is a reasonable thing, but there is no substitute for getting your hands in the pot and cutting the roots, and this is best done while the libs have their heads cranially located so that they can't pass regulations on root pruning or request an environmental impact statement.

8   Traditional moral principles have evolved over time, as have humans. Ancient biblical and other writings reflected these principles for the first time in written form, but they were not born there. Historically, morals were a matter of survival during times of starvation and other social stresses. Ethics are, for the most part, are common social standards that provide peace among individuals and cultures when times are more prosperous and survival is not an issue. Corruption is an organized violation of ethics.

9   For my thoughts on oxymoron, *please see* n2.

10 Perhaps I should have said that this is an *excuse* to be evil; we all justify the terrible things we do. What makes a person truly evil is not making an attempt to justify the behavior, because such an individual sees no reason to feel remorse. This is true *sociopathy,* evil in the ultimate, biblical sense.

11 For my thoughts on oxymoron, *please see* n2.

"CLIMATE CHANGE 2"

12 My balanced equation:

BS + (fear x media) = (panic + cash + control) − rational thinking ÷ gullible − (education x false theory)

This equation balances beautifully and has proved to be true; just ask any social control liberal. It always works until someone actually does the math!

"CLIMATE CHANGE 1"

13 I have had varying results with this test!

14 And now for our government at work:

As required, we hereby submit this environmental impact statement. Our conclusions are:

Government intervention is creating a great deal of unnecessary environmental impact as a result of regulations which require additional investment and a lot of additional resources. Those resources could have been used to complete the project, with a lot less pollution and environmental impact, except that an environmental impact statement was required. Meanwhile, we killed some gophers and cut down a tree or two to construct the government office building intended as a place to provide more office space to evaluate environmental impact statements. More resources were wasted on this project, because we could have done it two years ago for about one-third of the cost, except that a bone was found on the excavation site so an anthropologist had to be flown in from Africa, along with her staff, to do a scientific evaluation of the site, given that the local Native Americans were convinced that the location was actually an Indian burial site. The Native Americans petitioned the court for an injunction to suspend the project until the evaluation had been completed. The petition was not granted because the bone was said to not resemble any human remains. Further court action did eventually suspend the project when the Bureau of Indian Affairs flew in three experts who had been in China researching the possibility that Indians might be descendants of space aliens. It is estimated that this research will last for approximately ten more years, at tremendous cost and with a great deal of environmental impact. Before they could proceed with the evaluation they had to submit an environmental impact statement, which took about six months, cost $2 million, and created a lot of additional pollution, which had additional negative impact on the environment. DNA testing confirmed the rumors that the bone was the remains of a discarded pork chop left by the construction crew. Because of these difficulties, the office-building project has been completely abandoned, and all the related environmental impact was therefore rated "very severe," given that nothing came of the project. The construction of the office-building flagpole that is the purpose of this document should proceed as soon as possible, given that the $24 million funding allowance for the $2,400.00 flag pole will soon become unavailable.

Don't ya just love government?

"The Most Compelling Proclivity of All"

15 This concept actually plays to the female fantasy: "I am so hot that he just can't help but hit on me." Such things are common in movie scripts and play to both genders.

16 Don't assume that I am supporting and condoning the traditions of some extremist Middle Eastern cultures where marriage is little more than slavery for the woman!

17 **Fn,** Unpleasant reality of marriage, #1A; FOR MEN ONLY .

As mentioned, it is my observation that women are dominant in the majority of successful marriages. It is also my observation that the woman in control often puts herself in a "not negotiable" relationship. There is little or no bargaining. There is little or no consideration of a mutually beneficial relationship in which issues are addressed jointly. These certain women will take a rigid stand against the influences of their male partners, and they can do this because they will sacrifice the quality of the relationship in favor of control of the relationship. Having said that, this scenario is likely the best situation where the cultural institution of marriage is concerned. It also is possibly the natural scheme of things where marriage is concerned, given that female validation is a primary driving influence of the male psyche. Natural selection and anthropology are the reason this is true. Sorry, guys, but there is really not a damn thing we can do about it, and I will remind you of the favoritism that women have been shown in divorce courts across the land in recent history. This favoritism reflects the needs of our culture and families, as opposed to the needs of the individual male, and it also reflects the opinion of the population at large.

If you are curious about the problems and trials of male-dominated relationships, watch any daytime TV talk show. I also want to thank you ladies who continue to read every word in my book, in spite of my criticisms.

18 No government funds were wasted researching this study!

19 *Headlights, nip-ups,* and *pointers* are only three of the many slang references to the erect nipple. At the moment, they are the only three that I can think of.

"WORDS THAT START WITH N"

20   This footnote actually is bullshit. The only reason I included is that I was told I should have footnotes.

"QUANTUM"

21   FYI, I have no idea what the hell Einstein was talking about!

22   **Fn**, ! Every person should see, at least once, Saturn and its rings. through a telescope or with powerful binoculars. It is a life- altering experience and a much more than a science lesson. Seeing this planet and its exotic beauty through your own eyes will elevate you to a cosmic level of realization. Your world is now the universe. It is a transition humans first made 700 years ago.

"KRIB NOTES"

23   This phenomenon is also referred to as *play action fake*, that is, pretending to be doing something you are not. To fully understand the concept, think, *Obama.*

24   Candidate Obama said this during the 2008 campaign.

25   Al Franken (an embarrassment to my neighboring state of Minnesota) made references to the fact that corporations are not people, as a convoluted response to a comment by Dick Cheney (former vice president), who said that corporations were made of, and by, people. This is an abbreviated description because I just don't care to honor the comment more thoroughly.

Printed in the United States
By Bookmasters